DRAGON'S CAPTURE

RED PLANET DRAGONS OF TAJSS BOOK SIX

MIRANDA MARTIN

A COMMANDER NEVER COMPROMISES.

The beautiful, headstrong human female contests me at every turn. She is the leader of her people and they love and respect her. As do I, though neither of us admit it. I burn with the desire to claim her as my treasure.

My people revere the Edicts above all else. Together we are stronger. I must make her see that in order for my people and hers to be one, for she and I to be one, she must eliminate the threat that could drive our entire world apart.

Gershom. He has finally gone too far and I will not tolerate his continued presence.

The humans who mate with the Zmaj have been exiled and the confrontation has come to a head. This female who tempts my Dragon will find out how possessive and dominant a Commander can be.

ROSALIND

"*What* you've managed to accomplish is impressive, Visidion," I say, a tight smile on my face.

Visidion's smile is swift, gone as fast as it comes.

"It's a start Lady Rosalind," he says, waving his staff over the growing plants. "But it is not enough."

"No, it's not," I agree.

"This is amazing! Transplanting these here couldn't have been easy—how did you overcome the culture shock?" Calista asks, looking up at Visidion.

Visidion shakes his head and looks over at Astrid. Calista follows his gaze.

"Uh," Astrid says, perplexed. "We just, you know, did it?"

Calista smiles. "Sorry, I wasn't thinking."

"Please forgive her," Jolie chimes in. "She thinks everyone is a botanist."

Calista flushes and shrugs.

"So how often do you have to water?" Calista asks. "Illadon, no!"

Illadon pulls everyone's attention as he grabs up one of

the small plants and shoves it in his mouth. He looks at his mother, grinning, with a long green stalk sticking out of his mouth.

"Mama?" he asks, around the root, eyes wide and his tiny tail drooping behind him.

"I'm so sorry," Calista says, jumping to her feet to race over to Illadon.

"It's fine! That's what we're growing it for," Penelope says.

Illadon takes that for what it's worth and barely seems to chew before he's swallowing. He laughs as Calista sweeps him up into her arms with a grunt. I'm surprised she can still lift him—he's growing fast and must be pushing sixty pounds now, even though he's still a toddler. The human-zmaj babies are born big and grow fast. Illadon has been a toddler for a while, and now Rverre is doing her best to keep up with him. She giggles watching Illadon, and soon she's following along behind him.

The babies are almost always the center of attention. Everyone wants to know how they are, what they are doing, if they've done anything new. Stories of the babies are the meat and bread of the City. My interest in them is just as high but for much different reasons. They are our future. Neither of our races can survive on our own. We need each other.

"No, no, no, Rverre," Jolie says. "Just because Illadon got away with it doesn't mean you will."

She intercepts Rverre as she tries to uproot a stalk too.

"Perhaps we should go elsewhere?" I suggest.

"Of course," Visidion says, motioning towards the cliffs.

The Tribe has done an impressive amount of work turning these broken cliffs and caverns into a home. The side of the cliff is dotted with homes built into the rock. They've put up a rock wall to separate their area off from the rest of the barren plains. I assume it helps keep the wandering creatures out as well though it's not very tall, at least not yet. Maybe they plan to make it taller.

A spasm rips through my thigh when I step forward. Damn it, not now. Gritting my teeth, I will the leg to hold. The spasm passes and no one seems to have noticed. Good. I can't let them know, not yet. I wish Sarah was here with me, but I don't want anyone to know she works directly for me. There wasn't a good excuse to bring her along.

Things are going to come to a head with Gershom soon. If I can only hold him off a bit longer it won't matter if he takes control. I'll have laid the future of our races. A little more time. It's all I need.

Visidion walks beside me. Ladon and Sverre stand off by themselves. Three members of the Tribe stand a few feet from them, arms crossed. They're exchanging distrustful looks. Astarot walks out of the cavern and heads towards their group.

"Ladon!" Astarot calls out, apparently unperturbed by the tension between the two groups.

Good. I need Ladon to relax, and I hope that Astarot can accomplish that. Ladon uncrosses his arms and his tail stops slashing from side to side, which is all a step in the right direction.

"I'm glad you came," Visidion says. "Might I offer you refreshment?"

"We brought our own. I do not wish to be a burden," I say.

"Nonsense, I will provide for you. What kind of host would I be if I did not?"

Visidion's eyes are a deep emerald. When he stares at me it feels as if he's looking into my soul. There's something about his eyes and the way he locks his gaze on a person. I've seen him do it to others as well. The person he is focusing on becomes the center of the universe, and they know it. You can't help but feel it when interacting with him. It's an impressive skill, but a skill nonetheless.

"Thank you," I say, accepting his offer.

If only I could trust you. I push that thought aside and direct my attention to my surroundings. The Tribe has done amazing things in the short time they've been here. They've turned an empty cliff and cave into a home. Almost better than I've been able to accomplish with much longer in the City.

Astarot stands between the three Tribe Zmaj and Ladon with Sverre, making an obvious attempt to bridge the two cultures. As we pass by them he catches my eye and smiles. I nod my appreciation, and he breaks the eye contact first.

"Here," Visidion says, motioning with his staff.

A small table is laid out with snacks and clay vases of water. The table is a thin piece of metal that looks like salvage from one of the ships' wreckage. Wooden sticks have been worked through it to form legs. Twine is wrapped around them below the metal sheet and above to lock the table in place. It's an ingeniously simple design. The water vases hold most of my attention. They're hand crafted, functional but pretty. Designs are etched into the clay to create diamond patterns on one and swirls on the other. Functional dining ware is an area where we sorely lack. No one in the city, including me, had thought to find and use clay.

"How do you find the clay?" I ask, holding one of the vases up to inspect it closer.

"Clay is plentiful if you dig around an oasis or risk going into the caves," Visidion answers. "There is a skill to creating with it though."

"I'm sure there is," I say, setting the vase down. "Well, our trip has been productive, thank you."

"Of course," Visidion says, raising his glass before sipping.

"Our futures are intertwined, we must continue to strengthen the bonds between our people," I say.

"We don't need anyone," a smaller Zmaj mutters as he walks by the table. He's small by Zmaj standards but still towers over any human.

Visidion looks down but doesn't speak. His difficulties are not that different from mine, it would seem. This visit has shown, if nothing else, there is an underlying resentment among members of the Tribe, especially the Zmaj.

Time. I just need time. Damn it, Gershom, give me enough! My hand starts to shake, so I set the cup down before it becomes noticeable. Maybe I should be cursing my body for more time, though the tremors and weakness have been less than they were before. Time is my enemy in more ways than one.

"That is not true," I answer, but I'm looking at Visidion when I speak, watching for his reaction.

Visidion watches but now I've attracted more than just his attention. Good. They need to hear this. The small Zmaj who had muttered turns and glares as do other members of the Tribe, some more openly than others.

"What can you possibly mean?" Delilah, I think her name is, says stepping forward.

Delilah is a black woman of medium size. Though her height and build may be average, there is an imperial air in the sweep of her cheekbones and the way she carries herself. She thrusts her shoulders forward and tilts her head back, and there's an angry flash in her eyes.

"Together we are stronger," I answer her.

"Really? Were you not there when your people refused us entry into the City? After all the shit we went through, holding out a candle of hope, only to find out the light at the end of that tunnel was a damn lie?" she retorts, anger and sarcasm in every word.

"There are two sides to every story," I say.

"Sure," she says. "There always are, but what does it matter? We're fine here. We've got everything we need. Hell, life here is better than it was at the wreckage before I was captured. I don't need you. None of us here do."

The Zmaj close to her hisses his agreement. Squaring my shoulders I listen but her argument isn't new. I've heard it from my own people. They don't see the future because they're only looking at the moment. Visidion steps forward.

"This is not the time for such discussion," he says, tapping his staff on the ground.

"When is the time?" Delilah spits. "We welcome them in here like nothing happened? They turned us away!"

A redheaded woman steps out of the crowd and places a hand on Delilah's shoulder. She's a bigger girl, and I notice there's an unmistakable swell to her belly. I struggle to place her name. It's right there on the tip of my tongue. I never had this problem before. As Lady General, the entire fleet was under my command, and there was not a name and face in the entire force I could not put together on sight. That was before. It was the first thing I noticed failing. That led me to the doctors on the ship.

Olivia! That's her name!

"Delilah," she says, "please."

"Please what?" Delilah says, becoming angrier.

Tribe members move closer to the commotion. Ladon and Sverre appear behind me. Ladon's anger is palpable, coming off him in waves. Sverre is more in control, but neither of them are contributing to defusing the situation.

"This isn't the time," Olivia begs.

"Then when is?" Delilah asks.

This is getting out of control. The Tribe is gathering behind Delilah and my own people are behind me. There's an empty space between us, a few feet, but it might as well

6

be a galaxy. A gaping chasm of differences and hurt feelings.

"The choice to leave was yours," Ladon hisses over my shoulder.

"You refuse the Edicts!" a Zmaj shouts, stepping into the open space between our groups, his wings spreading, tail straight out behind him, his arms wide inviting any threat.

"Ragnar," Visidion says, slamming his staff into the ground.

The Zmaj who stepped forward stands down, his wings folding, tail lowering, and dropping his arms to his sides. He steps back but doesn't break his gaze with Ladon. Visidion steps into the middle ground, and on instinct, I move to his side. The two of us turn a slow circle in a silent accord. Staring at each person, locking eyes one after another, we connect with everyone until our unity makes the tension in each face, in each body, seep away. For now.

The crowd disperses leaving Visidion and me to face each other. Ladon storms off towards the wall where he's been standing watch for most of our visit. Sverre quietly joins him. Delilah stands alone at the end staring at me but turns and leaves too.

Visidion locks his stunning gaze with me, and that feeling of him looking into my soul returns. Despite it, the gulf between us is still wide. His worldview, shaped by the Edicts of the Tribe, are different. He shakes his head, smiling. The hooded cloak he wears, flapping in a light, hot breeze, pulls the fabric aside to further reveal his muscled chest. The red suns glint off his scales that have a soft blue tint to their edges. Something deep in my core tightens, stirring, interest rising. No, what am I thinking? It can never be.

"I apologize," Visidion says.

"I understand, but we must find a way to bring our peoples together," I say.

"I'm not sure that is possible," he says, sighing as he looks over my shoulder to where Ladon and Sverre stand. "We will not abandon the Edicts."

Chewing the inside of my lip, I nod my understanding.

The Zmaj, the natives of this planet my humans have crashed on, are a dying race, but proud. The devastating war that destroyed the planet happened long ago, leaving only a handful of male survivors. I've seen evidence of a time when they were plentiful. That was before. Now most Zmaj can barely stand to be within a hundred feet of each other. The handful of them in the City struggle to control an instinctive need to dominate.

The Tribe is different. So many Zmaj, living together, in peace, more or less. What they refer to as the Edicts is what makes it possible. Glancing over my shoulder at Ladon and Sverre, my stomach knots. Convincing Ladon of that is an entire project of its own.

Then there is Gershom. The constant thorn in my side, vying, subtly, for control of the survivors. He's a snake in the grass and I know it. Many times I've considered handling him with finality—but he has followers. If I moved against him directly, it would only fuel them, leading to a civil war among the humans. Something we can't afford. There aren't enough of us.

"How's it going?" Calista asks, interrupting my thoughts.

Illadon is on her hip, giggling as he pulls at her blouse. Jolie is just behind her with Rverre in her arms. The babies. That's where our future lies. Certainty fills my heart looking at them. Just one of the secrets I cannot share with anyone. Apart, our races are doomed. Together is our future. Fate, gods, the hand of the universe, or sheer blind luck brought us to this point, but no matter how, this is where we are.

"Momma," Illadon gurgles, pulling Calista's attention and bringing a smile to my face.

He may overall be Zmaj with his scales, wings, and tail, but the human in his features is clear too. His tiny budding horns grow out of a thick head of hair, and his sharp blue eyes and nose are all Calista. Ladon walks over, takes his son in his arms, and tosses him high in the sky. Illadon laughs so hard he's crying, flapping his tiny wings as he falls back into his father's grasp.

"Ladon!" Calista exclaims. "Careful!"

"Of course I'm careful," Ladon says, ignoring her as he throws the laughing Illadon into the air again.

This rift between our people must be healed. The epis, delicate, rare plant that extends the life of those who take it and has the miraculous effect of adjusting our human biology to survive the intense heat of Tajss, will not be enough for our survival on its own. There aren't enough of us. The balance of men to women is too far off. No, our only hope for the future is to bring our two dying races together.

"The future," Visidion whispers next to me.

My neck pops as I look at him so quickly. Was he in my thoughts?

He watches Illadon flying into the air and dropping into his father's arms. Ladon and Illadon are laughing and even Calista is. Rverre holds her tiny arms out, hands grasping and cooing, wanting the same attention. Sverre takes his daughter and plays with her, albeit in a much gentler way. Rverre revels in his attention, no matter it's not as rough as Ladon's.

"Yes," I agree, speaking softly too. "If we make it."

2

VISIDION

"It is late. You should stay, return in the morning," I say.

Rosalind stares out across the rolling dunes. The strong line of her jaw is set, and her smoky gray eyes stare into the distance, seeing things no one else does. Dark brown hair curling down past her shoulders to the middle of her back contrasts strongly with the white suit she wears. There is an imperial aura to her. She's a natural leader but I see the weight on her shoulders. She captivates me, but how do I say such?

My cock hasn't stirred in so many years that the sensations in my groin of desire and need take me by surprise. Only she has that effect, since the first moment I saw her standing on the other side of the glittering dome of the city. Tall, ramrod-straight back, the easy aura of being in charge— all caught my interest. Since then, what I've learned of her only makes my interest grow. She cares for her people and the Zmaj as well.

"I would not want to impose," she says.

"If it would be an imposition, I would not have offered," I answer.

She turns, her eyes locking with mine. Her head tilts to one side, and a hint of a smile plays across her lips.

"I admire your bluntness and honesty," she says.

My throat tightens, making speaking impossible. Her compliment has strange effects on my body. Unable to answer, I nod my head in response and turn away from her gaze. My stomach roils as if I've eaten a bad stajiss seed. What, am I a youngling? Swallowing hard, I force my throat open and calm my stomach through will.

"Thank you," I say. "It will give us time to discuss the future as well."

The future. I know what I would like, but what I would like and what I can and will most likely have are two distinctly different things. My people are first. The Edicts guide our lives. Without them we are nothing. Lose them and we lose ourselves. The Tribe would be more accepting of the City if Rosalind was willing to deal with Gershom.

That is an issue I cannot push. What would I do if the roles were reversed? Adopt a new and foreign system of rule or reject it out of hand? No, I could not give up the Edicts. Which leaves her and me at an impasse. For now.

"The future," she nods, pursing her full lips.

What would they taste like?

"Drosdan, find lodging for our guests for the night," I order.

Drosdan stares, hisses, then nods and moves to comply with my order. Drosdan is loyal even if he might grumble. Rosalind and I walk over to the wall together. There's an easy comfort to the silence between us. The setting suns cast their dying red rays across the wasteland that is my home. Tajss was never easy, but the devastation made it worse.

"Can you see it?" Rosalind asks, her delicate hand resting on the wall that comes just above her waist.

The bustle of evening sounds drifts past us as we stand, side by side, staring at the horizon. People talking, dishes rattling, the shuffle of life carrying on. A ray of light lands on Rosalind's face, accenting her strong jaw, casting an aura around her. In some ways, she reminds me of my father, Kaleessin the Seer. It was his vision before the devastation that founded the Tribe. He sees things no one else does. There is an air about him that is very much the same with Rosalind.

"What is it you see?" I ask, curiosity tingling along my scales.

"What we can be, what we must be," she sighs.

Boldly I place my hand on hers. We stand shoulder to shoulder, facing the setting suns together.

"That is a long road," I observe.

Her skin is soft under my touch, so soft. Desire stirs again, rising, clouding my judgment. She doesn't move her hand from mine, though in fairness she doesn't seem to notice it either.

"Yes," she says. "Fraught with peril."

"The future always is," I agree. "Only the strong can claim it."

"Are we strong enough?" she muses.

"Together we are stronger," I intone, the second of the Edicts.

She looks at me, eyes narrowing, mouth tightening.

"Your Edicts," she observes.

"Yes," I say.

"Tell me your history. How did you create all of this?" Her graceful gesture sweeps across the cliff homes of the Tribe.

"Ah, that is a tale, now isn't it? Shall I share it over a meal?" I ask, stomach clenching in anticipation.

Emotions flicker across her face in an instant, and then her eyes soften. She turns her hand under mine, palm up, then grips my hand tight.

"That would be nice," she agrees.

Chills run down my spine as we walk. When we reach my home, I pull the skins aside to let her enter. Before I step in, I see a few of the Tribe staring. Turning from their looks, I drop the skins behind me.

"Please, sit," I say, motioning to one of the two stools at my table.

She sits with a grace of movement that holds my attention. Every motion she makes flows from one to the next. A sensual beauty in action. Hospitality is rough here in our new home. Back at the Valley, I would have more to offer in both supplies and amenities. All of that we left behind when the Zzlo found us. The Zzlo, more than the hostility of the environment, weigh on my mind. They are the reason I believe we need an alliance with the City.

"Thank you," she says.

I take two clay cups and plates out of a small chest by the wall and set them on the table, then pour water from a vase. A woven basket has dried meats in it that I put on each of our plates before taking my own seat. She raises her glass holding it out over the table. My mind whirls, what is she doing? She's waiting, for what? What am I supposed to do to this gesture?

"It is a human custom," she says, smiling, "to touch glasses before drinking. It is a toast, an honor to the host."

"A toast?" I ask.

"Yes," she says, still holding her glass over the table. She searches for a word. "A toast is like... a blessing."

"Ah," I say, raising my glass and holding it out over the table too.

Humans have strange customs. She tilts her glass towards

mine until the edges clink together. Then she raises it to her lips and sips before setting it back on the table. I sip from my cup and put it down too.

"Your history," she prompts, picking up a piece of smoked meat and popping it in her mouth without further ado.

"Yes," I say, forcing my thoughts away from the fullness of her lips as they purse and relax with the chewing motions.

Thoughts of pleasure dance in my mind. Pleasure that is not mine to claim, but those lips. They appear so soft, so different than a Zmaj female's would be. What would they feel like on my... no. Focus.

"The Tribe started before the devastation," I say. "Kalessin foresaw what was coming."

"Kalessin is your father?" she asks.

Time stops, my hand halfway to my mouth with a piece of meat. Swallowing hard I tilt my head. Rosalind smiles, enjoying the fact she shocked me.

"You know more than I expected," I say.

"It's the only way to play the game," she acknowledges.

"Is that what we're doing? Playing a game?" I ask.

The air is thick between us. We stare into each other's eyes. My first cock stirs, stiffening, laden with desire. Thoughts race, my hearts thump hard in my chest. It's hard to breathe.

"Are we not," she whispers.

Her lips parting around the words, closing on each one, her beautiful eyes sparkling with hints of promise. I could lose my heart in those warm pools. She leans in, pulling me forward with her.

"Survival is not a game," I say, soft.

"It is the only game," she says, sensuous, closer.

I'm drawn in by her gravity. We're close, almost close enough to kiss. My cock throbs, pulsing need, clouding judgment. The Edicts.

"Survival of the group matters." Hoarse, scratchy words emerge from my too-tight throat.

"Yes, more than ourselves," she says.

Her hand touches mine on the table. Fire ignites in my scales as her fingertips brush against them. Roaring up my limbs and down to my core, fueling the inferno of desire and needs unmet in longer than memory. The piece of meat in my other raised hand drops to the table, forgotten.

So close. Her scent fills my senses, heady, spinning me deeper into desire. My tongue tingles, imagining how she will taste. Her warm breath passes over my mouth. Stomach clenching, I grip the table, bracing myself.

Focus. I am myself.

Her left hand rests on my clenched fist on the table. Her right rises, trembling, and she touches my cheek. Weakness strikes my legs—if I wasn't sitting I'd fall. A soft groan slips out of my throat. Never has a touch been so soft, sensuous, or more desired. If I were to purse my lips they would touch hers. I could, should… no.

"Why?" I ask.

It falls from my mouth unwanted, contrary to everything I desire, but I have to know. It breaks the moment. Rosalind leans back, leaving a vacuum where she was. I fall back onto my stool, and we stare at each other across the new-formed chasm. Was the moment real? Did she want me as I want her? The slightest shake of her shoulders as she settles on her stool, a quiver that fuels my doubts.

"Why?" she queries, staring at the table between us.

The raging of my cock subsides, softening with the missed opportunity. Regret dances in my chest, an empty ache, but my thoughts clear. I am Chieftain; the Tribe is first. Survival of the group matters. Focusing myself, I recite the Edicts in my mind before I answer her question.

One, I am myself. Two, together we are stronger. Three, survival of the group matters.

Inhaling deep, pushing desires aside, I exhale a low, slow breath.

"Yes, why. Why do you protect Gershom? What is this future you see in which you feel he plays a role? That's what it is, isn't it? You see a need he fulfills. Why else would you tolerate someone who causes so much trouble?"

Her shoulders slump. It's not obvious, only astute observation catches it. The weight on her returns.

"As you say, he fulfills a role," she sighs.

"What role, what future do you see?"

She looks up from the table, sharp eyes staring into mine, looking for something. I meet her gaze without flinching, opening to her. Her lips part; there is a heavy pause; then she shakes her head.

"Survival," she lies. "I'm just trying to make sure as many of my people as possible survive."

My chest constricts with pain. My hearts skip beats. Closing my eyes, I sigh and accept her answer. The trust between us is not yet enough.

"I see," I say, letting it go, my stomach knotting as if punched.

"You were telling me about your history," she says.

Smiling tight, I let her change the subject. Easier than facing the pain of distrust.

"As I said, Kalessin saw what was coming, but no one would listen. He went to the Councils, spoke against those who advocated war. He tried to get them to see, to believe his visions, but Zmaj are a proud race. They would not set aside their fixed views of the world.

Seeing he could not stop what was to come, he gathered those who would listen. They came together, collecting supplies, and then before his vision could come to pass, they went into the desert. A handful only, my family, a few others who would listen."

"The willfully blind do not see until it is too late," she mutters.

"Truth," I agree. "When it was over, the Tribe was but a few. Over time, survivors were found. Some joined us, others went their own ways. We were resigned to our end, but holding out hope. Kalessin often said there was hope. The future was clouded but not black. So we waited. We survived."

"The bijass?" she asks.

"What of it?" I ask.

"Tell me of it. I don't know that I understand it."

Breaking contact with her eyes I study the scratches in the thin metal top of the table between us. Bijass is shameful, not something to be discussed. Her hand touches my fist, insisting, pulling truth.

"It is shameful," I say.

"Yes, but what is it?" she implores me. "I need to understand. I lead Zmaj, but it is only by conjecture and observation. Help me, so I might better lead those who follow me."

Sincerity lies in her words. Gritting my teeth before meeting her gaze, I swallow hard.

"Zmaj are evolved for Tajss," I say. "A violent, savage planet. The bijass is our basest instinct, primal drives. A Zmaj struggles between rationality and the bijass, always. Hence the Edicts."

"They're a mantra," she observes.

"Yes, they focus the mind. Push back and help you to remain in control."

She purses her lips and the now not-unfamiliar stirrings in my crotch happen again. A tingle on my lips, desire to taste those plump entrances to her beautiful mouth.

"Why does Ladon reject them?"

"Because he's a fool," I retort without thinking, regret following immediately when her sharp eyes admonish me.

"Ladon is a lot of things, but not a fool."

"Are you sure?" I ask, holding the line now that the words have fallen.

"I am," she says.

"Then he is afraid."

"Afraid?" she snorts. "Ladon?"

"Yes," I say. "What else? He's either a fool, which you assert he is not, or afraid. Why else would he be unwilling to have tools to control his baser instincts?"

She doesn't say anything, looking thoughtful. One finger traces a pattern on the table, holding my attention. A tremor passes through her hand and she jerks it off the table to her side.

"Perhaps," she says, covering her strange behavior. "I will have to think about that."

"It is late, and we must be on our way early if we are to make the city tomorrow," she says, rising from the table.

"Of course, this way," I say, showing her to my small bed.

She tries to insist she will sleep on the floor, but the argument is moot. I will not bend on this point. And at last, she is lying in my bed behind a makeshift curtain I rig out of a couple of skins. I can just see the outline of her hip in the gap between them. With my back pressed to the wall, I study the curve of her. I contemplate what almost was between us until sleep claims me.

3

ROSALIND

"As you can see, trade is in both of our best interests," I say, picking a piece of smoked meat off the clay plate and placing it in my mouth.

"I agree, of course, but there are obstacles to be overcome," Visidion replies.

Chewing the tough piece of meat, I watch him and wait. He's left the statement open for me to reply, but often it is better to let the other talk more. Silence can be the greatest tool in my arsenal. Visidion is patient. Almost, I think he might win this game. I pick up the glass and take a long, slow drink, never letting my eyes break from his. A smile plays at the corners of his mouth.

My core tightens with an urge to throw myself across the table and taste his lips. Firming my grip on the cup, I resist until it passes.

"My people," he continues at last.

"Yes?" I encourage.

"We have lived on our own for too long," he says. "They do not believe we need you."

"What do you believe?" I probe.

Visidion sighs, leans back, spreads his arms wide, and shakes his head. His eyes close while he inhales deeply. His chest rises, expanding with the inhale pressing forward his impressive physique. Now-familiar tightness in my core winds tighter, his pectoral muscles tighten then relax as he lets the breath out. No. I'm not a schoolgirl. No matter how long it's been...

He opens his beautiful eyes, meeting my gaze with open honesty. His eyes are deep pools, unshielded access to his soul. My mouth is so dry that swallowing hard hurts my throat. His wings rustle on his back.

"Perhaps I have lived too long without hope," he says, his voice soft, placing a hand on the table halfway between us.

My hand is on his, unplanned, without thought. Instinct or driven by desire—I don't know. His scales are smooth and cool under my fingertips. I trace a slow circle with my index finger, my eyes never leaving his. The texture of his scales ignites my interest. A shudder passes through me as my body responds to the feel of him.

"And?"

His tongue darts out and across his lips. I lean, involuntarily, desire pulling me closer.

"I don't know what to do with it," he breathes, leaning.

"Embrace it."

"Then what?"

"Then we see..."

Our lips are so close his warm breath passes across me, a hint of spice to it. His emerald green eyes, pools of warm liquid, two inches away staring into my soul. He turns his hand under mine on the table and grips me tight. Closer, my lips tremble, about to touch his...

A scream cuts through the moment jerking us both to reality.

My heart pounds. Leaping to my feet, I bound for the

door, Visidion at my side. When I burst through the skins that cover the entrance, the bright suns assault my eyes. Spots dance across my vision, blurring everything to rough shapes.

Visidion's home is on the second level of the cliff homes. He pushes past me and is running down the ramp. I'm unable to follow without risking a fall until my eyes clear.

"Rawrrr!" echoes off the stone wall behind me.

I rub furiously at my eyes as I move down the ramp. The sounds of fighting are joined by shouts and more screams. My eyes clear at last and almost I wish they hadn't. The huge Zmaj, Drosdan I believe, is facing off against Ladon. The two of them circle each other, a crowd around them shouting and screaming. Blood is streaming down Ladon's face from a cut over his eye but he shows no sign of slowing.

In a sudden, surprising burst Ladon leaps into the air, wings spreading wide, arm cocked back, fist dropping towards Drosdan. Drosdan, bigger and slower, looks up and starts to raise his arms in defense but too late. Ladon's fist slams into him with a sickening crunch. Drosdan stumbles backwards, tail swinging wildly and wings batting at the air as he struggles to remain upright.

A round of gasps are accompanied by cheers.

"Kick his ass, Ladon!" someone yells, a human voice by the accent, but I can't see past the bodies to see who it is, now that I'm off the ramp.

"Drosdan!" a chant starts.

Feet pound the ground, creating a thunderous cacophony along with the chants of the name of the larger Zmaj. Visidion is just ahead of me, rushing for the crowd. The red-tan cloak he wears flaps in the wind behind him. He's stopped by the crowd.

"Make way!" he yells as I catch up to him.

The crowd parts around him. I follow in his wake, taking

advantage of the opening. Before we can pass through the cheering and chanting crowd, I hear another hard slam and more grunts of pain. My chest constricts as my heart beats faster. The crowd is too close, making it hard to breathe as we push our way through. My left thigh trembles, wanting to give way. No, not now. Gritting my teeth, I push past the pain, but the trembling of my hands isn't something I can control.

The problems have been less but are not gone. Every time they return it's a reminder of how precious time is and how little of it I have to accomplish my goals. Another loud crack and the crowd gasps. Someone screams. The chanting resumes.

Shifting bodies press in and out. How many people are there here? How can we not be through this crowd already?

Stumbling, I'm free of it. Visidion grabs my arm, steadying me.

"ENOUGH!" Visidion yells, his voice loud enough to echo off the cliff wall.

Silence drops like a blanket. No one speaks. I can't hear anyone even breathe.

Drosdan and Ladon face each other a couple of feet apart. Blood drips off both of them, pooling on the ground. Drosdan's left wing droops too. They're both panting but their fists are raised and ready to continue their battle.

Walking beside Visidion we move between the two men. Strategically I shift my position so that I end up closer to Drosdan, forcing Visidion to stand closer to Ladon. A quick shift of his eyes in my direction tells me he notes it, and the hint of a smile is his approval.

"What's going on here?" I ask, taking the lead.

"He called Illadon ugly," Ladon hisses.

"No, I said his father was as ugly as a bivo's droppings," Drosdan retorts.

The crowd laughs, and Drosdan stands straighter, grinning. Ladon hisses, balling his fists as he steps forward. Visidion stops him with a hand on his chest.

"Drosdan, we are guests in your home. Is this how the Tribe treats its guests?" I ask.

"Tribe," Ladon turns his head and spits the word. "Gathering of sismis is more accurate."

Sismis are tiny sand snakes with a very deadly poison. Calling the Tribe that must be a high insult in Zmaj judging by the reaction of the crowd. Drosdan roars, his tail springing straight up and his undamaged wing opening, the other struggling but failing to expand.

"Ladon," Visidion says, "is this the way you treat your hosts?"

Ladon locks eyes with Visidion as I turn to face Drosdan. Placing my hand on his massive chest I look up and stare until he glances down. Once he does our eyes lock and by my will alone I force him to keep his gaze on me. He's huge, with arms like tree trunks, shoulders wide enough I could stretch out across them and have room left. Still, he doesn't move from my touch or look away.

"No," Ladon says, defeat in his voice.

"And you Drosdan? Is this in line with the Edicts?" I ask.

His eyes widen, his jaw falls open as he shakes his head. His wings and tail drop and his hands unclench.

"We have differences," Visidion says, speaking to Ladon but pitching his voice to carry.

"But they are not so great," I finish his thought.

"There is enough in this world trying to destroy us," Visidion says.

"Storms, heat, zelmja, and Zzlo," I say.

"Do we need to destroy each other as well?" Visidion asks.

"Together we are stronger," I say, the crowd gasps and the tension lowers.

I know there is a power in the Edicts they follow. If only I could get my people to accept them. Soon, once Gershom is dealt with, it should be possible. The ideals they express are no different than my own but diametrically opposed to Gershom and his Human First movement.

"What about them? They don't follow our Edicts," a voice from the crowd.

"No, they do not," Visidion says.

"But not because we don't respect them," I continue.

"Are our ideals meant to be enforced? Should we make them follow our ways? Beat them down until they submit?" Visidion says.

"You are better than that, we all must be."

"Together we are stronger," Visidion repeats.

The crowd murmurs, the tide shifting. There are too few of us, even with the size of the Tribe and the new survivors who have chosen to live here. Too few for us to be at each other. The viability of both our races hangs in the balance.

"There is hope," I say. "Hope for a future for both our races. Open your minds and hearts and look forward."

"Yes," Visidion agrees. "Hope, that long-lost glimmer we have all but forsaken has come. In a new form, the form of the Humans and an alliance between our races. That is the future we see. Will you not follow me into it?"

"I will," Padraig says, stepping forward.

Padraig is as unmistakable as Drosdan, being second in size only to him. Big, burly—if Zmaj grew facial hair, I'd imagine him with a big, black thick beard to go with his bulging arms and chest. Even his voice is deep and booming. Other Zmaj follow suit, and then the humans among them are also agreeing. In moments, the near-riot passes as people return to their work, leaving Visidion and me standing between Ladon and Drosdan.

Both of the Zmaj are wounded from their fighting.

They're breathing heavily, and neither of them will meet the gaze of the other. Drosdan rubs his jaw, moving it back and forth until it cracks loudly. My stomach clenches at the sound in sympathy.

"You hit good," Drosdan says.

"You don't," Ladon says, wiping blood away from his eyes.

"Ladon, be nice!" Calista storms up.

She was probably blocked out by the crowd, but she's here now, and Ladon shrinks before his wife. Calista rises on her toes to look at the wound over his eye. Tsking as she inspects it, she pinches around the area. Ladon yelps, and Drosdan giggles in response. Ladon glares over his wife's head at the bigger Zmaj.

"You hit like a female," Ladon snaps.

"Go ahead, tiny man," Drosdan says.

Visidion and I exchange a glance, then leave the two men to work out the rest of their differences, the danger in the situation gone.

"We work well together," Visidion says.

He walks towards the wall. A short way off, two Zmaj and a woman are working. She lays a mud mixture down on the wall then the two Zmaj lift large stones up and place them, taking the wall higher.

"Yes," I agree.

"Perhaps we should do it more often?" he asks, staring out at the empty desert.

"Perhaps we should," I agree.

A slow smile spreads as he nods. We stand in comfortable silence, side by side, staring out into the great emptiness that is our home.

"You should leave soon," he says, but is that regret in his voice?

It couldn't be, could it? Focus, Rosalind.

"Yes," I agree, carefully controlling my voice so that my own regrets don't come out.

"We did not finalize the terms of our trade agreements," he says.

"Unfortunately no, we did not," I agree.

"Epis is vital to life, so there will be no restrictions but the supply is limited. We will have to control that," he offers.

"That is very generous of you," I say, though in fairness it's only right. They did claim our epis source without asking.

"I've instructed my hunters to range south of here. That will leave north of the City for your hunters," he says. "That should help with the food supply though it will take some time to let the balance return."

"Also very agreeable," I say.

"There has been a suggestion on that front," Visidion says.

"Oh?" I ask.

"It would be very dangerous but with a joint effort, it might be possible," he continues.

"You've got my interest," I say.

"A zemlja," he says.

"What about them?"

"They have enough meat to feed all our people for a long time," he says. "If we could survive killing one."

"Well, I know it's been done," I say.

"Yes, it's been done," he agrees. "Small ones."

"How big do they get?" I ask.

"They have no predators," he answers, as if that says it all.

"Sure, but I mean how big can they be?"

"Once, before the devastation, there was one that destroyed a city when it came up from its tunnel underneath the buildings."

"You're kidding me!"

He smiles and shrugs.

"Perhaps," he says. "It is a tale. Though all tales have some truth in them."

"Let's talk about this further," I say. "I'd also like to work out equitable trade for your craft goods. Plates, cups, the pottery, and baskets your people produce."

"Of course. No matter what my people believe, the City has things to offer us. Metal, glass, materials to ease our life."

"Good," I say, holding out my hand.

He clasps my wrist and we shake. I'm staring up into those stunning green eyes and wishing, for all the world, that I could kiss him. Regret causes bile in my stomach as I turn away from his gaze. As I suspected, we're being watched, albeit with some semblance of covertness.

"Round it up," I call out. "We need to return home."

4

VISIDION

Something touches my shoulder, jerking my attention away from the horizon. When I turn, Errol pulls his hand back. His face is grim, pensive, as he waits.

"Yes?" I ask.

"Uh, we need to work here sir," he says, motioning at the wall.

I'm confused for a long moment, still lost in thought, and then I notice that the workers have reached the point of the wall where I'm standing.

"Yes," I say, shaking my head.

My shoulders knot with tension as I turn away. I haven't been able to see her for some time, so there is no point in standing here any longer. Rolling my shoulders to relax the muscles, I head through my morning rounds. Padraig's hammer clanging echoes off stone, conversations mix, and life continues for the Tribe.

"Put that over here please," Olivia says, motioning Delilah and Bailey to set the crate they carry between them down.

"What is this?" I ask.

"Oh, hi," Olivia says, turning, her swollen belly sticking out between us.

It brings a smile to my face. Soon we will have a child among us. An image flashes through my mind of Rosalind, dressed in white, with her own belly swelling with our child. Ridiculous, how could we ever make that work? Our dedication is to our people, both of us, and neither group is accepting of the other.

"Hello," I say, motioning my staff at the crate.

"It's cloth," Bailey says.

"Cloth?" I ask.

"Yes, from the wreckage, we thought we could use it to make some other things," she says.

"We're thinking clothes," Olivia adds. "Ours are getting... thin."

She looks down at herself, and I take in the noticeable tears and holes in her outfit.

"Why not use skins?" I ask.

"Ugh," Delilah says, placing a hand on her hip. "Seriously? You have to ask? They're stiff for one; they're hard to move in; they have a weird odor; and can we just say no on style?"

I don't understand the way she is using some of the words, but her aura of righteous indignation is enough for me to gather her intent and to make it clear I don't want to insert myself into their project.

"Well, best of luck," I say, moving away to extricate myself from the situation.

"Thanks," Olivia says.

My rounds this morning go quickly. The Tribe members are all industrious in their own right. My inspections are for morale more than any other purpose. The gardens are growing nicely, the wall is coming along, and soon we will have a gate that Padraig is forging right now. A small protection perhaps, but better than none at all. My chest aches, an empty throbbing with each beat of my heart. The knots in my shoulders grow tighter no matter how often I roll my shoulders to ease the tension. Melancholy settles over me like a heavy cloth, weighing me down in its grip.

Climbing the ramp towards my father's chamber. I turn and look out over the Tribe's lands. Below, everyone is busy, working, talking, and they are happy. They squabble, they talk, life is happening. Everything is fine, good even, but it does nothing to touch the empty ache inside. Sighing, I turn and continue.

A dark, oiled skin covers the entrance. I pull it aside and slide into the cool dark. After walking down the short tunnel, I emerge into the circular chamber that my father has taken for his own. Falkosh, an elder in his own right, sits with my father. They both look up at my entrance.

"Welcome, my son," Kalessin says.

"Father," I greet him, grabbing a stool and pulling it over to sit in front of them.

"Hello, Visidion," Falkosh greets me. "Are the suns warming you today?"

"Yes, and may they continue to warm you," I respond, formal.

Falkosh more than any other has held on to things from before the devastation. My father stares at me for a long moment then turns to his friend.

"Thank you for your visit, Falkosh, perhaps we can enjoy supper together?" father says.

"Hmm? Oh, yes, I'd be honored," Falkosh says, taking the hint and rising to his feet.

Falkosh's chest is covered with old, puckered scars, scales torn from sections of his stomach and arms that was replaced by scar tissue. He makes his slow, shuffling way out. Once Falkosh was an amazing warrior, but it took its toll on his body. Only after he is gone do I speak.

"How are you, father?" I ask.

"Well, son, well, but the weight is heavy on you today," he observes.

"It's fine," I say.

He grips my shoulder and nods.

"I have had a vision," he says.

"Yes?"

"Darkness for you, a white light at your side. Trials. Blood and sand," he says. "Long, hard, arduous, trial after trial, you must persevere. Be strong, my son, your strength and your will are going to be challenged. The hope of our people rests on your shoulders."

"How is this different than what we've already come through?" I retort, red anger rising like a sandstorm cutting through me. "Since the devastation it's been nothing but a trial. One challenge after another. Tell me father, what is there new in your vision?"

He smiles, shaking his head.

"I tell you what I can," he says. "What I see is not clear, you know this. It must be interpreted, and often only in hindsight do we see the truth."

"You saw the devastation coming," I snap. "Why can you not see this more clearly?"

"I was lucky. I interpreted what I saw correctly," he answers. "That was not easier than this."

"Bah," I say, slashing my hand across the space between us. "I have not time for mysteries."

"A circle, surrounded by spectators, a monster roaring, crowds cheering, and a blue sky," he says.

"This is what you see?" I ask.

"Yes," he says.

"A blue sky? Where would such a thing exist?"

"I do not know," he says.

Shaking my head, my jaw clenched tight, I consider his words.

"It will be what it will be," I hiss, turning away.

"Yes, it will," he says, resignation in his voice.

Tingles run across my scales as my stomach churns, boiling in anger. Clenching my fist, gritting my teeth, I push down the bijass rising to engulf my thoughts.

I am myself, repeating the mantra until the red rage recedes.

Control of myself returns, the tension drains from my shoulders, and I take a deep breath.

"Do you see anything more?" I ask.

He sighs heavily, giving me all the answer before he speaks.

"No," he says.

"Well," I say. "Then I will face what comes."

My chest aches, an empty void needing to be filled. The stone under my hand is cool and hard, but my fingers long to touch the softness of flesh. Tingling runs up my arm, striking deep into my hearts, making them beat faster. Kalessin places a hand on my shoulder and I start. It's an unexpected gesture, an unusual display for my father. He grips tight, then lets go before turning and shuffling away.

Pulling the skins aside I step out onto the ledge. The warmth of the double red suns hits my scales. Staring out at the horizon across rolling red and white dunes of shifting sand, my eyes find the hazy edge of the world. Out there, coming fast, is our future. Everything is different now. The Tribe had resigned itself to our inevitable demise. Strangely, it had become comfortable, an accepted reality that our race had reached its end.

The humans changed everything.

I didn't know how much until we met the City. When we rescued the humans, it was an act of kindness, nothing more.

While some had an attraction, the pull to make a human their treasure, it wasn't for breeding. The human females are attractive. Resigning yourself to the end of your race doesn't override the biological drive to claim a treasure and hold it dear.

I never would have considered a merging of our races.

Rosalind sees a future as clearly or even more so then Kalessin does. It drives her, inspires her, and I feel it when I'm with her. Tickling along the edges of my mind, a rising feeling that swells in my chest and core. Hope. She brings hope. The babies...

Three shapes approaching the gates jerk me from my thoughts. The hunters are returning, dragging a carcass along behind them on the travois designed for the purpose. Good. Our meat supplies are running low, but it means more work to be overseen. Work is good, good for morale, good for keeping people focused. The only question is who to pull away from the jobs they are doing to butcher the meat.

"I'm going to need to go to an oasis," Ormarr the Tribe Healer says as I pass him on my way to meet Ragnar.

"How soon?" I ask, stopping to address his needs.

"Ten suns, maybe twelve," he says.

"I'll talk to Ragnar," I say, gripping his arm before I continue to meet Ragnar.

Olivia is at his side by the time I arrive. Bashir and Melchior pull the travois away, hauling the meat into the cavern.

"Welcome home," I say. "Good hunt?"

"Yes," he says, one arm around Olivia, holding her close to his side.

Olivia eyes shine with joy. The swell of her belly pushing out into the world. The cradle of our future.

"Go ahead," she says, when I meet her eyes.

She's used to it. All of us have the same urge. Smiling, I

step forward and place my hands on either side of her belly. The life growing inside of her is warm, shifting under my touch. It kicks my hand as if telling me to leave it alone. My laughter is joined by hers.

"I think you're annoying him," she says through her giggles.

"So it would seem," I agree.

"We need to talk," Ragnar says, serious.

When I meet his gaze, his eyes shift, taking a quick glance around. It's clear he doesn't want to talk where others can overhear our conversation. I motion with one hand leading the way to my home. Inside I offer seats to him and Olivia, but only she takes one. Ragnar goes back to the skins over the entrance, looking out, clearly making sure no one is close enough to eavesdrop.

"What is it Ragnar?" I ask.

"We found something," he says. "The Zzlo have a station. We know where they took the rest of the humans."

"We have to save them!" Olivia cries out, jumping to her feet and knocking the stool over.

"It is not so simple," Ragnar says, cupping his wife's face in his hand.

He places a hand on her stomach, kisses her forehead.

"Explain," I say.

Ragnar sets the stool back up and settles Olivia back on it before he continues.

"It's not just a base, it's a lift station," he says.

My breath is taken away, knocked out by the news. Pains in my chest as my hearts pound harder. Gasping for air, I take a seat myself.

"They can't be," I say, unable to say the rest of my thought.

"They have," he says.

"What? What does that mean?" Olivia asks, hysteria in her voice.

"They're taking those they capture off-world," I say.

"Off-world? They... can't... we're stuck..."

Emotions play across her face, and moisture drops from her eyes in that strange display the humans have. Wasteful yet strangely heart wrenching to see.

"This is what the Zzlo do," Ragnar says. "They're slavers. There is no one here to sell to, so they will take those they capture and sell them."

"But what about your brother? What about Ryuth? They didn't take him away," she says.

Rage rises in Ragnar's eyes but he pushes it down fast. Ryuth was captured by the Zzlo and turned into a berserker. They used him to lead the charge on our home. Ragnar has been working to undo what they've done to him, but it's a long, hard, and slow path.

"A distraction," I say, stepping in for Ragnar to give him time. "They used him for their own purposes."

"We have to save them!" she says, her voice cracking.

A void opens beneath me, threatening to swallow me whole. Could we?

"It's not possible," Ragnar says, a slashing motion of his hand cutting through the air. He looks at me for confirmation, but I shake my head. "You can't be..."

He doesn't finish the sentence.

I am. It won't be easy, but with help, maybe we can.

5

ROSALIND

*T*he dome sparkles, calling us home.

"They've done amazing," Calista says to Jolie. "I can't believe they were able to transplant so easily. I never would have thought it would take that well."

"I know, right?" Jolie agrees. "We should have thought of that instead of trying to adjust our own seeds to this environment."

The two of them haven't stopped talking about the Tribe's garden since we left. Ladon and Sverre are out to either side, ostensibly scouting. I can't help but wonder if they aren't escaping their wives' incessant chatter about plants. A smile forms on my face. Different species, millions of miles from Earth, but the problems of couples remain the same. Even with the Zmaj's primal claiming of their mates, males still go out hunting to escape from their wives.

It's been a good trip. We're closer to actual trade than we were, but more important, I know I have an ally in Visidion. My core tightens thinking of him. The rippling of his abs when he stands or sits, attractive, sure, but what holds my attention is his eyes. So deep green, but more—so piercing with a sharp intellect behind them. Visidion, I believe, could share in my vision of the future. Certainty fills me that together we could forge that future.

It's only a matter of walking the steps to get us to that point. Along with keeping Gershom at bay long enough. My stomach sinks thinking of him. He's moving faster than I expected, and that's a problem. I need a little longer. Long enough for the seeds I've planted to come to fruition. Then it will be past the point he can change the overall outcome. I will have won in spite of his self-centered efforts of personal aggrandizement.

A little longer. It's all I ask.

Reaching the dome, I punch in the code, letting the others go through the airlock first. Sverre and I are the last, waiting to enter.

"They're not wrong," Sverre says, while we wait.

"What do you mean?" I ask.

"We should deal with Gershom. He's growing bolder. We may not have time."

Sighing, I nod.

"I know," I say.

"Then why do you withhold us from acting? Please Rosalind, lift the restraints. Let us deal with him."

"And then what?" I ask.

"What do you mean? He'll be dealt with, it will be over."

"Would it?"

"Of course it would, how could it not?"

"Because he has followers. Those who really believe the crap he pays lip service to. Gershom uses the rhetoric but he doesn't believe it. What if the leader of the Humans First was a true believer? What then?"

"We deal with the new leader the same," he says.

"Sure, let's do that. While we're at it how about we deal

MIRANDA MARTIN

with about sixty percent of the surviving human race in the same way."

"It wouldn't be-"

"Yes it would!" I exclaim, cutting him off. "Sverre, you're smart, but you have to think this through. If we were to cull Gershom, in any manner, then he becomes a martyr. They'll rally around him. We'd lose control."

"We're already losing control!" he says, voice rising, hands balling into fists as his wings rustle.

"No, we're not. Barely, but we're not."

"How do you think that?"

"Because, Sverre, I have to. I'm looking at the future of both our races. We have to let this play out. We can't afford to lose that many people out of the pool of survivors. It reduces our odds of long-term survival by too much."

Sverre hisses and turns, staring out over the empty desert we just crossed. He turns his head and spits before turning back to me.

"Fine," he concedes. "But I don't like it. We both will regret this before it's over."

"Let's hope not," I say, entering the airlock with him.

The moment we enter I'm ready to eat my words.

"Rosalind!" Gershom says, his voice booming and full of himself.

"Gershom," I greet him, looking at the men with him.

All of them are armed with guns we confiscated from the pirates. Apparently he's no longer hiding where they had disappeared to. Bold, too bold. The others who traveled with me, including all the Zmaj stand in a tight group. Ladon stands at the front, his hands balled into tight fists, his tail up straight.

"I'm so glad you're back. How was your trip?"

"Fruitful," I say. "I'll make a full report to the Council."

"Oh, that, yes," he says, shaking his head and smiling from

ear to ear, sunlight glinting off his greased-back hair. "Well, you see, there's been a decision made while you were away."

"Oh?" I ask, arching an eyebrow.

"Yes," he grins. "There's to be an election. Something I'm sure you will agree is long overdue. We are, after all, a democracy."

"Gershom, this has been discussed already. It was agreed we would hold elections once we stabilized our position here on Tajss. Survival is more important than elections right now."

"We thought you might say that," Gershom says, shaking his head, shoulders slumping as if sad. "Didn't we discuss that?"

"Yes we did," several of the men with him respond, bringing their weapons up to mid-chest.

"Rosalind, that's a tired excuse. We're surviving just fine, here. In fact, the only threat we see is the one the Zmaj represent. So many people have come to me and expressed their concerns, their fears, that I can no longer ignore them. I, after all, have a duty as a member of the Council to listen to our people."

"You don't listen, you manipulate," I say through gritted teeth.

"Rosalind!" he exclaims, a hand flying to his chest as if wounded. "I can't believe you'd accuse me of that. I'm only looking out for our people."

"Raarrr!" Ladon roars, grabbing the man nearest to him and lifting him bodily into the air.

Guns rattle as the men wielding them bring them to their shoulders, all of them aiming at Ladon.

"Ladon!" I yell.

Calista jumps to his side, a hand on his face. He turns to look at her, the man still over his head, but I see the rage flowing out of him at her touch.

"Ladon, please," Calista says.

Illadon on her hip gurgles at his father. Ladon sets the man roughly down on the ground and steps back.

"That's better," Gershom says. "No one wants anything untoward. It's an election, a democracy. All we're saying is let the people have a say in the direction of their future."

Possibilities whirl through my thoughts, none of them ending well. The only option that has any viability is to play along. Gershom's supporters openly sporting arms from the pirates tilts the odds in their favor. The strength of the Zmaj had always weighed in my favor since his supporters outnumber my own. That advantage is gone and he knows it.

"When is the election?" I ask, conceding to him.

"Oh, did I forget to mention that? It's tomorrow," he grins, then turns and walks away, his men falling in behind him in a sloppy formation.

Bile rises in my throat.

———

STARING AT MYSELF IN THE MIRROR, I RESIGN MYSELF TO THE day. Gershom has planned it perfectly. I should have seen it coming, but hindsight is for the weak.

My hand trembles so I cover it with my other hand to stop it. Staring at my two hands, one covering the other, memories come unbidden. The first time my hand trembled I had dismissed it. Only when it happened so many times more that I could no longer dismiss it did I go to a doctor. I think even then I didn't want to know what they would say.

After they told me, I threw myself into work even more than before. That was on the ship, before the crash and all of this.

Someone knocks on my door and I jerk around knocking

one of my only small glasses off the counter to shatter on the floor.

"Damn it," I curse, bending to pick up the broken shards.

"Rosalind?" Sarah asks, entering at the sound of the breaking glass.

"It's fine," I say, not looking up.

She kneels down without a word and helps with the cleanup. One of the things I appreciate most about Sarah is that she knows when to keep her mouth shut. Sometimes silence is truly golden.

Picking up the last shard and adding it to the small pile in my other hand, I rise, then go to the small basket I use for waste. The shards catch sunlight and sparkle as they fall. Beautiful, tinkling shards dropping into oblivion. Suppressing a snort at the allegory of it, I face Sarah.

"Good morning," I say, straightening and squaring my shoulders.

"Morning, you okay?" she asks.

"Fine, yes," I say. "Anything new to report?"

She grimaces. "The voting is underway."

"Good," I say and give her a reassuring smile.

"You know... it's not looking good, right?"

"It's often darkest before the dawn Sarah," I say.

"And before a storm, a really big shit storm," she says, despondently.

"Sarah, no matter what happens, it will work out," I say, gripping both her shoulders.

"You're going to lose, Rosalind," she says, a tear making its way down her cheek.

I wipe the tear away then pull her into an embrace. She stiffens at my unusual display of affection then relaxes into my embrace.

"I know," I say.

"Then how can you let this go through?" she asks, pulling back.

"Because it is what they need," I say. "He's right. We are a democracy. Let them see for themselves what will be. They will choose and I will follow their wishes. My part in this play is easy. Yours will be the hardest."

"Mine?" she asks, eyes widening.

"Yes," I say. "He'll have to get rid of me if he wins."

"When," she inserts but I ignore her.

"Gershom is a snake, and he won't be able to stand the threat of my presence. Also, for him to appease his followers he will have to get rid of the Zmaj. He won't be bold enough for violence; his grip on the city isn't strong enough for that. This means he'll exile all of us."

"Oh Rosalind, he can't! I'll go with you," she says, tears flowing faster.

"No, you won't," I say, my voice firm.

"But—"

"No. No buts. You will stay here, in the City."

She shakes her head, tears streaming, swallowing hard then she pulls herself together. I see it in her eyes as she calls on the inner reserve of strength she has. She wipes her tears, shudders, then meets my eyes and nods.

"Of course," she says. "You'll need me."

"They will need you," I say. "But yes, I will too."

Squaring her shoulders, she accepts her role in what is to come.

"Now we have work to do. Go to Calista, Jolie, and Amara. Tell them I want them to pack for a journey. Have them get Shidan to take supplies outside the City. We might not have much time when things happen. We need to be prepared."

Sarah takes mental notes of all my orders, then rushes out of my apartment to set my plans in motion. I walk over to the windows and stare out across the city. I didn't have the time I wanted, but maybe I can make things work out anyway. I hope. It has to. If this doesn't work then the future of two races is over.

"THE VOTES HAVE BEEN COUNTED," BILL SAYS, STANDING ON the edge of the central fountain.

Bill is an honest, good man. I trust him to count the votes correctly. Election fraud of that nature isn't going to be the problem. The problem is not nearly as clear-cut as that.

Bill doesn't have to announce the results. The crowd around the fountain includes every citizen of the City. The divide among us is clear in where they stand. On one side is Gershom, his supporters and those who just want things to change. Gershom has enticed them to his team by buying them. He controls the water, has stolen supplies, anything he can do to make sure they think he's the man with a plan. Then there are those who support me. The numbers are not in my favor.

"Gershom wins by a landslide," Bill says, the crowd exploding into cheers and catcalls.

Gershom steps out of his supporters, armed men coming along behind him. The armed men line up, facing my group. Gershom makes his way to the fountain and I follow behind him. He climbs up next to Bill on the edge of the fountain, looking out at the crowds with his shit-eating grin.

"Thank you, citizens," he says. "I am honored and humbled by the trust you place in me."

Cheers and chants of his name. He basks in it, drinking in his moment. I stand watching, keeping my shoulders square, and my eyes locked on him.

"Congratulations, Gershom," I say, holding my hand out to him.

"Thank you, Lady General Rosalind," he says. Taking my hand, he shakes then lets go. "Now, for my first order of business I want to make good on my campaign promise!"

The crowd cheers even louder. My shoulders knot tight and my stomach clenches. This is it.

"This city belongs to Humans. We have to put our survival and the survival of our race first. So, all Zmaj are hereby banished. You have an hour to clear out of our city."

Ladon hisses and leaps. I drop, extending my left leg out to the side and touching the ground with the palm of my right hand to balance myself. Ladon passes over my head gliding towards Gershom.

Shots fire, buzzing through the air, the electrodes crackling to life.

"NO!" Calista's scream echoes as the crowd comes to life on both sides.

The electric bolts hit Ladon in mid-air, flipping him over. He lands hard on his back. Sverre and Shidan hiss, rushing forward to the fallen Zmaj. The humans who consider themselves on my side, woefully outnumbered, rush forward. The armed Gershom supporters bring their weapons to shoulder. Shots are fired before I can react, taking down several people.

Ladon leaps to his feet, ripping the tags out of his chest, spreading his arms wide and roaring in rage. The other two Zmaj at his side, all of them with wings spread, tails upright, arms wide ready to inflict damage.

Possibilities race through my mind. If I let this play out we have small odds of a 'win' but it will cost us dearly. Lives will be lost on both sides. Lives we can't afford to lose. The future depends on all of us. Our numbers are almost too few to be viable now. I can't let this happen. Decision made, I jump up from my crouch and land on the edge of the fountain next to Bill.

"STOP!" I yell, years of practice allowing me to pitch my voice to cut through the chaos.

The crowd doesn't have the discipline of a military, though. They clash, fighting hand to hand, too close for the weapons to come to bear. My stomach churns as cold chills race through my limbs. Screams, cries of pain and anger mix as battle erupts. Bloody faces distorting in rage, the crowd degenerating into a mob—I have to stop this somehow.

Scanning the crowd, I try to find a solution. The three Zmaj are at the front of the joined battle. Lifting humans bodily overhead and throwing them, they clear an area around the three of them by knocking the crowd back with their own members. A sound strategy for a physical fight but it doesn't allow for the guns that are in play. Three shooters hit Ladon who's at the front. His body is wracked violently by the shock tags hitting him. Shidan makes the mistake of trying to help, grabbing Ladon's arm. It sends the voltage through him too. The two of them are stuck together writhing under the electricity coursing through.

"SVERRE!" I yell, pulling his attention to me.

Rage dances across his face but his eyes focus on me. He's in control, I think. I hope. Motioning with both hands, I urge him to join me on the fountain while looking for my other target. There, surrounded by a circle of armored guards each carrying a shield and staff, I spot Gershom. He's grinning. Rage roars through me, I want to break him, wipe that sadistic grin off his face. He not only did this, he expected this result. The guards surrounding him prove it, I suspected this but to see it in fact... nausea grips me in a hard wave.

"GERSHOM!" I pull his attention away from the chaos he's so clearly enjoying.

He schools his face, fixing a look of shock and regret.

Ignoring the lie I motion him to come to me. He says something I can't hear to the guard in front of him and as one, well trained, they move to the fountain, cutting their way through the crowd with indiscriminate use of shields and staff. They don't care who they strike down as they cut through.

"Rosalind, we have to stop this!" Gershom says, his voice dripping with false concern.

Gritting my teeth to control my tongue I nod. Sverre makes the fountain, blood dripping from the side of his mouth, his left eye swelling shut.

"Climb up, both of you, I need both of you," I order and they comply.

Gershom's guards form a wall in front of the three of us holding the surging crowd at bay.

"The three of us, yell stop, count of three," I command, yelling to be heard. "Watch my fingers."

The two men nod. I hold up a hand with three fingers and count down.

"STOP!" we scream in unison.

It's just enough. Our three voices cut through the noise and pull people out of the reactive mob mentality. A few more punches are thrown as the insanity winds itself down.

"Citizens please there is no-" Gershom stops.

"Enough," I cut him off, slashing my hand through the air. "A vote has been held, the people have spoken."

Sarah's eyes stare at me out of the crowd. My throat goes dry, tears well in her eyes, swallowing hard I finish my thought.

"The Zmaj and I will be leaving the City. Those who do not wish to follow Gershom are welcome to join me."

Gershom inhales sharply. Good, I still have a few surprises up my sleeve, you stinking snake.

"Lady General," he says, but turning to him I glare and he stops.

"The survival of both our races is important. We cannot devolve into civil war. That is a sure path to both our destructions. I will leave, for now, taking those who wish to go. Those who wish to come along have six hours, then meet me at the airlock."

Cries of "no!" mix with the cheers of those who think they've won. Gershom struggles to keep the grin off his face. He extends his hand and I stare at it.

"This is very noble of you, Lady General Rosalind," he says, the hand hanging in the air between us.

"If doing the right thing is noble, then so be it," I say. "This isn't over. And I won't let it be solved with chaos and violence."

"Admirable," he says.

I turn my back on him and his extended hand.

"Rosalind," Sverre says. "What have you done?"

"The only thing we can, Sverre. You and Shidan get Ladon and get him out of here before he comes to. I want him out of the city before he wakes. He'll need time to understand, and we need him far enough away so his rage won't cause more problems."

Sverre grimaces, then nods.

It's done. Now to play out the game and hope I'm right.

6

VISIDION

"*I*f we build the wall just a bit more we should be able to fend off any attacks," I say.

"Yes, but if the Zzlo come, it won't be enough," Drosdan grunts, crossing his arms across his massive chest.

"True," I say. "We will need to continue constructing further defenses, but it is a start."

Drosdan shrugs then nods agreement.

The work continues, but he's right. It's not enough. If the Zzlo find us, we are in trouble. Knowing that they have a station set up and are sending slaves off world... bile rises in my throat. Somehow I had thought that their presence was less established. That they were remnants looking for quick easy prey and that they would move on. How wrong I was.

"We should destroy them," Drosdan says. "Go on the attack instead of waiting for them to find us, again."

He looks pointedly at me when he says again. Drosdan isn't subtle. He's not just big, he's blunt.

"We don't have the force," I say. "They are established. Ragnar scouted them and we would lose."

"We'll lose waiting here," Drosdan replies with a huff.

Placing a hand on his bicep, I shake my head.

"Time, Drosdan. We will win when the time is right. First let's make sure our people are safe. We have the females to care for," I smile.

Drosdan nods, his gaze shifting to the garden where several of the human females are working. Which one is his treasure?

"Incoming!" Samil, the youngest surviving Zmaj in the Tribe cries out.

Drosdan and I turn as one and run for the wall. Samil is at the gate opening pointing out at the horizon. After I close my outer eyelids to adjust for the distance and brightness of the suns, dim forms become clear. It's not Zzlo, there are Zmaj out there with humans.

"What is this?" Drosdan asks.

"I do not know," I say, a sick foreboding coming over me.

What twist has the future thrown at us now? They must be from the City, but they only left a few days ago. What could drive them to return so soon? I grasp for possibilities but nothing good comes to mind. Kalessin's prophecy drifts through my thoughts, but I don't see how it fits with this. Ragnar walks up with Melchior and Bashir in tow.

"What's happening?" he asks.

"The City is returning," I answer.

"Already?" he asks, frowning.

"Yes," I say.

"Let's go," he says to the other two hunters, breaking into a ground-eating run.

They fall in with him, their easy gait belying the speed at which they move across the red sand of Tajss.

"What now?" Drosdan asks.

"We should prepare for guests," I say.

"We don't have room for them—look how many of them there are! More than before!"

"I see that," I say, meeting his glare.

Drosdan puffs his chest out and leans in. Patient, I wait for him to have his moment without backing down. When he can't intimidate me, his chest deflates and his shoulders slump.

"They're not staying with me," he grouses, turning and walking away.

Word spreads quickly of the return of those from Ladon's city. Several tribesmen come to me and complain. Our resources are thin, but right now I don't know why they're coming back so soon. I reassure those who come while I wait. Standing by the gate, I watch the distant figures come slowly closer.

"Samil, go and get water," I order.

The small Zmaj runs off and soon returns with a jug full of water. Possibilities race through my mind as to why they are returning. Pacing back and forth in front of the opening in the wall becomes tiresome, so I pause and kneel, running my hands through the loose sand. I let it sift through my fingers until only a few pebbles remain. Rolling them against each other in my palm, I stand and look to see how close they are now.

Time crawls by as I wait. The distant figures come closer, but as they do, I see there are more than I expected. It's a larger group than was with Rosalind when she was here last. As they come closer, I see her at the head of the column. Her white outfit stands out sharply against the red sand. They crest a dune and I see her stop, shielding her eyes as she looks towards me.

The pounding in my chest aches as my hearts go into double time. Is she returning for me? Has she decided to resign her position and embrace the Tribe?

The idea is ludicrous. I know her too well to allow myself such a belief, but no matter how I try to suppress the idea, it lingers, dancing at the edge of my thoughts. It would be nice. Nice, I snort. She is the one my being calls to. I want to treasure her, but I cannot allow myself to have such a luxury. My duty to my people overrides that biological imperative. It doesn't matter that she triggers such feelings. I am myself. I cannot allow myself to give in to my desires.

"Visidion?" Samil cuts into my thoughts, breaking me out of their circling chain.

"Yes?" I ask, facing him.

His eyes shift around, not meeting mine. He swallows hard, kicks at the sand, then he meets my gaze at last.

"What's it like? How do you… know?"

"Know?" I ask, trying to ascertain what he is asking me.

His eyes break away, he rolls his shoulders, kicks the sand then clears his throat. Suddenly it hits me what he's asking. I forget how young he is, too young to have been mentored by his parents. He was a child when the devastation happened, and while now a man, in our male-only society that had no hope of a future… No one wanted to discuss things that could never be.

"Yeah…" he says, still looking anywhere but me.

Placing a hand on his shoulder, I grip tight, reassuring.

"You feel it," I say. "An emptiness in your chest when she's not there. A tightening in your core when you see her. An urge—to protect, to treasure, to never be separated. When you see her, your hearts speed up, your blood pressure rises, and you know, deep inside, that you will do anything for her."

"Oh," he nods, pursing his lips.

"Have you felt that?" I ask.

He shrugs, staring off across the empty sands at the approaching people of the City. I wait for him to answer but he doesn't. Instead of pushing him, I let him have his privacy and pat him on the back.

"We're going to need more water," I say,

"Sure," he says, setting down the one pitcher he brought and leaving to get more.

He's small and a bit weak. He's used to being abused by those around him, but even he deserves someone to love. I hope he does find his one. We need him to if we're going to survive beyond this generation. The empty ache in my chest recurs as I realize how much Rosalind has influenced my thoughts. I know that their coming back early is not a good thing, but I can't help but be at least a bit glad they're here. I miss her. They come closer as I watch with anticipation building, tingling, running along my scales.

"What are we going to do with them?" Ormarr asks, coming up beside me.

Ormarr is our resident healer. Once he was a doctor, skilled in the use of machines and able to save lives in almost any situation. Now he's a healer, medicine becoming more of an art than a science once technology was taken away.

"First I'll find why they've returned," I say.

"Send them packing," Padraig says, joining us.

Padraig is covered in soot from his work at the forge. His deep voice echoes off the stone wall. Arawn, the leather worker and pain in Padraig's tail, is beside him.

"Padraig the friendly, that's what we call you," Arawn teases.

"Humph," Padraig says, crossing his arms. "You know I'm not the only one feeling that way."

"So what?" Arawn asks. "We can't turn them away without offering our help."

"Sure we can, it's easy, just say 'bye' and turn them away. See how easy it was?" Padraig argues.

"Together we are stronger," Arawn answers.

Padraig's mouth snaps shut, unable or unwilling to argue with the Edicts.

"He's right," I say, looking at both of them and the growing crowd of others coming to see what's going on. "When have we turned away those in need? We are more than that. We are better. Protect the weak. Work together. The strong have responsibilities. We are the strong, so we must enable them to no longer be weak."

"They're not staying with me," someone in the crowd says, but I miss who.

"We don't have room," Errol says.

Errol is our mason, crafter of stone. It is through the magic of his hands that the small caves of the cliff have become homes. He, more than any other, knows the capacity of our homes.

"We are jumping ahead of ourselves," I say. "Go about your day, I will deal with this."

"What if we—" Padraig starts.

I cut him off with an icy glare. The bijass throbs behind my eyes, ready to pounce and grab control. Wrestling it into submission, I redirect its rage and use it. Stepping forward, squaring my shoulders, I enter his personal space. My wings slightly open and my tail rises in challenge, willing him to submit.

It works. Padraig shrinks before me, shrugging his shoulders.

"Fine," he agrees bitterness in his voice.

The crowd mutters, but no one is willing to challenge me for leadership. As they part and go their ways, Samil is left standing, holding another jar of water. His eyes are cast down, staring at the ground.

"Come Samil, you may join me in welcoming our guests," I say.

His smile splits his face, and he bounces over to me.

"Thank you!" he exclaims.

No answer is necessary. I'm doing him no kindness and

he knows it, for he may well pay for it later. The others will want to re-establish their dominance in our society. Still, he is grateful. No matter how far we've come, we still fight our primal need to dominate.

It's not long before the approaching group from the city is at the wall. Rosalind walks at the lead. Ladon walks beside Calista with their child on her hip right behind her, followed by Sverre, Jolie, and Rverre. Another Zmaj and a female I don't know, with a child, walk behind them.

My chest swells seeing the children. I can't look at them and not feel hope. Rosalind marches right up to me with at least thirty people behind her, fanning out in a group. She meets my gaze, but her jaw is tight and her face grim.

"What happened?" I ask without preamble.

"I ran out of time," she says, shaking her head. "I'm sorry to do this, but we need shelter."

Ladon glares over Rosalind's shoulder, anger coming off him in waves. Stepping past her, I walk up to him. As I approach he steps away from Calista and their child. His tail is down, his arms at his side, but still he meets my gaze in defiance.

"Ladon," I say his name.

The group around him holds their breath, waiting to see what will happen. Everyone knows of Ladon's temper, it seems. There are scorch marks on the scales of his chest. He's been shot by Zzloo weapons. His chest rises and falls with his rapid breathing, hands clenching into fists.

"Yes," he says.

"You will be our guest," I say. "Do you understand?"

His hard gaze bores into me, wanting to issue his defiance, but after a moment, he lowers his eyes. He looks at Calista and Illadon, and I see his shoulders slump. The weight of the situation is crushing. Having lost my home recently, I sympathize with him, but I cannot and will not allow that to make me weak. At last he nods his head.

"Of course," he says.

I clasp him by his shoulder before I turn back to Rosalind.

"The City is welcome here. Come, partake of water," I say, motioning to Samil who rushes forward and offers the pitcher.

"Thank you," Rosalind says, her face relaxing, but I see the pain in her eyes.

"Of course, we have much to discuss, but first let's get your people settled."

7

ROSALIND

"$\mathcal{E}$veryone has a place, for now," Visidion says, passing through the tanned leather door that blocks his home from the outside world.

"Good. Thank you," I say, not rising from the small table I'm sitting at.

An empty ache gnaws at me from my core. I should have been ready. I didn't think Gershom could move so fast.

Visidion sits down across the small table, his eyes boring into me, reading everything that I hide away from the world —or at least making me feel like he is. I can't let him see my pain. No one can see it.

My hand resting on the table trembles—damn it! The disease is still attacking, merciless in its assault. Pulling the hand off the table, I place it in my lap to hide it. A weakness I won't share with anyone.

"Well," Visidion says at last, giving no indication if he saw the tremble.

"Yes, well," I agree, sighing.

"I did warn you," he says.

The hairs on back of my neck rise as I grit my teeth. That's not what I want to hear right now.

"Yes, yes you did," I snap. "Congratulations."

"You kept a snake in your midst!" he snaps back.

"You don't see the bigger picture!" I yell.

"What does the bigger picture matter if you lose it all to what's happening today?" he asks, his fists balling on the table as he leans in.

"I'm looking at our long-term survival."

"Survival of what? A xenophobic culture that would see my entire race destroyed?"

"That's not what it's about!"

"Oh? Isn't it? I've heard the stories, and what's more, I've seen the results of Gershom's actions. He inspires hate in people. Plays on their fears. You were stupid to let him remain."

"Stupid?" I growl, rising to my feet and leaning over the table, fists resting on it.

"No, that's not what I mean—"

"Isn't it?" I cut him off. "You said the word."

We're close now, inches apart. Anger pounds through my veins but the scent of him, exotic with a hint of cocoa, fills my nostrils. Even through my anger it's enticing.

"Rosalind, I'm sorry," he says, apologizing without retreating. "That is not what I mean."

"Then explain to me," I say. "What do you mean?"

"You could have been hurt," he says. "Or worse."

The words fall between us as if weighted by a thousand pounds. Almost I can hear them crash into the silence that falls in their wake. His swirling green eyes piercing into my soul tell the truth. I see his fear, as clear as if it was a display of neon lights flashing in the night. My throat is dry, too dry to answer him. My lips tremble with anticipation and growing desire.

"You care," I state.

He remains silent, staring. Pain in my chest from my heart beating too hard. He moves closer, slowly, judging my reaction, as slowly as if he moved through thick liquid. Warm breath breezes across my skin. A citrus scent combined with the cocoa. I'm moving closer, being pulled in by the gravity of him. My mouth is dry, almost there, our lips just start to touch.

"NO!!!!!"

We both fall back onto our stools as the sound of pain and anguish cuts through the moment, ripping us apart.

"What now?" he barks, rising to his feet and whirling. Visidion storms out the door.

I follow. Fool that I am, falling for this man. What time do I have for such concerns? Stupid, girlish dreams. I am Lady-General, and my sworn duty is to safeguard the future of mankind.

Or it was.

On the ship, before Tajss, before Gershom. Is it now? To whom do I owe such allegiance now?

Doubt swirls through my thoughts, assaulting the rock that is my certainty. Pushing it aside, I step past the flapping skin door-cover just behind Visidion. Below us is a gathering of Zmaj and humans, standing in a loose circle in the open central area of the Tribe's home. A smaller Zmaj, Samil, cowers before a much bigger one who is beating him mercilessly. Samil's pain- and anguish-laden screams are the sound we heard.

Visidion rushes down the ramp to the ground. I catch up with him in a few long strides so that we arrive at the circle together. No one is stopping the spectacle. How can they be so callous?

"Steal from me again, will you?" the larger Zmaj roars, kicking Samil.

I recognize the larger Zmaj now that I'm closer as Padraig, the blacksmith of the Tribe. Samil is curled into a ball, trying to protect himself as the kicks rain in. Visidion steps past the clearing, and I move to stand next to him, expecting him to stop this insanity, but instead he crosses his arms and watches.

"Stop this," I say.

Visidion looks over, arching an eye ridge.

"Why would I do that?" he asks.

"Because he's small and weak! He can't defend himself!"

"He should not have stolen," Visidion says.

"This isn't the way to handle a problem," I say.

Samil's pitiful cries cut through me, a chilling ache that strikes into my bones. Visidion shrugs. Rage roars to life in me. One thing I've never stood for is bullies.

"If you won't stop this, I will," I hiss.

"It is our way," he says, shrugging.

My pulse pounds in my head and then the calm comes. The calm that has never failed me.

"It is not mine," I say, nodding sharply.

Stepping forward, I touch Padraig's shoulder just as he raises his arm to strike Samil again. He stops, looking over his shoulder, his eyes wide in surprise at seeing me.

"Enough," I say.

"He hasn't learned his lesson yet," he hisses. "This does not concern you."

The crowd around us falls silent. A warm gentle breeze blows, tugging at the white cape on my suit. Padraig turns, putting his attention back on Samil. His muscles flex under my fingertips as he moves to strike again. Quickly I pull my hand back two inches, then with fingers pressed together tightly, I jab into the muscles where his shoulder connects with his torso. His arm drops to his side halfway through his swing, suddenly lifeless.

He roars his rage, the sound of his deep bass voice echoing back to us from the stone walls of the cliff. The crowd gasps as one, an intake of breath loud enough to be heard over his voice.

As he spins on his heel, I'm forced to leap back and away to avoid his tail sweeping my legs out. Landing in a crouch, one hand resting gently on the sand, a slow smile spreads across my face as I meet his gaze. The cold calm embraces me. I've missed this.

Padraig's wings spread out behind him, his tail rises to stand straight, but his right arm hangs limp at his side. He raises the left, pointing accusingly at me. He looks like he's trying to say something but it comes out as a hiss.

"I said it was enough," I say, straightening.

He swings, a clumsy maneuver I duck under, dancing to the side. Rising, I lean forward, enticing him on. He takes the bait, swinging wildly with his one good arm. I duck and slam my left knee into his solar plexus for good measure. He doubles over as the air rushes out of him. The crowd responds with a gasp. Padraig stumbles forward, his one good arm sweeping back and forth, trying to grab me while he struggles to inhale.

A human would be down from that attack. The Zmaj scales offer him protection that a man would not have. His tail swings around at the exact wrong moment, forcing me to leap to avoid it—but that puts me in reach of his swinging arm.

His arm knocks into me while I'm in the air. My left side goes numb from the blow as I tumble through the air to the right. I struggle to inhale as I fly, then hit the ground so hard I bounce. It's surprising how hard the sand is. It puffs up, getting into my eyes. Padraig roars as he charges towards me. His steps are so powerful that the sand vibrates against my face.

I let him get closer, not moving, wanting him to believe I'm wounded. When his legs come into view, I move. I leap to my feet. Padraig stumbles back in surprise. I don't allow him any breathing room, striking him fast on the sides of his neck with side-handed chops, then bringing my knee up between his legs. He raises his one good arm, trying to defend himself, but to no avail.

As my knee connects with his groin he doubles over, bringing his chin into range. I slam my knee into his face, and at the same time I bring my elbow down on the base of his neck. One crack follows another and Padraig drops to the ground. The crowd gasps as he falls. Standing over my opponent I turn a slow circle, meeting the gaze of every person, judging their reaction.

I've won respect from most of them, but the shock on their faces is obvious. No one expected a human female to best Padraig.

Kneeling next to Samil I inspect him for any obvious wounds, trying to ignore the pain in my side where Padraig connected. Samil looks up at me with pleading eyes. His weakness calls to me, demanding I protect him.

I rise, then hold a hand out to Samil and help him to his feet. Visidion comes forward shaking his head.

"This is not our way," he says, holding his hands out before him.

"Then maybe it's time we find a new way," I reply, looking past him at all the crowd surrounding us. "The old ways will not take us forward."

"The edicts!" Someone cries out.

I square my shoulders and face all of those gathered.

"The edicts are fine," I say. "But they don't embrace all of our reality. We need each other. Is that not one of your edicts? Do they not state we are stronger together? And yet this is how you show it?" I motion towards Samil on his knees next to me. "Taking advantage of those weaker than you?"

"Only the strong survive," Ragnar says, stepping from the crowd.

"Only the strong survive?" I ask meeting his glare. "To what end? Why do the strong survive?"

"To survive! What other point is there?" Ragnar asks.

"Exactly," I reply, turning away from Ragnar, I lock eyes with Visidion. "Survival for survival's sake is not living. What future did you have before we came? What purpose was there to your lives?"

I see the doubts forming in Visidion's eyes. Murmurs run through the crowd as they absorb my words.

"What are you saying, Rosalind?" Visidion asked.

A cold chill runs down my spine as I stare at Visidion. A turning point opens before me. In one of those rare moments of life, I know everything hangs on this moment. Doubt assails me, but I can't let it control me.

"I'm saying we have to find a new way," I say.

"The Edicts are our law," Visidion says, shaking his head. "They are immutable."

"Nothing is unchangeable," I say.

The crowd watches the two of us quietly. Slowly they seem to be shifting, dividing back into the two groups, those from the City and the Tribe. This is exactly what I hope to avoid. We can't be divided again. If I've learned nothing from Gershom, it's that. His divisive tactics have landed me here.

"Bold words, Rosalind," Visidion says. "Especially for someone who has been kicked out of her own city."

My guts tighten at his words, and a shudder runs down my spine. Anger rises, but like any emotion, I push it aside. It has no place in these negotiations. What I'm doing is too important.

Ladon steps out of the crowd and comes to stand beside

me. He crosses his arms over his chest glaring at Visidion. Padraig stirs on the ground beside us.

"Right," I say, nodding agreement. "We can all learn lessons, valuable ones. Nothing is set in stone."

Visidion looks angry, but nods as his wings rustle and his tail lashes. He purses his lips.

"Perhaps," he says, turning to face the crowd. "This is over. Go about your day, there is much to do."

8

VISIDION

*T*he crowd disperses slowly. Long lingering looks before they go make it obvious they would prefer to stay. Crossing my arms over my chest, I watch and wait. When at last we are standing alone, I return my attention to Rosalind. Ladon stands next to her, silent, a brooding presence.

"You push too far," I say.

"Do I?" Rosalind asks, arching an eyebrow. "I would argue I don't push far enough."

"The Edicts define who we are," I answer her.

"Yes, they do," she says. "They also limit you."

The red rage of the bijass rises, threatening to claim my thoughts. I won't let it. I am myself.

Ladon's soft hiss cuts through my internal struggle. Locking eyes with him, I shake my head. Frustration grows from the anger. I make a slashing motion with my hand, cutting off the conversation and turn away. I head towards my quarters. Let them do as they will.

As I make my way up the ramp, I hear Rosalind's soft footsteps behind me. Consumed with the effort of fighting off the rage, I don't acknowledge her. When I reach the leather covers that serves as my door, I step aside and hold it open for her. She meets my eyes before entering, and no matter how I try to harden my heart, it softens. I cannot remain angry at her.

I step in behind her, offer her a chair and refreshment, then take a seat across from her. She sips the small cup of water and sets it down on the table with soft clink.

"It is not easy for us to change," I say by way of opening.

"Nothing before us is going to be easy," Rosalind says, staring at the table between us.

One hand grips the cup, and the other rests on the table. I see the free hand tremble. She balls it into a fist and pulls away.

"I'm not saying you're wrong," I say, changing tactics. "But nothing is more important to me than the good of the tribe. I have sacrificed everything to bring these few survivors together."

"Then why can't you see we need everybody," she says, a pleading note in her voice as her eyes lock with mine.

"If we allow weakness to breed, if we allow those who would undermine us to remain, we don't come out stronger. You let Gershom continue, knowing full well he was working against you."

"Yes," she says shaking her head. "I underestimated him."

"I tried to warn you," I say, and my gut knots. The last thing in the world I want to say is some version of I told you so. Still, if only she had listened to me, none of this would've happened.

"So you did," she says. "It doesn't change the fact that I need him. More than that, I need his followers. That's neither here nor there. Why did you not stop Padraig from beating on Samil?"

"That is not our way," I reply, shrugging.

"How can it not be? Is not the second edict 'together we are stronger'?"

"And three is, survival of the group matters," I respond.

"I don't understand how that addresses my question," she says.

"For the group to survive we have to be strong," I explain. "The edicts work together, interchanging with each other, they are the guiding rules by which we judge everything."

"I get that," Rosalind says, her jaw tightening in frustration. "Do not speak to me as if I'm a child."

"Rosalind, I'm not," I say, my heart pounding in my chest. As if of its own free will my hand covers hers. The small, balled fist of her hand is engulfed in mine, but all I can feel is the softness of her skin. "I would never treat you that way."

"Good," she says. "Then answer my question. How can you stand by and let someone like Samil take a beating like that. Where's your heart? Where is your sense of honor?"

"Because we sacrifice everything for the group," I say, anger rising, threatening to take control. "Nothing else matters. No one person is greater than the need of the group."

"What good is a group that sacrifices those who needed support?" She asks, her voice soft, her eyes imploring mine. "He needed you. He needed someone stronger than him."

"That is the difference between us, Rosalind," I say. "Sometimes we have to sacrifice the weak to ensure the safety and the future of the strong."

"I cannot agree to that," Rosalind says, shaking her head. "We have to be better than that. The society we create has to be one I can be proud of."

My scales tingle listening to her words, she speaks softly, but her voice is filled with her passion. My hearts beat faster, my hand tightens on hers, as I search for words to say.

There's a noise outside my door, and the skin is pulled aside. Ladon storms in followed closely by Sverre. Ragnar trails in behind them. Rising, I turn to face the newcomers.

"What is the meaning of this," I say, aggression rising.

"Has he told you?" Ladon asks, looking past me at Rosalind.

Sverre stands next to him, calmer than Ladon, but I can see in the tint of his scales that he is angry as well. Ragnar stands to one side, keeping a few feet between him and the other two. I turn my attention to him.

What is the meaning of this, Ragnar?" I ask.

Rosalind rises to her feet and comes to stand next to me. She has her hands on her hips as she looks between Ladon and me.

"Told me what?" she asks.

"Zzlo," Ladon says, making a slashing motion with his hand across the air between us before pointing at me accusingly.

"What about the Zzlo?" Rosalind asks.

"Ragnar and the hunters found their base," Ladon says. "They know where they are."

"Is that true?" Rosalind asks.

The weight of everything falls on my shoulders again. I hold up my hands palms out towards her.

"The information was just brought to me," I say.

"Are there survivors there?" Rosalind asks. Her voice sounds strange, but she's speaking softly.

"I don't know," I say.

"What do we know?" she asks.

"Too little right now," I say. "We only just found out right before you came back."

"Right," she nods. "Tell me what is known then, and let's go from there."

"We know the location," I say. "Nothing else yet."

"I saw their spaceship taking off," Ragnar adds. "It's obvious that they are shipping prisoners off world."

"What does that have to do with us?" Ladon asks.

"Because they took the other survivors," Rosalind says, whirling towards him in a rare display of anger.

"It's a tragedy," Sverre says. "That doesn't change the question though. If they've already shipped them off world, there is nothing we can do."

Rosalind looks the men over before turning and locking eyes with me. I can see the wheels turning in her mind. I know, before she says it, what she's thinking. The only question is what I do with it. I look at all the possibilities, trying to decide—what is the greatest good for the Tribe?

There are plenty of human females for every member of the Tribe to mate with. But that won't be enough, because not all of them will match. There is a disparity also in the number human females compared to the number of human males If we can rescue those human females it only increases the odds of a better future for the Tribe.

Rosalind stares into my eyes, waiting for me to respond. Coming to a decision, I give her the barest of nods. A smile spreads across her face. Warmth grows in my chest, starting in my hearts and pounding its way in a wave through my limbs.

"Perhaps that is not the case," I say.

"You can't be serious," Ladon exclaims.

"Why not?" Rosalind asked, jumping into the conversation.

"Because it's not worth the risk!" Sverre exclaims.

"Is it not more risk to allow them to operate without challenge?" Ragnar asks.

"We have responsibilities here," Ladon says, his wings

opening and hands balling into fists. "I've already lost my city. What else would you take from me?"

"Leaving the Zzlo to operate isn't wise," I say. "In any situation they are a future danger we're going to have to handle."

"And we need those survivors, human and Zmaj both," Rosalind says.

"Why?" Ladon asks, the edges of his scales edging red making it clear he's struggling with his bijass.

"Genetics," Rosalind says. Ladon and Sverre exchange a blank look before their attention returns to Rosalind. "How much do you understand about that subject?"

Ladon shrugs and Ragnar shakes his head.

"I understand," I say.

Rosalind inhales deeply, her brow furrowing in concentration. Silence sits heavy over all of us while she contemplates, then she nods at last.

"The future of our races is not assured," she says. "Neither human nor Zmaj. I think it's clear that we need each other. But even that may not be enough. If there is not a broad enough mix of genetics to pull from, we risk creating a short-term future that might only make it four or five generations."

"I don't understand," Ladon says shaking his head and wrestling his wings. "Illadon is doing well and so is Rverre."

"Yes, they are, for now," Rosalind agrees. "I said it would be three or four generations down the line before there are likely to be problems. Their great-grandchildren would be the earliest I would expect it to show up."

"What to show up?" Ragnar asks.

"Weakness in the genetics," Rosalind says. "Possible mutations or tendency towards diseases. No matter how it manifests, it would greatly shorten their lifespans, then continue to get worse as it extrapolates further down the line. Until at last, both of our races are doomed once more."

"You can't know this," Ladon says.

"I tend to agree Rosalind," I say, shaking my head. "How can you predict so far into the future?"

"I am the Lady General of a generational ship that left Earth four generations ago. A large portion of my training is to know things like this. The amount of science and work that went into the creation of the generation ships is beyond comprehension. They had to allow for every variable to make sure we would be viable when we reached our destination. All of that has been disrupted, but it is still my duty to shepherd the human race, and the survivors most especially, to a viable future."

A cold chill forms in my stomach as icy tendrils creep outwards.

"So you're certain that this is what will happen if we don't rescue them?" Ladon asks.

"No," Rosalind says. "Nothing in this is certain. It's all projections and conjecture based on educated guesses. I am saying that it greatly increases our odds of being successful if we rescue them. That alone makes it worth the effort to at least try."

Ladon and Ragnar lock eyes and I can feel the exchange going between the two of them without words. Ragnar nods, subtle, then Ladon does also.

"We'll go in the morning," Ragnar says.

"No, you won't," I say, shaking my head. "You and the other hunters are too valuable to us. We barely have enough food as it is. No, the ones who need to go are the ones who are most disposable right now."

"So what, would you send children? Perhaps Samil?" Ladon asks, sarcasm dripping from his words.

Rosalind and I exchange a look in which no words necessary. We both know what the other is thinking. The decision is right even though I know they won't see it at first.

"Rosalind and I will go," I say.

"No!" Ladon and Ragnar shout almost in unison.

"He's right," Rosalind agrees. "Visidion and I are the most expendable."

"You're our leader!" Ragnar says. "What are we going to do without you? Who will lead us into the future?"

"And without you who would feed us?" I ask. "There is no option. This is the way it has to be."

"This cannot be," Ladon says shaking his head, frowning and his hands clenched into tight fists.

"Ladon," Rosalind says. "You'll need to fill my role. Make sure everyone stays busy. Production is the key to morale. Keep them working and it'll keep their mind off the troubles."

"This is not my job," Ladon argues. "I am not a leader. They won't follow me."

"I think you'll be surprised," she says.

Ladon opens his mouth to argue further, but Sverre cuts him off.

"Rosalind, no. I understand the logic but the humans need you. Even those who left the City look to you for leadership. You're their inspiration. Visidion I know the Tribe feels the same about you."

Rosalind shakes her head, meeting Sverre's gaze head-on.

"No," she says simply. "It doesn't matter how you argue against this, it is the only way."

"She's right," I add. "Rosalind and I are more than capable of handling ourselves out there. The survival of the Tribe is all that matters, and that includes you who have been banished from the City."

"Ladon, Sverre, you both have children. Our future hinges on them as much as anything. You cannot go," Rosalind adds.

"Ragnar, you and the hunters are the lifeline," I say. "We would starve without your efforts."

"No one else can do this," Rosalind says. "Visidion and I are both well prepared for a reconnaissance mission. We'll go and gather information, then, when we return, we'll make a plan."

"I don't like it," Ladon hisses, shaking his head.

"I agree with him," Ragnar says. "This is stupid."

"They're right," Sverre says, crossing his arms over his chest and sighing.

The other two men look at him with surprise on their faces.

"You can't be serious?" Ragnar asks him.

"Yes, I am," he says. "Think it through. They're right. We can't let this operation continue but we can't stop it without information. We don't know what is going on there for sure. We can't send an army; we don't have one. It has to be a small, stealthy operation."

"Which is exactly what I do," Ragnar argues.

"Yes, but then who hunts? How many days of food do we have right now? Especially with the addition of us refugees?"

Ragnar opens his mouth to argue then snaps it shut. He looks grim, angry, but nods.

"You and I should go, Sverre," Ladon says.

"You would leave Illadon an orphan?" Sverre asks.

"Enough," I say cutting off the last of their arguments.

"It is decided," Visidion says. "We will leave in the morning."

The three men before us exchange looks, then shaking their heads, they silently and sullenly leave my quarters. At last Rosalind and I stand alone. She looks up, a wan smile on her face.

"This is a terrible idea," she says, her voice soft.

"Perhaps," I say.

An ache in my arms that feels like an empty void wanting to be filled consumes me. It's an effort of will to not grab her and take her into my arms. She shifts her weight from one leg to the other. Every line of her face is beautiful, perfect. Fingertips tingle with the desire to touch her face, my breath coming in shallow gasps.

We're inches apart but it might as well be miles. Something plays in her eyes. I can't read it. Desire rises in my core, need for her pounding in my soul. It's hard to breathe, my chest aches, and my hearts are in overdrive.

"We can't," Rosalind says.

"Why not?" I ask, my voice barely above a whisper, throat tight and raw.

"They count on us," she says, shoulders slumping.

"Then let us lead," I say, placing two fingers under her chin and lifting her face upwards.

Her lips quiver at the corners, her eyes narrow, and she starts to say something but I don't give her the chance. The pull between us is overwhelming.

I steal our first kiss.

Our lips touch. Sensation explodes like rockets shooting into the dark sky. My scales tingle and itch, my stomach tightens into a hard knot, and my first cock stiffens.

Her lips are soft, moving against mine. Her arms drape around my neck as she folds her body against me. When I wrap my arms around her, the empty, aching void fills—with her. A sense of completeness comes over me, the like of which I've never known.

We kiss, slow, drawn out, tasting each other until at last the need for air overrides desire and we part, gasping. Trailing my fingers lightly across her cheek, I lean in to kiss again, but she pulls back.

"No," she says.

"Rosalind," I counter.

"No," she says, holding a finger up between us. "We have

responsibilities to our people. That comes before our personal pleasures."

"So you did find it pleasurable?" I ask, grinning.

Her cheeks flush red and her eyes dance with light.

"You're terrible," she says, laughing.

9

ROSALIND

*W*aking up, stiff and sore, thoughts swirl as the first rays of sunlight creep past the leathers over the door. Visidion's breathe is the only sound.

It'd be so easy, I think, watching Visidion's chest rise and fall. *Just fall for him. What's stopping me?*

Everything, of course. Responsibility, expectations, all overriding my own wants and desires as they always have.

He's attractive, yes, but that's never been a deciding factor for me. His sharp mind, his leadership, his character, and his strength—those are what catch my attention.

Ridiculous. The City and the Tribe were barely getting along before Gershom. Now the Tribe resents the imposition of putting us up, but they're angrier about Gershom. The City thinks the Tribe betrayed them when they settled here on our epis source.

It would never work. If word got out that Visidion and I were lovers, both groups would revolt against us. The refuges from the City here might accept it, but I'd never regain control of the City itself. How would I then fulfill my duty? I can't ensure the survival of our race without everyone. My chest aches, an empty feeling. It pulls, growing, eating at my resolve. Closing my eyes, I take a deep breath and let it out slowly.

His view of the world is so different than mine. He may have gathered the Tribe together, and it's obvious he's the glue, but they're still barbaric. If I hadn't intervened, Padraig would not have stopped beating Samil. The Tribe, no matter their Edicts, works on a belief of might makes right. There is too much of an only-the-strong-survive mentality.

Genetically, yes the stronger genes will win out, but I cannot condone his approach, not when lives are on the line. There is strength in charity too, if only I could get him to see it. The Tribe watched and no one moved to interfere. No one cared if Padraig caused Samil permanent harm. In their eyes he is too weak to stand up for himself, so he deserves what he gets. How this complies with their Edicts I have no idea.

Heat rushes across my chest yet again. I clench my teeth and shake my head to try to clear the negative emotions. I handled the situation, but only for the moment. What if I'm not there next time? If Visidion doesn't change his attitude, the Tribe won't either. The chasm between our two worlds yawns wide between us as I watch his sleeping form, swallowing my desires and leaving me cold.

I close my eyes, wishing to retreat back to the irresponsibility of sleep for just a while longer. Duty. Visidion and I have a long journey before us. Perhaps during this time he will come to understand. I hope so. The future of both our races depends on it. Steeling myself, I open my eyes and sigh, resigned. Visidion stirs, his eyes fluttering open. A smile spreads across his face when he sees me waiting.

"Morning," he murmurs, sitting up and stretching his arms and wings.

The way his wings open and flutter is beautiful. It's attractive in an exotic, alien way. The dim candle light gives them a shimmer. My core tightens, body responding to primal desires that I will not give in to. He rolls his neck and shoulders then rises to his feet, looking at the packs I've set next to the door.

"Thought you were going to sleep the day away," I answer, grabbing my pack. "We need to go, before they start waking up."

"You are an impressive female, Rosalind," he says, opening the pack still there and glancing inside. He lashes it closed and hefts it onto his back.

"Thanks," I say, unsure how to take the statement. Ignore it, it's for the best.

Leading the way down the ramp, I make every effort to be as quiet as possible. We're passing the skins that serve as doors to individuals of the Tribe's homes. If anyone wakes and finds us slipping away they will have questions. Questions we don't have time to handle.

When we reach the point where the ramp turns back on itself and makes the final descent to the ground, a cough comes from the door we're in front of. Holding a fist up, I freeze in place. Only after we're both standing stock-still does it hit me that I'm using a human military sign and I'm lucky it didn't communicate something entirely different to Visidion.

Behind the stretched, tanned hide emerge the sounds of someone stirring. My heart beats faster as I continue holding my breath, not daring to breathe. The sounds stop at last but I wait another ten heartbeats before moving. The hairs on the back of my neck stand on end and I strain my hearing for any indication of discovery.

We reach the bottom of the ramp without further incident, and only then do I take a deep breath of relief. We exchange a glance, then walk across the open area at the base of the cliff towards the ever-growing wall they're building to separate their area of control from the rolling desert.

The dark is receding to gray as the suns begin their ascent, and it won't be long before the first rays break the horizon. As we pass through the gate Visidion pauses and turns around. A smile dances on his lips but sadness is in his eyes. His tail lashes sharply, betraying his agitation. It's too dark to see the tint of his scales, but I'm certain they're edged red.

"What?" I whisper, still afraid to make any noise that might betray our departure.

"Once, we were a great and proud people," he says, voice soft.

An ache comes back into my chest, and the longing in his voice pulls my heart to his.

"We've all lost a lot," I agree.

Silent, he turns his back on the Tribe community, and together we walk into the desert as the first ray of sunshine breaks the horizon. A red finger creeps across the rolling dunes of sand.

Traveling across the sand is difficult, but Visidion helps, wrapping an arm around my waist and using his wings to give us both lift. Without him I would sink with every step, but he uses his wings and tail to walk as light as a feather across the loose top sand that drifts with the warm breezes. Even slowed by the burden of me, we make good time. The suns rise and the temperature goes up along with them, rising exponentially higher.

"Tell me about your world," I say, as we climb yet another dune.

The trek is mindless, one foot in front of the other. The

best measure of our progress is the color of the sand we're crossing. The dunes are striated with shades of red towards white and are constantly shifting as we travel.

"What would you like to know?" he asks, helping me up the last few feet to the top of the dune, then we start down the new side.

"You said you were once a great and proud people. Tell me about that," I say. "What was Tajss like before the Devastation?"

"Different," he says. "Civilized. The cities were full of people. There were millions of us," he says.

"How many cities were there?" I ask. "Were they spread far apart? We haven't found the ruins of another besides Drakonov," I observe.

"How many?" he muses. "How many grains of sand on this dune? I do not know a number. Lots, a dozen or more the size of Drakonov or larger. Many more half the size of it or so, then hundreds or even thousands of small villages."

"What happened to them?" I ask.

"The Devastation," he says, the Zmaj answer to any questions of their past.

"And?"

He stops, looking down with surprise on his face.

"What do you mean?" he asks.

"Visidion, that doesn't answer what happened to them."

He frowns, stares ahead for a long moment then starts walking again.

"No, it doesn't does it?" he asks at last. "The Devastation destroyed . . . everything."

"I see," I say. "What about before? What was life like here before?"

"Hard but beautiful, like this!" he sweeps an arm out expansively gesturing around us.

He's right, it is beautiful, in a harsh way. The suns glinting off the sand dunes create sparkles of light like tiny diamonds have been scattered across the rolling hills. The striation of colors, shifting with the breeze, makes pretty abstract designs that are pleasing to look at.

"It is pretty," I agree.

"We had advanced technology, then" he says. "You've seen the City, surely some of it survives. You have the dome."

"Yes, but not much else is working," I say.

"Ah, I see," he says. "Well before, Tajss was the center of the galaxy."

"How so?" I ask.

"Epis," he says, shaking his head. "Always epis."

Frowning and wiping sweat away from my eyes I wait for him to explain. Silence sits heavy between us.

"What do you mean?" I ask, prompting him to continue at last.

He sighs heavily.

"Epis was our rise and our fall," he says. "Our entire planet, my race, served a single purpose. Harvest, prepare, and ship epis. The galaxy ran on epis. Whoever controlled epis controlled everything."

"But epis doesn't last long after being harvested, how?"

He stops, looking over his shoulder at me, sadness in his eyes.

"Technology," he says. "We stored it, shipped it—it was our export."

"Oh," I say. "But it's addictive…"

"Yes," he nods. "Yes it is."

"So they became dependent on it," I observe following the chain of logic.

"Just so," he says. "It was fine for years, lifetimes passed. No one dared disrupt the system. Everyone knew they depended on Tajss and we were protected. Occasional raids by the Zzlo but nothing that couldn't be handled."

"So what did happen?" I ask.

"One man, driven insane by his lust for power," he says, helping me climb yet another dune. "Prince Astirian decided he could take control of Tajss. He was a Krikian, a violent race barely civilized. He made his bid for control at a time my people were vulnerable from within, weakened by the Rebellion, Zmaj who claimed we were all slaves because of Epis. It started a war among the Twelve."

"It sounds awful," I say.

"Yes," he says, shaking his head, voice heavy with loss and grief. "Tell me of your ship. How did you come to be on it?"

"That's a big question," I laugh, grabbing the water bottle off my side and taking a swig. I offer it to him but he passes.

"Yes, but our journey is long," he replies.

"Right," I agree. "Those of us here are of the third generation on the ship. When it left Earth, our home, the situation was bad. Overpopulation, food shortages . . . the world was divided into the super-rich and everyone else."

"Your planet was overpopulated?" he asks.

"Yes," I nod. "Badly. They had started building into the ground it was so heavily populated. Many people never saw the sky in their lives."

"That is terrible," he observes.

"I guess it was," I agree. "It became bad enough that there were class riots. The inequality was too much, and the poor were rising up. So the very rich built the generation ships to off-load the population. Our ship was the twelfth. I don't know how many they built after ours or what happened. We lost contact with Earth before the first generation were gone."

"So they joined the generation ship in hopes of a brighter future, not for themselves but their children?" he asks.

"More or less, yes," I agree.

"That is a very bold move," he says. "What was it like, living your entire life on an enclosed space?"

"The ships are designed so you don't notice," I say.

"How?" he asks.

"Artificial gravity, artificial night and day. Everyone has a job. There were entertainment districts, shopping districts, apartments, it was all designed to keep your mind off of the fact we were on a ship."

"Interesting, did that work?" he asks.

"Yes," I say. "Especially by my generation. We never knew anything but the ship. Oh there were things to complain about, of course. There always are."

Visidion nods. "Humans are not so different than Zmaj."

"No, we're not," I agree.

The dune we're climbing is particularly steep. I'm struggling to make the climb more than with any other dune so far. Visidion wraps an arm around my chest, lifting me so my feet are barely touching the sand. His forearm under my breasts lifts them, causing them to rub against him as we move. Warmth spreads from that point of contact, and the tightness in my core pulses with pent-up need. I lean into him, letting him take my weight.

Suddenly he stops.

"What?" I ask, nerves causing the hairs on back of my arms to stand up.

He shakes his head, tilting it to one side and listening. Straining my senses I pick up a vibration, faint but growing louder.

Tightening his grip around me he leaps forward, sweeping me off my feet and carrying me along as if I weigh nothing. He squeezes so tightly it's hard to catch my breath. Reaching the top of the dune he sets me down and stares straight ahead.

"No," he exhales.

Shielding my eyes against the suns, I only take a moment to spot what he saw. A Zzlo transport, heading our way, fast. Before I can say a word he grabs me and drops with me to the ground, hitting so hard it knocks my wind out.

10

VISIDION

*P*ulling her down, I cover her with my body before she can react. She gasps as we hit the sand and I feel her struggling for air.

The transport rumbles straight for us, growing louder.

There is no time to explain.

Pressing down on her, I use my tail and wings to shift the sand, burying us in a thin layer of it.

Locking eyes with her, our lips barely apart, her body soft against me, her heart beats against my chest. My own hearts fall into time with hers. She wheezes, then her breathing smooths and becomes natural.

Her fleshy mounds on her chest, pressing out as the human females do, smash against me, enticing. The ground beneath us tremors as the transport comes closer, and it is an effort to focus my attention on it.

My body wants her, I want her.

My first cock stiffens, digging into her, desperate for relief. She wriggles beneath me, for comfort or from arousal I don't know.

Her breath, soft and sweet, passes over my face, pulling me into the vacuum it leaves behind.

Touching her lips with mine, soft, gentle, my hearts pounding in my chest, thumping so hard I know she feels them. My cock pulses in time with them, ready to explode.

Her eyes widen, she stiffens, then returns the kiss.

Her hips push up, into me, rubbing my cock through the fabric of my pants.

Nothing has ever felt better.

Staring into her eyes I give myself over to her, consequences be damned! She strokes my arms with her fingertips, light touches that entice me further, stroking, pulling me into her further.

This is bad.

I can't.

We can't.

I can't stop. She has to be mine. Bijass surges forward, pushing rational thought away, leaving behind only primal desires.

She is a treasure and I will make her mine.

Any who would stand in my way, I will destroy. Mine. She has to be mine.

Red fog, throbbing in my mind as my cock throbs between my legs with intense arousal. A treasure. My treasure. Give yourself to me Rosalind, be mine.

"Rosalind," I whisper.

Her lips purse, tongue darts out moistening them, I steal a kiss, then impulsively force my tongue past her lips, seeking hers. When they meet, stars explode, my body rocks with spasms of delight. The response opens her to me, pulling us closer together.

Warmth burns onto my back but I ignore it until the soft tremble in the ground becomes a rumble that cuts through primal needs.

We're exposed!

The approaching transports vibrations have shifted the sand hiding us. Darting a quick look, I see that it's close, close enough that we could be seen if anyone is looking.

Rosalind lifts her head, coming in for a kiss, but I shake my head no, hissing softly. Working quickly, I shift the sand back over us, holding her still.

"They're close," I whisper.

Bijass retreats letting thought return, but not lessening the burning need in my loins, the tightness in my lower stomach, or my aching need for her to be my treasure.

She is the one. How, why, it doesn't matter. Every Zmaj knows there is one for him, fated the day we are born, there will be one who opens a male's inner soul, his treasure. When Ragnar found Olivia and they were mated, I wondered if perhaps he didn't understand or had forgotten our ways. In loneliness, it seemed perhaps he only sought solace. That, perhaps, she was not truly his 'treasure' but merely a love.

Meeting the pairs from the City did nothing to change my thoughts. The Zmaj males were lonely. We were a dying race—of course they wanted comfort. How easy it would be to confuse comfort for the connection of a treasure.

I was wrong.

How, why, these females from a planet so far away we could not reach each other in three lifetimes would be our treasures.

Rosalind is mine.

The vibrations increase, the transport comes closer. Peeking out, I see that it's close but worse—it's turning, coming towards us. Damn it.

"Hold still," I whisper.

"Close?" she asks.

"Yes," I say.

She shifts her hips, and I almost explode. Surely, she did

that for her own comfort, but it presses her against my cock in such a delightful way my thoughts disperse under the onslaught of pleasure.

Edicts!

Focus. I am myself.

Yes, I am, and I want her. She is mine, my fated, my treasure.

The press of her soft mounds against my chest, her hips against mine, sensations burning through my body.

The Zzlo transport is coming closer, driving straight at us. Did they see something? Are they coming for us?

Rage dances around the edge of my thoughts. I will destroy them. They will not harm her; she is mine.

MINE!

Chest tightening until it is hard to breathe, hearts pounding, desire warring with rationality and impending rage. Rosalind's bright eyes dance, alight with sharp intelligence and strength. Her beautiful lips purse, and she blinks, breathing shallow. It focuses my thoughts, helps to push aside the pulsing need of my cock trying to control my mind.

Two, together we are stronger.

Yes, we are. Rosalind and I together, we would rule this planet. None could stand against us. My cock pressing into her throbs and involuntarily I shift my hips, rubbing it against her. There is no stopping the soft moan escaping my lips.

Survival of the group matters, I think, reciting the final of the Edicts to myself.

Cold races through me, damping both desire and rage.

The group, the Tribe. I cannot betray the Tribe.

My cock softens as thought clears. The transport adjusts its path, not much, but it puts them even more on track to pass right over us.

Rosalind does not uphold the Edicts. Claiming her as my

treasure would divide the Tribe. Some might follow me still but it would be under duress. She betrayed the Edicts by allowing Gershom to remain, and now he's grabbed control. Her beating of Padraig, stopping him from establishing his dominance over Samil—no, the Tribe will not accept her.

This cannot be.

No matter how much I want her. She is my treasure but my duty is to the Tribe first, not myself. No matter how I wish it were not so, I cannot give myself over to primal instinct. It would be a betrayal of all I am. The Edicts are the fabric of the Tribe. Betraying them, I betray myself.

An empty ache, an unfillable void opens in my stomach, spreading until it swallows my heart. A cold chill runs down my spine and I shiver.

Concern passes over Rosalind's face, an instant that I barely catch, but it's there. A passing moment that she hides away. The gulf between us widens proportionate to the chasm between our beliefs. No matter how much I want her, I cannot take her as my treasure without destroying the Tribe. That I cannot do.

Now is not the time, our mission and survival are at stake.

The ground beneath us rumbles harder. The transport is so close now I can smell its exhaust. It's climbing the very dune we're on, heading straight for us but it's not slowing.

It adjusts direction, small shifts, making it difficult for me to judge whether it will pass us by or run us over.

Tensing, ready to move if necessary, I inhale deeply and hold my breath. Rosalind's eyes bore into me. She can't see what's happening; her trust is fully in me.

Moving slowly so as not to disturb the sand hiding us, I get a grip on her sides, using my elbows to keep myself pressed up. If we have to move, I'll need a good grip to pull her with me.

Closer, it's halfway up the dune.

Too damn close.

It's going to hit us.

Shifting my right leg, I press my knee down, finding purchase, ready to roll out of the way.

The transport is so loud I can't hear anything but its rumbling sound, coming closer. The sand of the dune vibrates, shifting under its approach.

Tightening my grip, watching, waiting, the timing has to be perfect.

Almost.

Now!

Gripping tightly, I tilt to the side, taking her with me as I roll. Sand flies into my face, my protective lids close so I see flashes of the transport passing over where we were a moment before.

Clutching Rosalind to my breast, one leg hooked around her keeping her close, I don't stop until we're tumbling down the side of the dune, away from the transport and any possible sighting by those inside. We pick up momentum as we roll. There's no way to control it. We're bouncing down the dune, and all I can do is shield her with my body, absorbing the impacts the best I can.

At last, we come to a stop at the bottom of the dune. My muscles ache, and there will be bruises, but none of that matters.

"Are you okay?" I ask, as she gasps.

"Yeah," she exhales, shaking her head. "Hell of a ride."

"More than I expected," I chuckle.

She extricates herself from me, crouching on her hands and knees. Lying on my side, I let the dizziness pass before rising too.

"Are we safe?" she asks, looking warily around.

"For now," I say, after listening a moment.

"They're heading for the City," she says.

"Gershom will deal with them," I answer.

Rosalind's jaw tightens, her eyes narrow, and her brow furrows. It's may not be the answer she wants to hear, but it is the truth. One she needs to come to terms with.

"He's a fool," she growls, gritting her teeth.

Anger comes off her in waves. She stands up, wavers once, then steady, she turns and walks a few feet away, keeping her back to me. Standing up myself, I stare at her back.

"You should have dealt with him when I told you to," I say.

She whirls around. Her normally warm eyes are now cold and hard and locked on mine.

"You don't see the bigger picture, that's your problem. All you worry about is your Tribe, but there's no future. You're too stubborn to see it."

"The Tribe is fine, and we won't tolerate a traitor in our midst," I respond, wings opening as my tail goes stiff.

"No, they're not fine," she says. "None of us are fine. You need to listen to the words of your edicts, together we are stronger."

"Yes," I answer, moving closer, looking down at her. "The Edicts bind us together but still only the strongest of us will survive. We all must contribute."

She stares up at me, cold, imperious, unshaken by my greater height or size. The lines of her face are regal. Touched by the red rays of the suns, her eyes flash. My first cock springs to life, hard and pounding with desire for her with every beat of my hearts.

"Short-sighted," she says. "We need all of them. There are not enough of us. We need every single one of us."

Her chest rises and falls in rapid succession, her soft mounds pushing out with each rise, and her perfect, beautiful skin glows. A light sheen of sweat covers her face. There is barely space between us.

My core is so tight I'm about to explode. My cock strains, urging towards freedom, towards her.

"At what cost, Rosalind? How far do you let your vision take you? Take us?"

"As far as it takes," she says.

She inhales deeply and her breasts press against my stomach. Desire claims me. I can't control it.

Grabbing her in my arms, I lift her off her feet, bringing our lips together. The soft mounds of her breasts crush against me, kindling my desire. Her arms wrap around my neck, her legs hook across my hips, our tongues meet and dance together, and so I take what is mine. My treasure. Mine.

She breaks the kiss, her legs drop, and she pushes away.

"Put me down," she says. When I set her back on her feet, she stares up at me, but then she turns away. "We need to keep moving."

She walks away. My throbbing cock softens, but my desire is only flamed higher. She will be mine.

11

ROSALIND

*F**ool*, I admonish myself, walking away from him.

Fool or not, the heat between my legs isn't being denied. The fire burning low in my stomach is a raging inferno needing satisfaction. Satisfaction I won't give it.

The way he grabbed me, taking what he wanted—the nerve of it! Exactly why I can't be his lover. A display like that in public? I'd lose every ounce of respect and all ability to lead.

Tingles run through my body, remembering it. Damn if it didn't feel good. Wrapped in his arms, his massive, hard cock digging into my stomach, begging for me. He may have been physically dominating me, but his desire for me was dominating him, giving me a degree of control still.

If only he'd open his damn eyes!

The ground rises and I start up another dune. Sand slides from beneath me with each step making it take three steps forward to gain the equivalent of one step. As I struggle, Visidion catches up to me and silently lends his aid.

I stiffen at his touch, then push that instinct aside. I'm not a fool. I can't navigate this world without him, no matter how angry I am with him. Or how much I want him, which is the deeper problem. My skin burns where he touches it, and visions of his touch in more intimate places dance at the edge of my thoughts.

After an hour, the desire has tamped down, but the anger is still there.

If only he would open his damn mind. Everything is there, if only he would see it! The Tribe could go in a new direction, a better one. One that would help ensure the survival of all our people.

"How much further," I ask, stopping for a drink.

"We should arrive tonight," he says. "At our current pace."

I cap my water bottle then start forward again. The suns beat down mercilessly, relentless, as harsh as anything else on this desert planet. This is so far from the ideal world for which we were bound. That empty rock will be halfway done with its terra-forming now. Two more generations and it would be ready for our arrival, which wouldn't have been for another generation after that.

It doesn't matter. This is where we are.

"Rosalind," Visidion says.

"What?" I ask, not bothering to look at him.

He doesn't say anything for a long time. We continue walking, my curiosity growing as I wonder what he's thinking. His strong arm hooks my hips as he helps me out of another bog in the sand. When I look up at him at last, he's staring ahead, either not looking or avoiding looking at me.

Curiosity gets the best of me.

"What, Visidion?" I finally ask.

He stops, rolls his shoulders, and at last meets my gaze.

"Nothing," he says.

"It's not nothing," I snap. "Say what's on your mind."

"Gershom could have hurt you," he says.

"Yes, he could have," I agree. "But he didn't."

Back to climbing the dune, we walk in continued silence.

The sand shifts suddenly, pouring down from the top of the dune, burying my feet. I'm sliding backwards, even though I'm leaning forward as far as I can. There is no stopping my backwards motion.

Visidion holds me by my waist, struggling to move forward too.

"What is happening?" I ask.

Visidion doesn't answer, spreading his wings and using them to stop our retreat. The ground trembles beneath our feet, reminiscent of the transport's approach. Visidion stiffens, his wings snapping shut. He looks around, eyes wide, frown on his face.

"Damn," he exhales. "Zemlja, hold still."

My heart pounds in my chest as we both stop struggling. The sifting sand carries us backwards until we're at the bottom of the dune. I'm afraid to breathe. Zemlja, the giant worms that crisscross Tajss beneath the surface, are the most dangerous thing on the planet. This on a planet where even the plant life is trying to kill you.

They're massive. Even the babies are over a hundred feet in length and twenty to thirty feet in diameter. Relentless hunters, they travel constantly, hunting and eating, never stopping.

The best encounter with one is the encounter you avoid.

I focus on controlling my heartbeat. Zemlja hunt by vibrations. The slightest sound can attract one if it's close. The sand continues shifting but slows.

Visidion is turning his head around looking for something. Following his gaze, I try to figure out what it is he's watching. When he stops turning and stares at a spot for an extended period, I figure it out. The ground where he's staring is jumping. The sand shifts like the waves of an ocean. That is where the zemlja is passing by. I start counting, trying to estimate the size of the beast, guessing that each second is about one foot. By the time the last of it passes us by I'm up over four hundred.

A massive worm, definitely not one we want to confront with just the two of us. We stand silent a while longer, letting the minutes tick past while the double red suns beat down on us. The warm breeze does nothing to cool my burning skin. My mouth is dry and my throat raw, but I don't want to risk getting my water bottle. Not until I'm sure it's passed us by.

Visidion relaxes and I take my first deep breath, letting it out in a sharp exhale of relief.

"That was close," he says.

"Too close," I agree.

We resume traveling, silence still hanging heavy between us.

Why is he being stubborn?

He's right, I should have dealt with Gershom sooner. It was a mistake but it doesn't change the facts. Gershom has followers, too many for me to lose. If I took action against him it would solidify the divide among the survivors. What would that gain us?

My people are scared and how can I blame them for that? There are only a handful of us left. The ship housed almost quarter of a million souls. Now there are so few of us left I'm worried about the gene pool. No one else thinks that far into the future, but I have to. It's my duty, entrusted to me, no matter that everything has changed.

If I don't care for them, no one will. If I don't guide them, they won't survive.

What I need him to see is that I need the Tribe too. Bringing our two races together increases our odds of survival exponentially. Together we can survive.

"Why can't you see that we need everyone?" I ask, exasperation pushing me to break the silence.

Visidion glances over, arching an eyebrow.

"Why can't you see that we can't include those who aren't strong enough to add to the group?" he asks in return.

"Because in the end that doesn't matter! Human decency if nothing else?"

"What is 'human decency'? An excuse for the weak?" he asks.

"No, damn it, it's being human."

"But I'm not human, Rosalind," he says. "I'm a Zmaj male. Our duty is to be strong, to claim and protect our treasures. This is my home—do you see softness here? Do you see this 'decency' anywhere in my world?"

"Just because it's not here now doesn't mean you can't embrace it," I respond.

"To what end?"

"To the end of the survival of all of us," I answer.

"You keep saying that, but what would then survive? A weak group without the strength to survive the planet. You would breed us down to nothing."

"That is not true, and you know it," I snap.

"Isn't it?" he asks. "How do you know this? This is not your home. You do not comprehend what it takes to survive here. Weakness and divisiveness cannot be tolerated. Survival of the group matters. It overrides the rest of the Edicts. You're a leader, as am I. We are the ones who must make the hard choices, the ones who dictate survival for the many versus the needs or wants of the few." His eyes drill into me before he goes on.

"That is where you went wrong with Gershom. You should have stopped him in the beginning. Look where it has gotten you."

The truth in his words cut deep. Icy rage consumes my thoughts, but I cannot give in to it. A lifetime of controlling my emotions, pushing them aside, remaining rational in the face of impossible odds keeps me in control. It doesn't matter how much his words hurt.

"Fine," I say, marching away from him.

I won't argue further. If he doesn't want to see the truth then so be it. I'll continue without him.

"Rosalind," he calls after me.

Ignoring him, I continue walking. There is nothing more to say. His mind is set and so is mine. Anger pounding through my thoughts drives me to walk faster. Focus on the mission to hand. I need to know if there are more survivors. That's what's important. I'll deal with Visidion when the time comes. If he won't come along of his own free will, then I'll find another way. Our races will survive.

A hand grips my arm with the power of a vise, forcing me to turn around. Pulling me into his arms, smashing me into his broad, muscled chest, he wraps his arms around me and lifts me off my feet. Desire pushes away anger. I'm wet, ready, muscles trembling as he crushes me against him. His lips find mine and his tongue invades my mouth. Resisting, I push back with mine.

Hands on my ass, squeezing, pulling me even closer. Hard to breathe, heart pounding, core tight and ready to explode. Wetness pours out of me, feeling his erection pressing hard against my silk tunnel.

Wrapping my legs around his waist, I grind against his erection; arms around his neck, I push his tongue out of my mouth and drive mine into his. Pushing back against his dominance, I take control from him. He groans, his cock spasms between us, encouraging me. His tail rises up behind him, swaying in the air, his wings open as our tongues wrestle, neither of us submitting.

Nipples hard as diamonds shoot thrilling jolts through me as they rub against the scales of his chest through the thin cloth of my blouse. Grinding harder, faster, he's groaning, his body relaxes into me, his cock harder, pulsing.

Breaking the kiss, I pull back, look into his eyes. We gaze into each other, looking deeper than our mere physical bodies. Our connection and desire for each other are deep and strong, but I won't give in to him. Not yet.

"Put me down," I say, unhooking my legs and dangling in his arms.

He jerks me tighter to him, thrusting his hips up, driving his cock hard against the cloth that separates us. He's hissing, grunting with desire, but I shake my head.

"No, Visidion," I say, controlling my own need and desire.

No matter how much I want him, I can't. Survival of our people is foremost. Giving in to him now puts everything in jeopardy. I can't, I won't.

He sets me down on my feet.

"How many times?" he asks, breathless.

"Until it's right," I answer, not needing him to clarify the question.

I want him every bit as much as he wants me, but the greater good overrides personal desire.

He shakes his head. His cock is sticking straight out, tenting his pants. An impressive member. I've heard about the Zmaj cocks, and I can't say I'm not curious for the experience. I'm so wet my panties are soaked and uncomfortable. Nothing would be better than to give myself to him and take our pleasure of each other.

No, it can't be. Our mission is first, then the survival of our groups. Somehow, we have to come to an agreement. Somehow, some way.

Until then, no.

VISIDION

*M*y balls ache. My first cock keeps twitching, stirring every time I glance at the sway of her ass, the swell of her chest, the curve of her hips. Even the moisture dripping down her face is erotic and arousing.

When she tilts her head back to drink water, the way her throat works stiffens my cock. It's distracting, clouding my thoughts. Desire, need, every moment is a reminder of how much I want her. She is my treasure. The most primal part of me wants to claim her fully. Consummate my desires.

There are no words between us, and we travel in silence. Heavy quiet, full of unspoken thoughts and desire. Her body responds to me, so she wants me as much as I want her—that much is obvious. How she maintains control in the face of our mutual attraction and rising needs is beyond my comprehension.

My thoughts won't quit circling around her. Desire, need, pulse pounding, cock stiffening, time passes by unnoticed. Rosalind stops, hip cocked to one side making her ass the most enticing, desirable thing I've ever seen. My palms itch with desire to touch her, to feel her bare skin under my fingertips.

"What is that?" she asks.

It's an effort of will to tear my gaze away and follow her pointing finger. Even so my gaze traces the perfect line from her shoulder to the tip of her finger before I can focus my eyes on her target.

"That's the camp," I say.

Sticking above a not-so-distant sand dune is the tip of a spaceship, barely visible from our current position.

"We need to get closer," she says.

Smoke drifts up into the red tinted sky. I catch the scent of it on the wind. Fuel, burning fuel.

"We have a problem," I say. "That ship is preparing to leave."

"How do you know that?" she asks.

"I don't, for sure, but there is the scent of fuel in the air," I tell her.

She nods, frowning.

"Let's move," I say, leading the way forward.

Rosalind falls in with me. We move slowly, stopping often to listen and look. The suns are low, sinking fast below the horizon as we make our final approach towards the Zzlo camp. The shadows give us some cover. The Zzlo chose their location well, an especially barren area where even the surrounding sand dunes are relatively low.

After crawling on our bellies to the top of one of the dunes, we look down on their camp.

It's a flat area, a rare feature on Tajss, with an oasis close to hand. The camp is surrounded by a temporary fence marking their area. Well-armed guards patrol along the fence. We watch in silence and I count three guards working the perimeter. There is a gap in their coverage where we might be able to penetrate past them if we time it well.

The ship dominates the landscape, towering over even the highest dunes. I know from experience it's only a shuttle, but it's been long years since I've seen its like. Once, before the Devastation, such ships were common, and the memory of them, vague under the fog of the bijass, is still with me if only as a concept. The ship has a ramp open leading to the ground. A Zzlo stands guard at the base of the ramp too.

The engines of the transport are warming up. Smoke drifts from them at regular intervals as they heat the fuel for takeoff. So many of my memories from before are dim and hazy because of the bijass. The origins of this memory are lost to me, but I know it's true.

"There," Rosalind whispers, pointing.

Following her finger I see what she spotted. A pop-up shelter with two guards in front of it, located close to the fence on the far side of the compound. A Zzlo emerges from inside, pulling a struggling figure along with him. A human, male. Hands bound behind him, still he fights against his captor. Kicking and screaming, trying to break free.

Cold spreads through my chest, running through my veins. When the door opens, I catch a glimpse of several other humans in there. One female with red hair and pale skin stares out the open door. Her eyes are sunken, skin red and peeling, and now moisture pours down her face from her eyes. My stomach tightens into a hard ball, and I can't swallow. Her despair drives into me across the distance. I'm shaking with pent-up anger. It's clear that they have found a lot of slaves and they're shipping them off-world.

I tap Rosalind on the shoulder, nod, then point back down the dune. Together we slide towards the base.

"We don't have time to go back to the Tribe," I say, keeping my voice low.

"Why not?" she asks.

"That ship is preparing to leave, a day, two at the outside. It would be gone before we can get help and return."

"Shit," she exhales. "We have to save them."

Mind racing through the possibilities I try to find a way to say no. Images of that forlorn female drift through all my thoughts. No one will rescue her, no one but us. We are their only hope.

"Yes," I agree.

"How many of them did you count?"

"Fourteen," I say.

"Same," she says. "Damn it."

Her lips purse as her brow furrows. Touching her face before I think about it, my fingertips trail along her jaw, smoothing the tension away. When I stare into her eyes, the ache in my chest and stomach yawn wide, emptiness that only she can fill. I want to say something, find words that will set things right between us but nothing comes. She places her hand over mine then the moment passes.

"We'll have to be smart about this," I observe.

"We need a distraction, something that can pull most of them away," she says.

"The oasis," I say, an idea coming to me.

"What about it?"

"Majmun," I say, a smile breaking across my face. "We can use them!"

"How?" she asks.

"Come with me, I'll show you an old trick," I grin.

Crouching low, we make our way out and around the dunes. Full dark falls as we slowly skirt the Zzlo camp. As the temperature drops, my body slows, aching with the cold. Rosalind doesn't seem to be affected by it, but the cold always bothers me, and tonight seems particularly cold. We're moving, still in a crouch, around what should be the southern-most dune when I hear something.

Grabbing Rosalind, I jerk her close and drop flat to the ground, covering her with my body. An initial gasp comes from her, but then she doesn't resist as I cover us with sand using my tail and wings.

A Zzlo appears at the top of the dune. He holds something up to his eyes and looks out with it. Only my eyes are watching him. My thoughts are consumed again with her. I'm not sure how long I can resist the lure of her soft flesh. My first cock digs into her, relentless, wanting more, needing to take her. My hearts pound against the soft mounds pressed against me.

Her heart beats against my chest, rapid and strong. Her hands rest on my shoulders, burning points where her bare skin contacts mine. Unbidden my hips shift, thrusting into her, instinct and desire controlling my body without conscious thought. I want to bury myself inside her, giving her both of my cocks and leaving my seed to grow. Together we could create the future we both dream of. Our children could be numerous.

The Zzlo turns and makes his way back down the far side of the dune. I count to one hundred, making sure he's had time to be a good distance away before I roll off her. We both rise, and her gaze lingers on my erection holding my pants out. All my will is consumed in not grabbing her and taking her, even breathing is held off as I struggle to maintain control.

She signals that we should move and I agree, if for no other reason than if we stay here any longer, I'm going to claim her, risk of capture or no.

Crouching, we continue towards the oasis. The moons are dim tonight, and long shadows creep across the dunes that we dart between. Coming around the edge of a dune, we see the oasis lying before us. Now to implement my plan.

"Be careful," I whisper. "Follow in my footsteps only."

Rosalind nods understanding, not risking more words. The imminent threat of the Zzlo is too close for comfort.

Leading the way into the oasis, I avoid the most dangerous plants that grow along the edges, ready to capture unwary visitors. As we move deeper, there is the soft sound of water moving. This oasis must have a small waterfall. The baoba trees grow closer together until we have to squeeze between the massive trunks, easier for Rosalind than me by far.

Ahead is a cluster of a dozen trees, all close together. I study the branches that are far overhead. As I expected, I notice the signs of the majmun making their home up there.

"Stay here, be ready to run," I whisper.

"What are you going to do?" she asks.

"Something stupid," I grin, moving away.

Gripping the base of the closest tree, I climb up the trunk towards the high branches. Silence is a must. Alerting them to my approach will ruin my plan. Almost there. The trunk of the baoba trees are smooth. I shimmy my way up the bole until the first of the massive limbs is within reach. I'm twenty feet off the ground by the time I reach it, and now I smell them. Majmun mark their territory giving it an offensive odor.

Pulling myself up onto the limb and positioning myself in a crouch, I look around for my goal. The majmun are sleeping just over my head, but as I expected, the weaker young ones are lower. Taking a deep breath, I stand and stretch for the next branch up. As my full weight presses onto the branch I'm on, it bends down. My fingertips brush the branch but I can't get a grip on it.

Damn it.

There is no other option. Crouching, I take one deep breath, then I leap, spreading my wings for lift. Rosalind's gasp reaches me just as my fingers close over the top of the branch. Hanging by my fingertips, body swaying, my muscles strain as I pull myself up and over, scrambling on top of the branch.

I hold still, listening, alert for any stirrings of the majmun. Fighting them in the trees would not go in my favor.

Silence.

Good. Getting my feet under me, I make my way along the branch towards the nest that is my goal, a collection of limbs covered with leaves where I know I'll find a baby majmun. Majmun are strange creatures—the babies are not kept with their mothers. They set them up in their own beds for the night and leave them, but if an alarm is raised by one of them the entire pack will come to its aid. A strange display of indifference balanced by rabid protection. Which is what I'm counting on.

The baby majmun is curled into a ball, sleeping. Positioning myself carefully next to the nest, I cover its mouth at the same time as I carefully grab it up, keeping it from crying out. It struggles in my arms but doesn't make a sound.

Opening my wings, I drop out of the tree, landing with a thump close to Rosalind. She's staring at me wide-eyed but doesn't break the silence. I take off, and she falls in with me as I make my way back to the edge of the oasis. Once the Zzlo camp is in sight beyond the edge of the oasis, I crouch and watch for the patrol, struggling with the baby in my arms who is fighting for its freedom. Rosalind at my side, I watch the guard march slowly by, my hearts thumping in my chest, ready to spring into action.

He passes, and I count to twenty. I mouth silent instructions with gestures to Rosalind, and she nods when she gets I want her to stay hidden. Satisfied it's time, I race across the barren land between the oasis and the fence of the camp. As I reach the fence the baby in my arms manages to bite my hand. The sharp pain blinds me for an instant, and I lose my grip on it. It cries out, a loud, pitiful sound that carries through the night. When I put it on the ground, it races away from me, through the fence into the Zzlo camp.

Perfect.

I race back to Rosalind, take her hand, and pull her along. We run out of the oasis and north, parallel to the camp. Before we clear the oasis, I hear the cries of the majmun, and the treetops are rustling. Rosalind looks over her shoulder. When she looks back, she finds me grinning.

"What?" she asks.

"A distraction," I answer, as the commotion grows louder.

I grab her arm as I slide to a stop and crouch behind a small rock. The majmun pack bursts out of the oasis in a mad rush, led by their alpha. The cries of the baby from deep in the Zzlo camp are calling them on. They barrel forward, leaping over the fence. Cries go up from inside the camp.

13

ROSALIND

*T*his is insane. The strange-looking creatures pour out of the oasis like a moving, screaming river of fur, claws, and rage. The cacophony is an assault on my ears. The fence around the camp collapses beneath their onslaught. They storm into the camp, and the Zzlo scramble to face their attack.

"Now," Visidion says, rising and running forward.

His plan is obvious, and it is a brilliant distraction. The sounds of lasers zing from within the camp as the Zzlo organize. Our window of opportunity is small. Running side by side, we cross the fallen fence. The creatures are racing around attacking anything that gets in their way, building or Zzlo makes no difference. At the ramp of the ship the Zzlo are gathering to resist the invasion. They fire randomly into the crowd of attacking animals, dropping those they hit, but there are so many of them leaping around that the odds seem stacked against them.

Visidion leads the way to the shelter where we saw the captives. As we reach it a Zzlo steps around the corner, weapon at the ready.

"Hey!" Visidion yells, pulling the guards attention.

As he turns, Visidion swings, connecting with his jaw. A loud crack echoes as his fist hits. The Zzlo stumbles backwards. I step forward, drop, and sweep my right leg, taking his out from under him. He lands on his back, but his weapon fires as he does.

Visidion steps over him, opening the door to the shelter.

"No!" a female voice cries out, and something hits Visidion, forcing him to step back.

A man, haggard looking and too thin, attacks him. Slamming against him and trying to drive him back through force of will more than strength.

Visidion tries to get a hold on him without hurting him.

"Stop!" I order in Common.

The crazed man doesn't listen, attacking with wild swings and kicks.

"Kill you!" he screams.

We don't have time for this.

Stepping behind the man I hit him three times at strategic points causing the muscles of his arms to go numb effectively ending his assault without causing any lasting harm. He spins around, gnashing his teeth, then his eyes clear when he sees me.

"Lady General?" he asks, voice quavering.

"Stand down," I order.

He instantly obeys, standing at attention with his numb arms limp at his side.

"Yes, Lady," he responds.

I don't recognize him immediately. He's gaunt, hair grown long and wild, and there are heavy bruises and swelling on his face. It's obvious that he was a soldier, though.

"Help us," I order, and he nods weakly, obeying.

Visidion pulls the door to the shelter back open. Screams emerge again.

"Allow me," I say, placing a hand on his shoulder.

Frowning, he nods, stepping aside to let me enter first.

Those inside look terrible, with obvious signs of neglect and abuse. Clothes shredded, dirty, underfed, and some of them barely alive, but there are a dozen of them, all human. They huddle together in the far corner, ten women and two men, not counting the one out front. They cower when Visidion steps in behind me.

"It's fine," I assure them. "He's with me."

They look at each other, fearful, cowed by their experiences.

"We need to go Rosalind, our distraction is dispersing," Visidion says, urgency in his voice.

"Move, come with us," I order.

Visidion steps back outside and I follow. The captives hesitate then come out after us. The noise of the animals attacking is quieting and there is only the occasional sizzle of Zzlo weapons firing. Visidion is right, we don't have long.

"Name and rank," I order the man who attacked Visidion, still standing where I'd left him.

"Lieutenant Draker, ma'am," he answers.

"Right. Lead these people north, through the broken fence then march by the stars. Don't stop until you see a massive cliff that dominates the horizon. You'll see a man-made wall and others who look like him," I nod at Visidion. "They will help you. Tell them I sent you."

"Rosalind, what are you planning?" Visidion asks.

"We have to buy them time," I answer him in Zmaj.

Visidion looks at the captives, a deep frown forming on his lips, then he nods.

"Right," he says, resigning himself, knowing without saying it that this is a bad idea.

The captives move like a herd of wounded animals. Huddling tight together, moving as if in slow motion. Closing my eyes, I count to five, then turn away from them. All I can do is give them a shot. The rest is up to them.

Scanning the camp, I see that the beast herd is retreating and a handful of Zzlo are following, shooting them. Their attention is focused on that threat, and no one has yet noticed we've set their captives free. The ship is an open target, and I only see a single guard at the ramp. Visidion follows my gaze and hisses.

"Bold," he says.

Grinning, I shrug and then crouch to move forward quickly. The odds of our success are so low as to be minuscule, but if it works it will turn the tide in our favor.

Visidion runs at my side. Hiding behind a stack of crates, I look the area over again. The guard is standing at the top of the ramp with his attention on what his fellows are doing against the majmun. I sift through the sand until I find a rock. I throw it, putting all I have into it. It sails up and over, clacking on the far side of the ship.

The guard turns towards it, and Visidion runs up, grabbing him in a choke hold. The guard struggles, but the larger Zmaj has him, keeping him silent by cutting off his air. Visidion drags him up the ramp and out of sight. Staying low, I race up the ramp and join him inside the ship.

It's an open cargo area, much as I expected. Crates are fastened to the floors and walls with straps as they prepare for takeoff. Stairs lead up to a catwalk that crisscrosses the area. The only door out seems to be on the second tier.

"What now?" Visidion asks.

"Know how to fly a ship?" I grin.

"No," he shakes his head, then his eyes widen as comprehension dawns on him. "You can't be serious?"

"Why not?"

His mouth drops open, and he looks like he's about to protest, but then it snaps shut and he shrugs.

"Right," he agrees.

We make our way up the catwalk towards the door. The design of the ship is unfamiliar to me, of course, but ships are ships, and I know the technology intimately. Space is at a premium in a spaceship of any size. The design always follows the logic of that overriding rule.

When we reach the door further into the ship, I stop and try to figure out the panel. It's similar to the ones on the generation ship, but different enough that I'm not sure how to work it. I try every idea I can think of with Visidion looming over my shoulder.

"Bah," he exclaims, his fist flying over my shoulder and smashing the control panel.

Glass breaks, wires hang loose, and sparks fly but the door slides open. All I can do is stare, but he shrugs, grinning.

We make our way into the ship, following the tight passages, passing doors to rooms until we come to a crossroads and have to choose. The path to the left ends with a ladder, so I choose it, certain that the bridge has to be up.

The ship is quiet, too quiet. I find it hard to believe we haven't come across any of the Zzlo yet. My skin crawls and the hairs on my arms stand on end, as I get the distinct feeling we're walking into a trap. Pausing the forward advance and looking over my shoulder at Visidion, I arch an eyebrow. He shakes his head, lips pursed, his concern obviously going in the same direction as mine.

Steeling my resolve, I push forward. We've come too far now to do anything else. My hands itch for a weapon, but we have what we have. The hall we're in extends on for a few more yards then we're at a T. Before I can glance around the corner, I hear a sound from the left. Both of us press flat to the wall. The sound of hard boots ringing against metal echo down the hall, coming closer. Counting the steps in time to my heart pounding in my chest, I wait until they come closer still. As I think they're about to appear around the corner, I drop low, swinging my leg out and around, but Visidion is faster. His arm darts over my head around the corner. There's a loud yelp as he grabs the Zzlo and jerks the alien towards him. Lifting the poor bastard clean off the floor, he slams him into the wall so hard the metal reverberates. The Zzlo's head leaves an indentation as deep as the thickness of my thumb.

The Zzlo is limp in Visidion's grasp. Visidion shakes him, I assume to make sure he's really out, before grinning at me. Closing my eyes, I shake my head.

"We could have pumped him for information," I observe.

"He'd have screamed," Visdion says, practical if nothing else.

"I'm sure no one heard the entire ship ringing when you bounced his head off the wall," I say wryly.

When Visidion looks at the indentation on the wall, his face falls and he shrugs.

"Yeah," he agrees. "That could have been done better."

"Take his weapons," I say. "We might as well charge forward. Either this works, or we're screwed."

Visidion takes the gun off the limp body. He's so broad chested that the gun looks tiny in his hands. Stepping around me, he stands in the T-cross and looks both ways before looking at me.

"I think left," I say. "Hurry."

He nods and heads that direction without another word.

Picking up the pace since we're no longer concerned with being quiet, it's a matter now of making it to the bridge before they can dig in or get reinforcements there. Visidion's feet clang with every step, giving away our position, loud enough to cover the clack of my boots on the mesh steel floor. We make it to the end of this hall, and there's another ladder. Visidion doesn't bother with the rungs, crouching and leaping up to the next deck in an impressive display of strength and agility.

I take the more acceptable method of actually climbing the ladder, if for no other reason than I can't leap eight feet into the air. This deck is open, a wide hallway that must be at least half the width of the ship itself that goes forward. There's a double door to my left with markings. That should be our destination. Visidion moves towards it, and I follow. The hairs on the back of my neck are on end again. A last deep breath to calm the nerves. Visidion and I exchange a long look, then he smashes the control panel, and the doors slide open with a hiss.

I do a shoulder roll through the doors before they finish opening, landing in a crouch.

Bolts of electricity shoot over my head, and Visidion cries out in pain. There are five Zzlo under cover behind the flight console shooting at the door. They're at least fifteen feet away and behind cover, while all I have is a smile and my bare hands to take on all five of them and their weapons.

"Run!" Visidion hisses, his voice echoing off the metal walls of the bridge.

I don't know if he thinks I should run forward or run away. It doesn't matter—there's only one option, a full frontal assault.

Leaping up, I somersault forward then jump into a handspring to the right. I do cartwheels from that point forward until I'm past the end of the console they're hiding behind. It's not a matter of being pretty or showing off. The bolts they're firing would stun me, and my gymnastics makes me an unpredictable target.

"ARRRGGHH!" Visidion yells, as I crouch to get my bearings.

They're focusing on him. I don't know how many hits he's taken but he's moving forward like Darth Vader at the end of *Revenge of the Sith*, screaming with both arms held out in front of him. He's firing the two-handed rifle with one hand, not bothering to aim. The muscles of his chest and arms are spasming from all the electrical volts pumping through him, but he refuses to go down. My heart leaps into my throat seeing him in so much pain. I know he's doing it for me, damn fool that he is.

This is the worst idea ever.

It's all mine too, damn it.

I'm no better than one of those fool women in a romance novel. If someone was reading this as a story I'm sure they'd be screaming at the book what an idiot I was for walking into this. It's always easier from the outside to see that someone is being too stupid to live than when you're living it.

Desperate times and all that.

"Allons-y!" I yell, running forward.

The Zzloo closest to me turns, his gun dragging behind him. Dropping to my side, I slide into him feet-first.

As I slam into him, taking his legs out from under him, he falls into the one behind him. Two out, for the moment, but the first one and I are tangled together, and I can't get free quick enough. He's grunting and has somehow managed to hang onto his weapon.

"Rosalind!" Visidion roars over the sound of rifle fire and the struggle of bodies.

A crashing sound jerks my attention up in time to see Visidion land on top of the flight console. One massive hand grabs a Zzlo by the head. He tries to lift but three more bolts of electricity hit him from the side. His muscles spasm, and he loses his grip. His eyes lock with mine, and in that moment the deepest sense of loss I've felt since I rode the ship down to this planet opens up in my core and swallows the world around me. He reaches for me, his hand jerking uncontrollably. Convulsions take over his entire body. He goes rigid, straightening up to his full height, and then he falls backwards off the control panel landing with a bang that breaks my heart.

"Visidion!" his name rips out of my throat, tearing tissue with the force of it.

Grief and rage pour out in the syllables of his name. Pain in my chest, something ripping apart.

I kick my way free of the bastard that I'm tangled with and I plant my boot in his face. Something crunches and a dark, almost black blood runs down his face.

Rolling backwards, I get to my feet, low, then leap forward into the Zzlo rising behind the one whose face I just broke. I drive my shoulder into his neck until he falls back under the force, and I hear him trying to gasp in air. I don't know their anatomy, but it's similar enough to human to know that they need to breathe and the throat is the passage for air. His trachea is collapsed, so good luck with that, buddy.

Three remain. Things are happening so fast that they're only now taking their attention from Visidion.

A glimmer of hope alights deep in my core. A chance, small, but it's there.

The closest one of them turns, time is moving in slow motion, he turns, and I'm kicking at his knee in the same, stop-action motion. Before my boot reaches his knee pain blossoms like a delicate flower in my left side. Shockingly cold and numb until the petals open and my nervous system explodes. Convulsing, with one foot on the ground and the other swinging through air, I lose my balance.

When I land on my back, the air is knocked out of me as a fresh bout of numbing pain starts in my right thigh. My head bounces off the metal floor, more than once, as I struggle to take control of my body, but I'm betrayed. Control has been taken away. It's too hard to think.

Through my uncontrollably blinking eyes, the last thing I see is three Zzlo standing over me, dark rifles pointing down. They fire as one.

14

VISIDION

*D*im awareness of something heavy. A weight that is too much, more than I want to deal with. Easier to stay here in the darkness, let that heavy, awful weight be someone else's problem.

Rosalind.

Yes, Rosalind. Perfect, my treasure.

Where is she?

Hmm, have to find her.

Have to reach Rosalind.

Danger!

Danger?

That damn weight intrudes again. It's like it's calling to me, pulling me in.

What was I thinking?

Thinking, hard to hold a thought.

Everything is…

"ROSALIND!" I scream, leaping to my feet as I grab control of my body and slash my tail.

Clanking sounds, loud in my ears. Scrambling, dragging, metal on metal.

Eyesight is blurry, can't bring anything into focus.

My arms are heavy, pulled down, by... something.

"ROSALIND!"

"Stop it," a strange voice growls. It sounds like two rocks rubbing together.

"WHERE IS SHE!" I yell, turning blindly toward the voice.

"There, sit, shut up," the voice grumbles.

Rushing forward, towards the sound, the sound of metal dragging on metal, then suddenly my feet stop but I'm still intent on going forward. Falling. I land hard, smashing my face against the cold steel of the floor. The air is pushed out of my lungs.

"Hah!" a different voice laughs.

"Stupid," the gravel voice says.

I get to my knees. Fumbling, still unable to focus my eyes, I feel my way down my legs to my ankles, the point where something stopped my forward progress. Cold metal meets my fingertips. Tracing its circle around my leg, I find the point where a heavy chain connects me to something.

"Where is she?" I hiss.

"Quiet, no trouble," gravel voice says.

I blink rapidly until my vision clears enough to make out blurry shapes.

"Answer me," I say, listening to figure out which one of the blobs is the speaker.

"There," a blob says and motions to my left.

I grab for him but my fingers come up short of being able to reach him.

"Hah!" the other one laughs again. "You he get, Cenar."

"You, shut up," Cenar says. "There."

He motions again to my left. Unable to grab the source of my frustration, I place my hands on the metal floor and feel my way to the left. Chains clank as I move. Muscles hurt, every fiber of my body is in pain, but it doesn't matter. Rosalind is all.

My fingers touch something soft and cool. Leaning down, close, I see her face. Her perfect, beautiful face. I move a hand in front of her mouth, and a puff of air warms my palm. Dropping to the floor next to her, I let out a breath I didn't realize I was holding. She's alive. My treasure is alive.

I lie there for a long time. There's no way to mark the passage of time, but I lie there until my eyesight clears at last and it hurts less to breathe. Rosalind doesn't move, but I'm content resting my head next to her chest. The steady beat of her heart in my ear, her soft breath passing over my face, these things help me find my center. Knowing she's alive is enough. I give my body time to recover while she rests and recovers too.

As time passes, occasional thoughts form and then disperse. I let them go. All concerns are pushed aside as I bask in certainty that she's here with me. I'll deal with what comes next when I must. Until then, I'm going to rest. I know we're captured. I'm certain we've already been taken off world, so there is no rush.

Ragnar and Ladon will have to care for the Tribe. I know they'll lead them well. Rosalind and I will meet whatever comes our way. Her steady heartbeat pulsing in my ear makes a smile spread across my face. While I never could have imagined being where we are, I'm happy we're together. My treasure and I, free from the responsibilities that kept us apart. There is nothing in our way now. What was before doesn't matter any longer.

My vision clears at last. Every muscle hurts still, but it's a steady, throbbing pain that I quickly become used to. There is a soft vibration through the floor, the ship's thrusters engaging. Soon I'll deal with that. Right now I'm happy to enjoy the moment. The rise and fall of her chest and the sound of her life lulls me to a restful state. A certainty fills me. No matter what we have to face, we'll conquer it. Together, nothing in the universe can stop us for long. This is a temporary setback.

Chains rattle, pulling me out of my thoughts. I take my first real look at our surroundings. It's what I expected, a metal box of a room. Heavy chains connect Rosalind and me to the walls. There are others with us, none of them human or Zmaj. The one across from us looks like a rock that has taken on a vaguely bipedal shape. Massive, at least twice my size, he has rocky outcroppings protruding from his arms, legs, and chest. His mouth is a hard line, and nothing in his face looks any more expressive than a stone. He has dark, black eyes that stare at me with an air of resentment. This must be Cenar, guessing by his location and associating the voice I heard earlier with his appearance. He glares at me, his mouth opening and closing with a clacking sound of two rocks smacking together.

Left of him is a thin, gangly creature, covered with matted brown fur. It has a long snout for a face, sharp teeth, and beady, bloodshot yellow eyes. Two pointed ears, one of which looks like it was bitten half off, judging by its jagged edge. There's a furtiveness to the way it moves. The rotting, dirty rags it wears add to its overall air of decay. Its thin arms extend longer than it seems they should to hands with sharp, dirty claws that could easily tear through flesh.

Twisting my head to the limit, I find two more aliens. The first is small, even smaller than Rosalind, with deep blue skin and dark green eyes. Bright red hair with streaks of yellow decorate its head, sticking up in different directions. It is bipedal, shaped a lot like Rosalind, but half her size. Its head is between its legs, hunched over, staring at the floor in front of it.

The last one is lying on its back. A huge belly protrudes

so high that I can't see its face. Yellowish skin with blue striations and black swirls is exposed where its clothing pulls up over its distended stomach. Each of its legs look as big as my chest, and its feet are as big as my head. It doesn't have any footwear, but it doesn't need any—its feet look hardened and have long, green-yellow toenails that come to sharp points.

Only Cenar, the rocky creature, seems to be paying any attention. Staring at me with those black eyes, mouth opening and closing with soft clacks. When I meet its gaze, its mouth drops open, then we stare at each other for a long moment.

"You," Cenar says.

"What?" I ask.

It shakes its head, its mouth hanging open then snapping shut with a louder clack than before. It rolls its shoulders, and even that simple motion is accompanied by an echo of rocks sliding against each other.

"Trouble," Cenar says.

"Yes, ha!" the higher-pitched, fur-covered thing adds. "Trouble, you are, much trouble."

Cenar looks over, then back at me, shakes his head once more, then goes still.

"What trouble?" I ask.

"Make mad," Cenar answers.

"Ha! Mad, yes, mad," the other thing adds.

Rosalind's breathing shifts and her heart rate picks up. Sitting up to give her all my attention, I touch her face with the palm of my hand, smoothing her hair away from her eyes. Perfect. Tingles run from my fingers deep into my chest, her skin so soft it thrills me to touch it. Her eyes flutter then spring open. She sits straight up, eyes wide, mouth open.

"Visidion!" she cries out.

I take her into my arms where she struggles for an instant

and then collapses against my chest, holding me tight. A perfect, beautiful moment, that couldn't have been any better if I'd planned it in full. She inhales deeply before pulling back and looking me up and down.

"You're okay?" she asks.

"I'll be fine," I say, ignoring the deep aches.

Pursing her perfect lips, she nods and turns her attention around the room.

"Mmm, female it is, is pretty, yes," the fur thing says.

Rosalind looks at it, arches an eyebrow, and then shakes her head.

"How does that thing speak Zmaj?" she asks.

"I don't know," I respond.

"Zmaj? What Zmaj is?" it asks.

"The language you're speaking," Rosalind says.

"No speak, no," it shakes its head emphatically. "Translators it is."

She touches a hand to her ear. A small trickle of dried blood is on her cheek. I hadn't thought anything of it in the mix of her other wounds and the beating I was sure she'd taken after they'd dropped me, but obviously it means something to her.

"Interesting," she says. "How long was I out?"

"I'm not sure," I answer.

"Cycles, many," the fur creature says.

Cenar's mouth clacks several times, loud, pulling Rosalind's gaze to him. He shrugs, shifts, each movement loud and obnoxious.

"Seven sun cycles," Cenar adds, after all his noisy motions and clacking.

"Damn," Rosalind exhales, locking her eyes on to mine. "How screwed are we?"

An urge to lie rises from deep within me and I almost do. My mouth opens, the words are right there, but when they come out the truth is there with them. No matter how much I want to protect her, I can never go so far as to lie.

"Bad," I say.

"We're off the planet, aren't we," she says, not asking.

I nod agreement. She shakes her head again then grabs the shackle around her leg. The effort it takes her is obvious as she hefts the chain closer to her. Each link is as big as her fist. She examines it closely, her brow furrowing as she does. She drops it with a dissatisfied grunt.

"No escape," Cenar adds, helpfully.

"Escape you won't," fur creature says.

"What is your name?" Rosalind asks, looking at the fur creature.

"Mesto, I am," it answers.

"Rosalind," she says, then points at me. "This is Visidion."

"Cenar," Cenar says, pointing at himself.

"Well, we're all well and truly screwed. If we work together, we have our best chance of survival," Rosalind says.

Cenar and Mesto exchange a look making it clear they know something we don't.

"What is it?" I ask.

Cenar shrugs, rocks grinding, then closes his eyes and leans back against the wall.

"You don't know," Mesto says. "Bad place, we go."

"What bad place?" I ask.

"Krik," Cenar answers, not opening his eyes.

"No," I exhale.

"Krik?" Rosalind asks, looking at me. "That isn't where that Prince Astirian was from is it?"

Mouth dry, I nod.

"They can't have survived the War of Twelve—surely they were destroyed!"

Cenar grunts, the deep rumble of it echoing off the steel

walls and bouncing back to us over and over. It is the sound of despair, echoing.

"Dead, no," Mesto says. "No dead. Arenas. Many fighters, many many."

"How do you know that's where we're being taken?" I ask.

"Trouble," Cenar says. "Always troublemakers go Krik."

"Because you're big, and apparently they think she can fight," a new voice says. It's the blue creature, looking up for the first time I'm aware of.

"You are?" Rosalind asks.

"Not your friend," it answers.

"You have something better to do?" Rosalind counters, arching an eyebrow.

The blue creature stares at her, frowning. The tips of two small tusks stick out of the corners of its mouth.

"You, I like," it says. "I am K'sara."

"Nice to meet you," Rosalind says.

"It is nice for now, not so if we meet in the arena," K'sara says.

"Cross that bridge when we get there," Rosalind responds.

"Right," K'sara nods.

"What do we know about Krik?" Rosalind asks.

"Fighters bring the best price, but if you're good enough you can live well," K'sara says. "It's all about winning matches. The more you win, the more valuable you become, until you lose," K'sara says.

"Hah! Well live, die well," Mesto adds.

"What about escaping before we get there?" Rosalind asks.

"Escape where? We're in space," K'sara says.

"Why don't all you noisemakers shut up," the last creature in the room says without bothering to sit up.

"Hah," Mesto says.

"Todd," Cenar says. "Shut it."

"You'll be first on my list, Cenar," Todd says.

"List?" Rosalind asks.

"Oh yes," Todd says.

"What list?" I ask.

"The list of who I'm going to kill first," Todd responds. "Now shut up and let me rest."

"Wouldn't it be smarter if we come together?" Rosalind asks.

"Smarter for who? You, tiny female?" Todd asks. "I don't need anyone. This is my fate. I will embrace it."

Silence falls across the room as everyone contemplates his words. Rosalind scoots close to me, lying her head on my chest. I stroke her soft hair, lean against the wall, and close my eyes, letting my body heal. Soon enough I'll be put to the test. I won't be found wanting.

15

ROSALIND

e have no way to mark the passage of time. On the generation ship there was artificial day and night, built into the ship itself. One of the many things our ancestors considered in the design. Human bodies run on cycles of awake and asleep triggered by the external cues of day and night. In our small room there is no consideration of that. The only break in the monotony is when food shows up. A small section of the door to the room slides up, a bucket is shoved in, and then the section slams shut.

Those of us chained further from the door depend on Cenar to reach the bucket then share it around with us. When the first bucket shows up, my stomach grumbles loudly. I don't know when I last ate, but it's been a long time. Cenar grabs the bucket and pulls it to him. He scoops out a thick gruel with his hands and shovels it into his mouth. He licks his fingers clean each time before dipping them back into the bucket. A disgusting habit, and if I wasn't so damn hungry, I'd skip eating because of it.

I close my eyes and do my best to ignore the sounds of his eating. When he takes his fill, he passes it to Mesto, who has no such concerns, taking to it with a gusto that is loud and sloppy. Mesto passes it to K'sara and so it goes until at last Todd slides it to me. Closing my eyes and forcing my hand to move through an effort of will, I eat the slop. It's bad but not terrible. It's tasteless, mostly. What taste it does have is similar to dirt and ash mixed together to form a paste. When I finish it, I hand it to Visidion.

Once we finish eating, there is nothing left to do but to stare despondently around the small space at each other or to sleep. As time passes, I make small talk with our cellmates, learning what I can about them. Todd is the hardest to engage with. Of all of us, he seems the most resigned to his fate, embracing it with no interest in taking control of it. It might be a stretch to say we become friends or allies even, but there is a definite connection that I actively work to develop. I don't have a plan but the one thing I'm certain of is that if we're to escape we'll need help. With that end in mind, I work to build trust among the captives.

Assuming we all end up in the same place. Assuming there is a chance to get free. Assuming, assuming, assuming, lots of assumings because I have no data to work with. It doesn't matter, because I know what I'm doing right now is the right thing. Focusing on the now keeps despair at bay. Counting the meals and assuming that they feed us three times a day, two weeks pass by my estimation. Long, boring days, but I make a lot of progress in that time. Even Todd is opening up, if only a little.

The vibration of the ship's engines changes, going from a constant background thrumming to a violent shaking of the floor. All of us sit up, taking notice, except Todd who sighs loudly as his only response.

"What it is?" Mesto asks.

"We're slowing down," I answer, recognizing the feel of the thrusters reversing from my training as a fighter pilot.

"Ha!" Mesto says. "Krik, here we are!"

"So," I say, pulling the room's attention to me. "Are we in agreement?"

"Agree?" Cenar asks, the grinding sound of his body as he shifts positions almost drowning out his words.

"Yes, agree. We work together and find a way to gain our freedom back," I remind them all of the things we've talked about during the last two weeks.

"Free, together," Mesto nods so enthusiastically it looks like it could break his neck. "Mesto free. Yes, ha!"

"If we meet in arena? What then?" K'sara asks.

Over our time together I've learned that K'sara is practical to a fault.

"Are all arena battles to the death?" I ask, looking around to see if anyone actually knows.

"No," Todd says, sitting up and scooting around until his back is against the wall.

Todd's shirt rides up across his protruding belly, revealing more of the swirling black tattoos that cover his yellow skin, intertwining around the blue striations. He scratches himself, coughs loudly, then turns his head and spits.

"Then we do what we have to do," I say.

"Some will be though," he says. "Blood Fights make the most money, but they're rare. Usually for troublemakers. Like you."

"Good to know," Visidion says.

"I'll kill you, if I have to," Todd says. "But I don't want to. Not anymore."

"Thanks," I say, glancing over at Visidion.

Visidion can't hide his anger, not from me. The edges of his scales are a bright red, a sure sign he's pissed. Todd is big, but he doesn't seem to be quick or well muscled, both of which Visidion is. A match between them would probably go to Visidion. Putting a hand on Visidion's shoulder, I smile, trailing my fingers up his neck to cup his face. Now is not the time for him to be consumed by rage.

"What say you all?" I ask.

"Cenar agree," he grumbles.

"Mesto free, Mesto want," he says.

"Why not," K'sara answers.

All of us shift and stare at Todd. He's leaning his head back against the wall, eyes closed, apparently oblivious to all of us. We wait, bated breath, until I have to breathe.

"Todd?" I prompt.

"What?" he asks.

"Are you in?" I ask.

"What about wings? Haven't heard him speak," he says.

"I'm in, of course," Visidion says.

"What do you mean, of course?" Todd challenges.

Visidion hisses, rising to a crouch, the chain clanking. Anger rolls off him in hot waves.

This is a terrible moment for the bijass to turn him into a raging alpha male asserting his dominance.

Shifting quickly to put myself between him and Todd, I put both my hands on his face. His eyes are clouding over. I can see the rage taking control of him. Behind me chains drag across the floor as Todd shifts, ready to meet Visidion's attack. I have to stop this. Visidion grips my arms, his muscles tense, and in a moment he'll move me aside, and everything will be ruined.

Leaning forward quickly, I kiss him. I smash my lips into his so fast I hit with a bruising force. Ignoring the instant of pain, I shove my tongue into his mouth. His mouth resists, a moment, then his hard lips relax and move against mine, his tongue rises to meet mine as he returns the kiss in full.

Gasps surround us, then I hear Mesto cheering, jumping

up and down by the sound of his chains clanking, and clapping his hands.

"HA!" Mesto cries out.

The tension drains from Visidion. His lips, soft and warm against mine, his tongue dancing with mine, make my body respond, core tightening as my heart rate increases. His strong arms embrace me, pulling me tight. Molding against him, I open myself to him, forgetting our audience. His wings open then close around us, shielding the moment from view.

"Ah, fair not! Ha!" Mesto grouses.

Parting for air, I smile and Visidion returns the same.

"Better?" I ask.

"It's always better, with you," he whispers.

"Good," I smile.

Pushing away he folds his wings back and I turn to face our fellow prisoners.

"I'm in," Visidion says, gaze locked on Todd.

The tension rises while Todd stares back at Visidion. I don't know if Todd is being deliberately difficult or not. It's hard to read him. Mesto's head is turning back and forth between them, a stupid grin on his face showing the sharp teeth along his long mouth. It almost looks like he's panting. Does he want to see these two throw down?

"Okay," Todd says finally.

"You're in?" I ask, pushing him to state his intentions.

"For now," he shrugs.

Anger shoots through me, and almost I open my mouth. I manage to snap it shut before I say sharp words that will not help me accomplish my goals.

"Good," I say.

It is good. Good enough, anyway, and the most I can hope for right now. The ship bucks and shimmies, sure signs we're entering a gravity field. We'll land soon. I hope my vague plan of escape will work. Until we land, I lean back to the wall and close my eyes, letting the rough vibrations rock me into a mindless state of resting.

THE DOOR TO OUR CELL SLIDES OPEN WITH A CREAK. FOUR Zzlo guards stand outside it in full space armor, weapons at the ready. One of them enters, walks over to Cenar, and unlocks his chain from the wall. The other three have their weapons focused on him the entire time. Cenar stares at me as the Zzlo prods him with its gun. Slowly he climbs to his feet, and subtly I shake my head, letting him know it's not time yet. I'm watching for an opportunity for us to escape. I don't think, even if we all go together, we can take the ship. I'm hoping a better option appears.

Once Cenar is on his feet, the Zzlo drags Cenar's chain over to Mesto. Before he unlocks the chain holding Mesto to the wall, he attaches a collar to Mesto's neck, then hooks Cenar's chain to it. Instead of unlocking Mesto's chain from the wall, he walks out into the hallway. Another one of the guards there steps into the doorway, grabbing a small box that was attached to his belt. He raises the box before him, holding it out as if offering it to us. His thumb smashes down on the box and Mesto screams, eyes wide, body convulsing. An instant later Cenar drops to his knees, his deep rumbly voice screaming in pain.

"Stop it!" I scream, pain tearing through my chest, watching them suffer for no reason.

The guard with the box looks at me, grinning. The dreadlocks-like tentacles that serve as hair, each decorated with metal rings, clatter when he turns. A smile spreads across his grotesque face, his dead eyes shining with inner delight. He holds his thumb down longer, watching me. Hands balling into fists, I fight with every fiber of my being the instinct to go into action. Closing my eyes, I will my hands to unclench and my jaw to stop grinding.

When I open my eyes, he's still staring at me with that nightmarish grin. At last, he lifts his thumb and the screams stop. Mesto and Cenar both drop to the floor, panting heavily. Mesto is whimpering in pain, Cenar suffers silently.

The guard with the box steps back out into the hallway. The first one returns and continues his work of placing collars on each of us and then attaching the other prisoners' chains. When he comes to me, I meet his eyes and swear silently to myself that I will end him. Somehow, someday, I will destroy these evil bastards. Gershom had been my standard of bad but the Zzlo put him to shame. Gershom is power hungry, but underneath that he's scared. I've always known that about him, which allowed me to be compassionate towards him. Looking in this monster's eyes, I don't see anything but emptiness. No pleasure, no joy, almost no life—nothing but pure empty evil.

The collar clicks around my neck with a soft snap that sounds much louder in my ears than it actually is. Focusing, I keep my breathing even, making myself appear calm despite the storm raging in my heart. He moves on to Visidion and attaches the final collar, then goes to stand with the other guards.

"Move," one of them orders.

Cenar climbs to his feet, and then gives a hand to Mesto. He turns at last and walks. Two of the guards move back down the hall and the other two hold the chain leading all of us, pulling us along. My hopes of escape diminish. The chain gives them an edge that I hadn't expected. I'm certain that it can kill us if they want. Heart sinking, I move forward, struggling to keep a glimmer of hope alive.

16

VISIDION

*T*he bijass ebbs and swells at the edge of my thoughts as we're led off the ship.

"Visidion," Rosalind whispers, glancing over her shoulder.

"Yes?" I respond but forming the word takes an effort, pushing past the urge to destroy our captors.

"Trust me," she says.

Her soft voice cuts through the red fog, appealing, calling me to reason. Trust. Can I? She's been wrong before. Gershom is her mistake. She was blind to him despite my warning.

One mistake doesn't change who she is or my feelings. Trust her. I do.

The chains clank as we walk. She's right, now is not our chance. Focus on surviving, and we'll figure the rest out.

As we are led down the ramp off the ship, the air outside is cool on my scales. We emerge onto a decaying spaceport. The processed material of the pad is pitted with holes, and cracks run across the entire surface, clear signs of long neglect. Directly ahead of us sits a row of buildings that have metal infrastructure sticking out of the stone walls. Multiple other ships dot the spaceport but none of them appear to be in good repair.

A dozen different aliens move about the area, whether they're doing work or wandering aimlessly isn't clear. The four Zzlo guarding us herd us forward towards one of the buildings. There's a black gaping hole that might once have been a door but is now a broad opening. Emerging from the black hole comes a massive, hulking creature that puts Todd to shame for size. It's at least twice my size, maybe more. Its purple skin covers rippling mountains of muscles. It walks hunched over at the waist, shoulders rolled forward. A heavy protruding brow gives it the appearance of being barely more than an animal. On its shoulder is a creature no more than two feet tall with big eyes that dominate its round face. It seems to be lashed to the monstrosity of a walking mountain and guiding it by pulling on its ears.

"Far enough!" the small thing yells.

The Zzlo stop their forward progress, while the three not holding the chain prod us into a line with the butts of their weapons.

"Gladiators," the one holding the chain says. "Good ones."

"I'll be the judge of that, won't I?" the small creature says, tugging on the thing's ear.

The purple monster moves to the end of the line then leans even further over until I'm surprised it doesn't fall over. The small creature leans forward and inspects Todd at the end of the line.

"Hmm," he muses. "Not bad. Bit worn, though, isn't it? What did you feed it to make it so fat?"

"It's not fat, it's mass," the lead Zzlo answers. "Good for holding position in the arena."

"Hah!" Mesto exclaims.

The small creature jerks hard on its mounts ear and it turns so that he's now facing Mesto.

134

"Like that, did you, scrawny thing? It's pretty clear this one ate your share. What good are you going to be in the arena? You'll not last two microns," he says.

Mesto straightens to his full, scrawny height. The rags he wears shift in the wind to show his ribs.

"Mesto fights mightily," he says. "Hah! Mesto you take, Mesto skilled."

"At what, boring them to death?" the little buyer says.

"Hah!" Mesto responds, baring the rows of sharp teeth in his snout.

"We'll see," he says, frowning. He walks down the line, inspecting, pausing at me. "Zmaj?" he asks, looking at the Zzlo. "Nice."

My scales crawl, and my hands clench tight, because I'm fighting the urge to grab it and smash it under my foot. Now is not the time; I know it; but every instinct screams for me to fight. Rosalind's calm becomes a rock for me. She stands tall and straight, her head held high, an aura of control about her, despite our situation.

He moves down the line, coming to Rosalind.

"Female?" he says, looking at the Zzlo. "What do I do with a female, huh?"

"She's a fighter," the Zzlo answers.

"So you claim," he says. "Last female you brought me didn't last three fights."

"She's better," he says. "Best of the lot."

"I'll judge that," he says, manipulating his ride until his face is so close to Rosalind they're almost touching.

My core tightens, muscles tensed, knees bent. It's a feat to keep myself from leaping on him now. Rosalind doesn't move, doesn't blink, doesn't show any sign of discomfort as he leans around her face.

"If you don't want her, I'll sell her to Vin'taris," the Zzlo says, indifferent. "He'll be happy to pay a good price for her."

The Zzlo pulls a device off his belt, holding it in the same hand as the chain, poking at it with a finger.

"Heh? No!" the buyer responds. "No, I'll take them all."

"Two hundred fifty," the Zzlo says.

"Robbery!" he exclaims. "Seventy-five!"

"The Zmaj alone is worth more," the Zzlo answers.

They barter back and forth. Acid fills my stomach, creating nausea, as they dicker over our price. At last they come to an agreement, and the chain holding us all is passed over to the hand of the purple creature.

"Come," the small thing says. "You belong to Bacca now."

Rosalind catches my attention and nods almost imperceptibly. Calm comes with that nod. Now is the time. We're going to make our break. A thrill of excitement bursts through my nerves. Taking two steps forward, using the slack in the chain, I pass Rosalind, intent on the big creature. If I take it out, the small one won't be a threat.

Rosalind puts a hand on my arm as I pass her, and I look down to her. She shakes her head.

"Not yet," she mouths the words.

Hissing, I shake my head, looking at the creature's back in front of me, assessing its vulnerable spots.

"The female's right," the thing says without looking back. "You don't want to do that."

Waves of shock run across me.

"How?" I ask.

He turns his ride around towards the slaves. One tiny finger taps against the side of his head. "I know," he grins.

Cold creeps from my core and out to my limbs. It pushes the bijass aside, leaving nothing but reason in its wake. I step back into line. No matter how smart he thinks he is, every enemy makes a mistake. It's only a matter of when and being ready when he does.

"Hah!" Mesto says.

I shoot a glare at him, but he grins bigger and shrugs.

We're led through the dark opening and into the building. My outer lenses snap open, adjusting my eyes to the change in lighting. The interior is in an even worse state of decay than the exterior. The walls have so many openings blasted through them, they can barely divide the space. Sunlight streaming through holes in the ceiling is the only source of light.

Our despondent group treks through the wreckage, climbing over small piles of debris while moving around large ones, until at last we emerge on the other side—a busy city street. A wide variety of animals are leashed to posts along the roadside, while hundreds of different beings walk, run, barter, yell, and interact for as far as I can see in either direction. Yellow dirt forms the street, and the dust of it covers everything and everyone.

It's noisy, too noisy, an assault on my ears. It's been so long since I've heard the sound of so many living beings in a small area. Rosalind slows her walk until she's closer to me. She gives me a tight smile.

"It's okay," she says, so softly that I read her lips more than hear her words. "Stay calm."

A grimace is all I can manage in return. Warmth in my core flickers knowing she is picking up on my emotions. It's tempered by our situation. The collar around my neck chafes against my bare skin, a heavy reminder that we have nothing, not even our own freedom.

"Hurry up," our captor says, and then the being he rides jerks the chain forward. Cenar is pulled off his feet, slamming to the ground with a loud crack, crying out in surprise if not pain.

Mesto falls as the chain around his neck pulls tight with Cenar's collapse. Seeing it coming, I move fast. Grabbing the chain in front of Rosalind, I wrap it around my arm then pull back, bracing myself. The chain jerks, but I absorb the force from it, keeping it from hitting Rosalind. Protecting her.

As Cenar climbs back to his feet, Rosalind places a soft hand on my arm, smiling. She mouths her thanks to me as I let the chain go. The warmth grows in my core, having protected her at least that much.

We resume our march through the city. I'm surprised no one gives us a second look. Those whose gaze does pass over us seem to not even notice we're there. We're not the only ones with collars, though I don't see any others chained together as we are. Similar collars adorn at least half those I see. Watching them I see they act subservient to anyone without a collar on.

It would seem that slaves can reach a state of being able to roam freely. I assume they are on their masters' errands. None of the ones I see look like fighters. They don't have the build for it. Rosalind nods her head to the right. Following her indication, I see four creatures with collars. One of them, bigger than the other three, has a lighter chain connecting them all to a box in his hand. He walks with an imperious air, and the crowd is parting before him. Even those without collars step out of his way as he walks.

The three slaves following him are all obviously female and barely dressed. Each of them is bare chested with breasts exposed, all of them having the swells on their chests that I imagine are similar to Rosalind's, though none of them are human or have her coloring. The three keep their eyes cast down but sway their bodies in a way that shouts sex.

Bijass rages, rising inside me and grabbing control. My hands ball into fists, and I step to the side, with redness closing on the edges of my vision. This cannot be.

Spreading my wings as I bend my knees, I leap, not caring about the chain on my neck. Landing in front of the haughty creature controlling the females, I slam a fist into his thin, bony face. A satisfying crunch sounds, and then blue-green blood spurts from his broken nose. He screams, a high-pitched sound like an injured bivo calf.

Stumbling back, he drops the box controlling the slaves' chains. I grab it before it hits the ground, while the females cry out in fear. I crush the damnable box in one hand. A soft shock runs up my arm but only slightly numbs it. The bleeding male creature shouts something unintelligible, and then others are racing forward. The first to reach me is covered head to toe in rags with some kind of goggles over its eyes.

I punch it in the throat area before it gets within its own arms' reach, and it drops to the ground gagging. Something moves at the edge of my vision, and I swing my tail, making solid contact. I turn in time to see another flying up into the air and landing on its back with a whump.

Three more close from all sides, approaching with more caution. They have long sticks crackling with electricity and jab them in and out as they approach. Roaring my defiance, I turn back and forth keeping them all within my sight.

"Visidion!" Rosalind cries out in pain.

The purple creature our new owner rides has her, its one massive paw gripping the top of her head, holding her in the air, her feet dangling off the ground. Her face is red, eyes wide. The rage burns hotter. Rushing forward, I slam into one of the defenders with his electric stick, knocking him to one side with the force of the impact.

"Yes, Visidion, come my strong one, you'll be a champion for sure. Once I break you," our owner says, smiling.

Rosalind's mouth moves, but the blood rushing in my ears drowns out sound. Red covers my vision, and rage consumes me as I leap into the air. Wings spreading, catching a draft, carrying me forward. I'm already cocking a fist as I arc down at the monster holding my treasure.

White. Everything turns to white and pain. Can't control my body, convulsing on the dirt, every fiber burning. Distantly, the sound of Rosalind screaming my name. Her voice pulls me through.

I rise to my knees, muscles quivering as electricity pours through me. Gritting my teeth, I force myself to stand no matter the pain, no matter the betrayal of my body. No one will hurt her. She is my treasure. I am her guardian.

"This one will be my champion!" the small creature cackles.

"Stop, fool," Todd says.

One step forward, the pain increases, vision flashes on and off.

"Come my champion, show us all you have. Let us see if Noki won't break you," the creature says, smiling and bobbing up and down with excitement.

Rosalind still dangles from the huge creature's hand. I take another step, and Noki touches the box in its hand again. The pain is so intense there is no thought. My legs tremble as I force another step. Almost... there.

Water streams down Rosalind's face, stoking my rage higher. Another step, last one. A touch on the pad and the pain goes to heights unbelievable.

Balling my fist, blind with pain, I jab, striking the place where the purple monster's shoulder meets its arm. It cries out in surprise and pain, dropping Rosalind. The convulsions become less when I touch him, as the electricity moves through me to him. I leap forward, arms wide, and then grab onto the purple creature with both arms, enclosing it in a hug. It screams, and letting go, I scream too.

Together it and I fall to the ground, taking Bacca with us. The pain rises further, blinding, until I can't see or hear. Pain is all there is. Rosalind is free. When I know that, the pain spikes, and I lose myself to the darkness.

17

ROSALIND

"Fool," I mutter, crouching next to him, wetting the cloth again, and then wiping it across Visidion's forehead and cheeks.

"Impressive, he was," Mesto says, looking through the open door to the small room where they laid Visidion.

"He's a good fighter, stupid, but good," Todd adds, standing behind him.

The two of them move away from the door. After Visidion's resistance on the street, he was carried by the purple creature, and the rest of us were taken on a forced march out of the town. The walk to our new home was long, tedious, and boring. This planet isn't devastated like Tajss but it's not beautiful by any means. Barren, sparse brown weeds and grass, scraggly trees, and a bright yellow sun in an azure sky were all I saw.

A long, yellow dirt road led the way to a large estate. The estate consists of low mud-and-rock buildings surrounded by a mud-and-rock wall. It rests on the edge of a cliff beyond which is a sound that I think might be an ocean. I didn't see it, and haven't seen one in real life, so I'm guessing by the

MIRANDA MARTIN

sound from vid sticks in various entertainments I've
watched. My hand trembles as I wipe the damp cloth across
his forehead. Gritting my teeth, I will strength into the
muscles.

The tremors have been less than they were on the ship,
coming less often, but it's still a weakness. No one can know
the truth, so I have to hide them. Too many questions.

Or there would have been. On Tajss, with my people, who
are now on their own.

The realization hits with a weight that forces me back
onto the ground. It doesn't matter anymore. An empty void
pulses in my guts, aching like the throbbing of a painful
tooth. Despair threatens to push its way into my mind. It
would be so easy to let that dark, empty abyss swallow me.
To allow myself to abandon all I am, all I believe, everything
that I've fought for all my life. It doesn't look bad or scary, it's
. . . welcoming. A release. Letting go of all responsibility.

I close my eyes as the dark emptiness yawns, and I stare
into it, contemplating the ease it offers. Temptation. Living
for myself, alone. Spending what time I have left doing what
makes me happy. I could explore my feelings for Visidion.
See if there is more to this desire.

Tempting, so damn tempting.

But I can't.

That is not who I am. In my mind, I step away from the
abyss, refusing its dark gift. I glance around to make sure no
one is watching before I slip a hand inside my suit. There are
small pockets hidden throughout where I have small stashes.
I pull out a piece of epis. It's browning at the edges, the glow
almost completely gone. I slip it in my mouth and chew, but
its flavor is pale in comparison to how it should be. Another
problem that will arise soon. Without epis, I'll go into withdrawal eventually. It's as inevitable as Tajss's two red suns
rising.

A problem for another day. One moment at a time.

Visidion's chest rises and falls steadily, his hearts beat strong—he'll recover. There's nothing more I can do for him except wait and keep him comfortable. I've been forcing the broth they feed us down his throat, to keep his strength up. It's been a day since we've arrived at the estate. We were herded into one of the stone-and-mud buildings and left on our own ever since. The building has a single common room with several doorways that give onto smaller rooms. We've each laid a claim to one of them. The floor is yellow dirt, hard packed so it's almost like a real floor. There were a few blankets and pillows, and the central room has a small fire pit in the middle of it that was complete with stoked coals.

When I step into the main room, the others are sitting around the fire.

"What happens next?" I ask, taking a seat in their circle.

"Ha!" Mesto answers, unhelpful as usual.

"Soon we'll be trained, then we'll fight," K'sara answers. "Then eventually, we'll all die, and new slaves will be purchased, and they'll repeat the cycle."

His shoulders are hunched, and his voice is as heavy as his words.

"I won't die," Todd says, confident.

"Ha! Right, Todd no die, ha!" Mesto adds.

Cenar shifts, sounding like a small avalanche as his rock joints rub together.

"We all die. Sooner or later, we die," Cenar sighs.

"No, we don't," Visidion says, and everyone turns to look at him. "We fight, we win."

He's leaning against the door frame. He inhales deeply, grimaces, exhales heavily, then pushes off the door frame. When I rush to him, he smiles and accepts my help, leaning on me, if only partially. My heart pounds in my chest, just from being close to him. Together we walk to the circle. Everyone scoots to the side, making room for us.

"There is no winning," K'sara sighs. "Even if we do, eventually they'll pair the best of us off against each other."

"We'll figure it out," Visidion says, his eyes locked on mine. "I've seen it."

"Ha! A seer?" Mesto asks.

Visidion nods, but our eyes never leave each other.

His father claimed to have visions. His visions led to the creation—and survival—of the Tribe. They claim he foresaw the devastation and gathered those who believed him, and together they escaped the brunt of the war. I've not given it much thought, but visions aren't something I would consider a reliable way to plot my future. Mostly I'd considered it a convenient fable, something to help bring the survivors together, more than anything close to the truth. Visidion's eyes beam his conviction and belief in his words. A smile spreads on his face as he reaches over and takes my hands in his.

"Together," he whispers.

My chest aches, pulse pounds in my ears, and I'm light-headed. As if I'm a schoolgirl experiencing my first crush. The palms of my hands tingle resting against the rough edges of his scales. Fire rages in my core, a rising urge that comes with a desire to throw myself at him. Let him have his way with my body and take his pleasure of me.

"You have a plan to go with that vision?" I ask, throat so dry the words are hard to push out.

"No," he smiles, shaking his head. "I have faith, in you. In us."

"Faith," I repeat.

"Yes," he nods.

"You've gone insane. That blow to the head must have been too much," I say.

"I'm fine," he says. "I see more clearly now than I have for a long time. These trials before us, that's all they are. Trials meant to test us, to forge us. Padraig could tell you about the forging of steel, tempering, making it stronger. This is our forging and I have seen that together we will succeed."

"You and I?" I ask, arching an eyebrow, feeling the weight of the others' intent stares.

"All of us," he says.

"Ha! Mesto too?"

"Yes, Mesto too," Visidion answers.

"Definitely a blow to the head," Todd says. "Todd is first for Todd."

"Of course," Visidion says.

His conviction is infectious. Strong, pulling me to him.

"A fool's errand, we're all doomed," K'sara says, despair in his voice.

"No," Visidion says, breaking his gaze with me for the first time, and turning his gaze to each of the others in turn. "It's going to take all of us. Together, we can survive."

Boots hitting dirt approach our door, followed by the sound of a key in the massive lock that hangs off it. A grizzled man walks in. He's almost human looking, but his skin is onyx black, too black for a human, and his eyes are bright orange. Buzz-cut gray hair covers his head, and his face is wrinkled, worn, and scarred all over. Two leather straps crisscross his chest, and a red kilt rests on his waist. Sticking over his shoulders are the hilts of two swords. He stares at us with eyes that look like raging infernos.

"What a sorry lot of losers," he growls.

"Todd no loser!" Todd yells, leaping to his feet, fists balled at his side.

The newcomer looks at Todd and grimaces.

"Oh look, baby wants to cry," he taunts Todd.

Todd looks apoplectic, shaking in place, staring wide-eyed at the newcomer. Strange, because I've never seen Todd not in control of himself.

"Who are you?" Visidion asks, climbing to his feet.

"Sir, to you, scrub," he says, not taking his eyes off Todd. "Maybe, one day, you'll earn the right to learn my name. Until then you will all call me sir."

The hairs on back of my neck bristle, but patience is key, so I bite back on my smart remarks.

"Okay, sir," Visidion says. "Who are you then?"

"Your trainer," he says. "All of you, outside. This is the first day of the rest of your lives. We have to get you ready for the arena, and I've only got seven turns to make sure you at least die with enough grace to return the master's investment in you."

He turns his back, arrogant to a fault, and stalks out the door. Exchanging looks with the others, we follow him out.

"Line up!" he barks, and we form a rough line.

The central area of the estate is an open, hard-packed circle. The largest building is to the left of us, and I assume that it's the main house. There is a balcony running the length of it, and shadowy figures on it watch the proceedings down here. There are dummies along the far wall and several crates of weapons rest along the sides. Our building butts up against the exterior wall. There are three other buildings that are duplicates of the one we stay in. Three doors in the surrounding wall give access to the areas outside this space. One of them is a large double door, big enough for wagons to come in. The other one is the obvious one, but I notice the third one tucked away in a corner by the big house, covered in shadows.

Noting the exits and possible escapes, I file them away in my memory for later use. Sir walks down the line of us, inspecting each of us with a critical eye. When he reaches me, he turns his head to the side and spits, shaking his head.

Looking over his shoulder up to the balcony he arches an eyebrow.

"What am I supposed to do with this?" he asks the shadows.

He waits as if expecting an answer but nothing happens. Sighing he turns back to me.

"You'll be first to die," he says, stepping on.

"I don't think so," I answer.

He whirls on one foot and shoves his face into mine.

"You don't think so, what?" he yells, dank breath that smells of raw meat assaulting my senses.

"Sir, I don't think so, Sir," I answer, coming to full attention as my military training kicks in.

"Good, scrub," he says. "Then you'll go first in proving yourself."

"Fine, sir," I answer.

"No, I will," Visidion says, stepping out of line.

"You will do what you're told, scrub," Sir barks.

"You, female, forward, let's see what you got," he orders.

Glancing at Visidion, I mouth to him that it's fine.

The tension in his shoulders, his fists balled at his sides, the anger and frustration flashing in his eyes are there for anyone to read. Visidion isn't subtle. I step out of line and stand at attention. Right now we must do what we have to, play the game until the way out becomes clear.

Sir paces around me in a circle. Forcing my mind into a state of relaxation and preparedness allows me to push aside everything. It's a pure state. Years of training brought me to it. Every sense is heightened, information is processed at increased rates of speed. I'm ready for anything. The sound of his boots grinding into the dirt as he paces around me tell me a story. When he shifts his weight from his right to his left and his hand balls into a fist, the shifts in sound and the way he feels behind me gives me warning.

I duck, and his fist swishes through the air where my head was. Crouching, I spin on my right heel, swinging my left leg, sweeping for his legs. He's fast, leaping over my sweeping leg and landing neatly behind it. His fist swings down, aiming for the head again, but I roll backwards over my left shoulder and spring to my feet in a ready stance. Fists before him, his dark gaze looks me up and down. A deep, throbbing pain in my left thigh threatens to betray my display of strength, but I hold it at bay through a sheer effort of will.

Sir lowers his fist, straightens, and then gives a sharp nod.

"Not bad," he says. "The rest of you sorry lot could learn from her."

I catch Visidion's eyes. Worry and anger war in his face, but I also see his pride. He's going to have to come to terms with my being able to take care of myself, or he's going to get us both killed. Stepping back into line next to him, my heart rate returns to normal as I take a deep breath and feel the adrenaline fade. My left arm trembles, and not from the after effects of the conflict, so I clasp my hands behind my back in a parade rest hoping no one caught the moment of weakness. At the same moment I see Sir staring at me, and his eyes narrow. He purses his lips, and my heart pounds in my chest.

Shit!

"Okay scrubs, pair off," Sir orders. "I want to see what each of you brings to the table. Work hard if you want to earn your dinner."

Snapping out orders, he pairs Visidion off with Todd, K'sara with Cenar, leaving Mesto for me.

Mesto is shorter than I am, with long, gangly arms that end in sharp claws and he also has a snout full of sharp teeth. While he appears small and possibly weak, I'm not going to underestimate him, even if this is only supposed to be sparring. Mesto stares at his feet, moving to stand four feet in front of me, then shakes his head.

"Ha! Sorry, Mesto is," he says, not looking up.

"Start!" Sir barks.

Mesto becomes a flying blur of fur and claws. It's all I can do to block blows that seem to come from all directions at once. Claws scrape against my space armor suit making loud noises as they try to find purchase. I'm a fraction too slow. Pain flashes red through my brain, and fire lights up on my left cheek where his slashes make contact. Backing up, I'm on full defense, unable to land a single offensive blow. Blood drips down my cheek, staining my white suit.

"Rosalind!" Visidion screams, jerking my attention to him.

He's staring at me instead of watching Todd. Todd's massive fist connects with Visidion's jaw, and there's a sickening crunch. Visidion staggers under the force of the blow, stumbling to the side as he struggles to stay upright. Mesto connects with my stomach, and my breath rushes out in a blast, leaving me gasping as I stumble backwards and trip over something, landing hard on my ass.

Mesto lands on top of me, a blur. Raising my arms, trying to protect my face, I turn from one side to the other, trying to dislodge him.

"Enough!" Sir barks.

Mesto stops, leaping backwards to land softly on the balls of his feet. Todd is storming towards Visidion. Visidion has his balance back, his right hand balled into a fist, close to the ground. He's watching Todd's approach and pulling him in closer. As Todd closes, Visidion swings, a wild haymaker, but it has his full force behind it.

Sir catches Visidion's fist right before it connects with Todd. Pushing Todd back with his other hand, he throws Visidion's arm through the motion, forcing Visidion to follow through with it. Visidion spins, Sir using his own momentum against him, stumbling the other direction. Visidion spreads his wings to catch his balance then turns towards Sir, red rage in his eyes.

"Try it, scrub," Sir says, his voice low and dangerous.

His arms are at his sides, and he seems relaxed, but I have no doubts that he is ready for Visidion's attack.

Visidion shudders, his tail standing straight up behind him, the edges of his scales tinting red, visible signs of the rage storming in him. He doesn't move, glaring, as the red tint fades and his tail lowers back to the ground. He closes his wings, then nods his head.

"Smart," Sir says. "Back in line scrubs."

We shuffle back into a loose line. As everyone shifts I run a hand down Visidion's bulging bicep and we share a quick glance. Survive. We have to survive and bide our time. His almost-imperceptible nod in response is all I need.

"Okay, not bad," Sir says, pacing up and down our line. "Rule one, in sparring never go for permanent damage. Your value is in the arena. No one is paying to watch you train. If you cause permanent damage to your sparring partner, you will be immediately put in for the Blood Games. Understood?"

"Yes sirs" greet his question, but I don't answer.

"What are the Blood Games?" I ask.

"Ha, she knows not," Mesto barks.

"Battles to the death," Sir answers, not breaking his stride.

Okay, good to know. Avoid the blood games. Visidion and I exchange a glance. One day at a time, wait and watch. Sir continues laying out the rules. We listen to them all, and then we're arranged into new pairings. The training begins in earnest.

1 8

VISIDION

"All right scrubs," Sir barks, marching down the line of us. Outside, the roar of the crowd reaches a crescendo. In here, dust falls from the ceiling and there's a thumping as they stomp their feet. "Make a good show of it out there! Earn out what Master paid for you."

"Sir, yes, sir," we answer in unison.

Though I hate to admit it, he has made me a better fighter. We've been sorted into pairs, and Rosalind is my partner. K'sara and Mesto are matched, and Cenar and Todd are the other pair. Sir looks us over with a critical eye. I'm still trying to get used to having the leather bandoliers criss-crossing my chest. Once we're in battle it will be useful, but I hate the feel of it against my skin. It's restrictive. I roll my shoulders and neck to ease the tension.

"Look," a new voice says. "Thrace has a new batch of scum."

We all look out the door of our prep area. The gladiators prepare in a room under the arena. Wood slats form the ceiling, holding the dirt of the arena floor up. Rough walls divide the space into rooms off a central gathering area where the medics have workstations. Two men stand outside our door looking in. The first is bright purple with bulging muscles and a heavy, protruding forehead, and the other is as red as a majmun's ass and smaller than I am. He has a rugged look to him with sharp features and piercing eyes that are just as red as his skin.

"Step back, Brisong," Sir says, stepping to the open door of our area.

"Why, you going to do something, old man?" Brisong, the purple one, answers while cracking the knuckles of his hands in Sir's face.

"Save it for the arena," Sir answers him.

"How's it feel?" Brisong asks.

"Tell us, Thrace," the red one says. "What's it like to be such a has-been?"

They're obviously baiting him, but Sir doesn't bother responding. In the ultimate show of disrespect, he turns his back.

"Scrubs—" he says, but then Brisong grabs him by his shoulder.

Sir moves with a blinding speed, grabbing Brisong's hand and twisting. Turning into him, he forces Brisong to his knees as he twists his arm. Brisong cries out in pain as he drops. Sir brings his right leg up against Brisong's neck, holding the arm by the wrist extended, his gaze locked on the red one.

"Try it," Sir says. "You'll lose your partner."

"You wouldn't dare," the red guy says. "We're third on the ladder!"

"Try me," Sir says.

"Stand down," Brisong says, pain in his voice.

Red guy is leaning in, eyes burning hot with rage, fists coming up, ready to make a move. All of us step forward, making a semi-circle around Sir. It's strange, because I don't think about it. Over the week, Sir has earned our respect. I have every intention of escaping and taking Rosalind away from here, but that has nothing to do with the grizzled onyx warrior. He's a cog in the machine, a warrior like us, surviving day to day. The red guy's gaze shifts from Sir to us and he takes a step back unclenching his fists.

"Fine," he says.

Sir nods and lets go of Brisong, stepping back as he does. Brisong rises, holding his shoulder and massaging the muscles.

"You'll pay for that," he hisses.

"For what? Being a 'has-been' who just kicked your ass?" Sir taunts.

Rage plays across Brisong's face as he splutters, unable to form words. Red guy grabs his arm and pulls him away.

"We'll see your people in the arena," Red guy says over his shoulder.

The two of them swagger off. My scales itch and my palms burn with the desire to beat them both.

"Who was that?" Cenar asks.

"Number three team on the ladder," Sir says, turning to us. "Dangerous and dirty. If any of you are lucky, you'll rise to face them," he says. "When you do, I'll expect you to kick their asses, again."

Murmurs of agreement rise from us.

"As I was saying," he continues. "This is your first show-ing, so don't you disappoint me. You're at the bottom of the ladders, so no one is going to expect much. Don't over show. Hold back."

One of the lessons he's stressed over the past seven turns is to not do more than you must to win. The arena is as much about show as it is about skill. We'll be playing to the crowds. Please them and we advance; displease them and we end up in the Blood Games.

153

"Today should not be difficult for any of you. You're not the sorriest lot I've ever had to work with."

The closest he's come to complimenting. Pride swells in my core taking me by surprise. How can I feel pride when I'm a slave? Rosalind leans close as Sir dismisses us.

"We've got this," she whispers.

"Yes," I agree.

Dirt falls from the ceiling as the crowd above goes crazy. Screaming and stomping, making the ceiling vibrate so hard that I wonder it doesn't collapse under their excitement.

"Seven widows' brides!" someone outside yells and the other gladiators rush into the center area.

"Tanir is hurt!" someone yells.

Rosalind and I exchange a look, and then we look at Sir. He's standing with his arms crossed, shaking his head.

"That can't be," he says.

The gate that blocks the prep area from the arena floor clanks as heavy chains lift it. Two big creatures like the purple monstrosity that our new owner rides rush down the sloping hall to the main room, carrying a stretcher between them. Medics rush over, taking the stretcher and putting it on one of their tables. A heavily muscled, yellow-skinned creature with long black hair lies on top of it, green blood oozing from long, deep cuts that race across his chest. He grunts as they tend to his wounds.

Whispers and murmurs pass around as the gladiators gather to see how bad it is. Rosalind takes my hand, pulling me back from the crowd until we're next to Sir, who watches with an impassive frown on his face.

"Who is that?" she asks.

"He's the number-one ranked gladiator, top of the ladder," Sir answers.

"What happened?" she asks.

"Was I there?" he barks.

Rosalind stares, not responding to his gruffness. He meets her steady gaze until his shoulders drop.

"Looks like wounds from a trinfar," he says at last.

"What's a trinfar?" Rosalind asks.

"Supposed to be illegal," he mutters.

"That doesn't answer the question," I say.

"No, it doesn't," he says as a long low cry emerges from the center of the crowd. "Curse the Seven Widows."

"Thrace," Rosalind says, using his name. "Please."

That jerks his attention to her, the frown on his face deepening.

"Animal, claws and teeth," he says. "Green, orange stripes, weighs three to four hundred stone. Its claws ooze a poison for which there is no antidote, which is why they were banned. If that is what he fought, then someone is changing the rules."

The high-pitched cry becomes a scream that cuts off, leaving a heavy, empty silence in its wake. The silence weighs across all of us as we exchange quick glances. Rosalind clenches my hand in hers, and instinctively I place an arm around her shoulders, pulling her close. The ceiling above vibrates as the crowd screams in excitement.

"NEXT!" the cry echoes down the tunnel to the arena.

Thrace taps me on the shoulder.

"You two are up," he says.

Nodding, throat tight, I walk up the ramp with Rosalind. The two wooden swords strapped to my back clap against me as we walk. Rosalind has a wooden staff that she taps the dirt of the tunnel with. We reach the heavy iron gate. Two wooden doors are closed on the other side of it, blocking our view of the arena, but now I hear an announcer, his voice echoing and doubling over as it reaches me.

The crowd oohs and aahhs as the announcer plays up the spectacle they are about to see. Rosalind shivers.

"Are you okay?" I ask.

This is the first moment we've had to ourselves since our capture by the Zzlo. She glances up, frowns, then nods.

"I'm fine," she lies.

"What is it?" I ask. Her shoulders tense and the line of her jaw tightens as she continues staring straight ahead, as if willing the problem, whatever it is, out of existence. "Rosalind?"

"Epis," she says at last.

The world falls out from beneath my feet. How could I have forgotten it?

"How much do you have left?" I ask.

"What I have is no longer effective," she answers.

Two, maybe three weeks. That's all we have. A sense of urgency makes my scales itch. Irrationally, I look around hoping to spot an escape, as if there could be one conveniently waiting for us.

"Okay," I say, numbness creeping in and replacing the sensation of falling.

"It's fine," she says.

"For now," I add.

"Yes," she says.

"We have to escape," I say.

"Of course we do," she says. "We will."

"Yes," I answer as the gate clanks and then starts to rise.

The wooden doors swing open, and bright yellow light stabs into the dim tunnel, creating flashes in my eyes. My outer lenses snap shut, filtering out the light and clearing my vision. The arena is a giant circle surrounded by a wall behind which rises seats crowded with aliens of all shapes and sizes. When I step out first, the crowd roars so loud it's deafening. Rosalind comes a step behind me, as we practiced. My larger size makes me an obvious target, which we plan to use to our advantage.

On the opposite side of the arena, our opponents emerge. They're big but not huge and look enough alike that they must be related. Yellow-skinned humanoids with large heads and massive tusks sticking up from the corners of their mouths. One of them has a trident and net, the other is wielding a large club. They raise their arms as they march straight ahead, waving at the crowd who responds raucously.

Rosalind and I march forward, but our opponents start jogging, picking up speed as they approach. Rosalind breaks to the right as I go left, making a V away from each other. Our opponents look at each other without breaking their run, then cross paths. The net and trident heads for me, while the club heads for Rosalind. I can't suppress my smile, exactly what I'd hoped for.

Trident swings his net in a lazy loop around his head as I run sideways keeping myself facing him while moving farther away from Rosalind, forcing him to turn to follow me. He stabs towards me with the trident, growling. Facing him fully, I dance sideways to keep him moving, but now I'm slowly looping around towards Rosalind again as she does the same.

Trident throws the net, which I expect. It flies through the air in a slow-motion arc. Ducking my chin, I dive forward and roll across my left shoulder, continuing the roll until I'm close to him. I leap out of the roll, spread my wings, and pull the wooden swords. Trident turns, dumbfounded to find that I'm airborne. With surprise on my side, I have plenty of time to swing my weapons. I slam the wooden swords on either side of his head. With the loud crack still echoing through the stadium, his eyes widen, his mouth falls open, and then he drops the trident.

As I land over him, he slams down, unconscious.

"Visidion!" Rosalind cries.

Club has her on defense, swinging wild, forcing her into

retreat. She dodges his clumsy swings, but he's bigger than she is and has a greater reach. I throw the sword in my left hand. It circles through the air, hilt over blade, but misses my target, going by his ear. He glances to the side and Rosalind attacks. Ducking under his swinging club, she comes up inside his reach and lands multiple blows to his core. Her knee comes up between his legs with so much force I feel sympathy pain for him.

He screams at such a pitch it makes my ears hurt as he falls over backwards, curling into a ball on the yellow dirt.

The arena is silent. Too silent. I could hear the whisper of a distant star in this silence. No one moves in the stands. The crowd is stunned, and if it's a good thing or a bad thing I don't know. I go to Rosalind's side and take her hand. Built above the crowded seats of the rest of the arena is a lavish raised box. Massive purple banners hang in front of it, each with a white hand painted in a red circle. The raised box has fancy seats in it, and a huge, fat alien sits there, staring down.

The crowd is staring at him, waiting, so Rosalind and I stare at him too. Thrace told us about him. This is the new king of Krik. He rules by brute force and fear. Nothing happens on Krik without his approval. The few stories I've heard about him make him seem little more than a bully. Looking at him doesn't change my opinion.

Rolls of fat hang over the fancy robes he wears, and his face is pale to the point of almost seeming translucent. He's so big his arms seem too short to reach his mouth, and indeed he has servants to either side, one holding a massive cup and the other a leg of meat. Others hover close to him, patting his face with towels, brushing crumbs from his belly, and fanning him. On either side of him sit those in favor with the crown. One of them catches my attention. A Zmaj sits there, wearing rough leather armor and staring down at me with cold eyes. His scales are edged yellow with hints of blue. A potential ally?

"Gladiators," the king says, his voice a whining sound that makes my bones ache with the desire to punch him in his fat face. "You've fought well. Almost... too well."

He lets that hang in the air, unclear about what that means for our fate. Slowly his massive head turns towards the Zmaj at his side.

"What say you, Arcan?" the king asks.

Arcan stares down, frowning, his wings rustling.

"They are undermatched," he says at last.

"Yes, yes they are, impressive. They shall be moved up the ladder, four, no... six rungs!" the king declares.

The crowd erupts. The noise is deafening. Rosalind says something, but I can't make out the words. We walk out of the arena, ears ringing with the excitement of the crowd. Now to find out what such a jump on the ladders means for our future.

19

ROSALIND

"Don't let it go to your heads, scrubs," Thrace says. Standing at attention in the practice yard, Visidion and I wait under his stare. "All of you made a good showing, but good isn't good enough."

He pairs us off and we train.

We're worked so hard every day that it's almost easy to fall into an acceptance of it. End the day too tired to hold your head up, eat, and fall asleep. Wake up early only to start the same again. Thrace is a hard trainer, fair but hard. He pushes us beyond our limits until those limits expand.

We have fourteen turns until our next match. Fourteen turns, but that's longer than I have. I'm out of epis. Any day now I'll start feeling the effects of withdrawal. How will my body react? I only hope I can hold the worst of it at bay.

At the end of the day, we all sit around our common fire and eat our meal. Now that we've made a good showing in the arena, our food is better than when we first arrived and includes actual meat, though God knows what it's the meat of. No one is talking. All of us are exhausted.

"Ha!" Mesto says, at last, setting his plate aside and lying on his back. "No escape. No hope."

"Don't say that," I mutter.

"Why not?" Todd asks. "How do we escape? You have a ship hidden in that suit of yours?"

"We don't give up," Visidion says. "I've seen it."

"Seen it, ha," Mesto says.

"I'll believe it when I see it," K'sara sighs. "I'm too tired to think about it right now."

Cenar watches everyone with mild interest but doesn't say anything. The depression in the room is heavy, an aura of despair threatening all I've built.

Rising to my feet, I meet the gaze of each of them.

"It'd be easy," I say.

"Easy?" K'sara asks. "Nothing about our lives is easy."

"Yes, it would be," I answer him. "Easy to give in. Go into agreement with it all. This is where we are, what we are. Gladiators. Train every turn, fight every fourteen. Eventually we'd lose, but maybe between now and then, we would build some prestige and get to retire in something resembling comfort."

"Doesn't sound bad," Todd says.

"No, because it's easy," I answer him, rolling my shoulders and feeling the moment. They're all staring at me, counting on me. "Easy, you see? It's how they win. Breaking us down with the lure of easy, going through the motions. No time to look at the big picture. No time to think clearly."

"Ha, this easy not," Mesto says.

"But the promise is," I insist. Visidion's eyes dance with an internal fire flowing support to me. "The promise of a brighter future, do the routine, fall into it, and agree. We can't do that! We can't go into agreement because the moment we do, that's the moment we lose."

"Lose?" K'sara asks, leaning forward.

"Yes. We lose, they win. That's what you have to see. They've designed an entire system around future rewards, pushing you to agree. There has to be a way off this planet. We have to find it. We can escape. We can be free."

"What do you know?" Todd grumbles.

Todd and I lock gazes. Cold sweat runs down my back, and then a tremor races through my right thigh. A reminder of what is waiting for me. A race. Which will be the end of me first, epis withdrawal? Or the other. . . the big secret I haven't told anyone.

"I know," I say, throat dry, eyes scratchy. "I'm sick, very sick. I'm dying. Every day I wake up wondering if this is the last one. Every day I face the ease of going into agreement with the 'way it is' or doing the hard thing. Making the hard choices."

Purposefully I avoid Visidion's gaze, but I feel it boring into me. My arms shake, and I can't look at any of them anymore. The words sit heavy between all of us.

"Rosalind," Visidion says, his voice tight with unexpressed emotions.

"No," I say, pulling my hand away before he can grasp it. Tears well in my eyes. "You all have to see what I see. I don't know how long I have. It may not be long—or it might be. All I know is that every day I don't have the luxury of easy. We have to escape. I don't want to die on this godforsaken shit-hole of a planet, far from my people. They need me. And so I need you."

Turning my back on them I walk out the door into the cool night air. When I'm released from their gaze, my tears fall free. I haven't cried since that day in the doctor's office. The day he said the words, giving me my diagnosis. Cancer. The tremors, passing weaknesses, and occasional moments of being dizzy. I'd thought it was exhaustion from pushing myself too hard. How wrong could I be?

Cancer, an almost unheard-of disease. Dr. Traven said he had to dig deep into the ship journals to identify what it was. The forefathers of everyone aboard the generation ship had gone through extensive genetic testing to screen out all possible defects. Somehow, whatever made me susceptible to this had gone unnoticed. He told me then I had a year, maybe two. Tumors were growing in my body, slowly affecting my nervous system, and the symptoms would only grow worse until one day I would be too weak to stand.

The door to our hut opens and shuts. Wiping away the tears, I cross my arms over my chest, bracing myself. Bulging arms wrap around me, and Visidion rests his head on my shoulder, pulling me tight against him but not saying a word. I stiffen, waiting for the sympathy or the questions, or any of the myriad things that come when someone finds out you're dying. All the things I avoid because I don't want to deal with them. He tugs me closer, tighter to his chest, and remains silent. Holding me.

The tension grows until my muscles tremble. Any moment now he'll say something.

Warm breath breezes across my cheek, and still he's silent. My resistance crumbles, and I melt against him. He takes my weight, holding me up. As the tension fades, the elasticity of my muscles goes with it, and I collapse into him. I turn to face him and meld to his hard muscles, and then rest my head on his shoulder. Unbidden, the tears return, and I let them fall, soaking his shoulder. I cry until there's nothing left, and still soft sobs wrack my chest. I don't know how much time passes in silence. His hands stroke my hair and rub circles on my back, until at last I'm empty. All the pain and fear is exhausted.

The truth is out there. He knows.

Straightening, I wipe my cheeks dry, unable to meet his eyes. Shaking my head to clear it of the cottony cloud filling it, I take several deep breaths until my lungs fill and empty without catching on the last of my emotions. Feeling back in control at last, I rest a hand on his chest, staring at the chiseled muscles. I let my fingers follow the lines, their tips tingling as I trace the edges of scales that overlap across his skin. One of his large hands cups my cheek, and I nuzzle into it without further thought.

His other arm is around my waist, and it strikes me that I'm encircled by him. Not just physically, but emotionally too. Soft but intense waves of love and concern wash over me, and somehow it's a physical sensation. My skin burns as it washes over me, warming to his feelings. Slowly I raise my eyes towards his. My stomach is clenching as a cold ball of fear forms, fear of what I'll find in his eyes. I don't want to see it, but it'll be there. Sympathy. The one thing I don't need. Unable to avoid it any longer, I meet his gaze.

It's not there.

Not a sign of sympathy. Concern and what I can only label as love shines from his eyes, but not a hint of sympathy. His fingertips trace the line of my jaw and cross my lips, pulling them open as he passes across them. Soft, gentle, a touch filled with desire, but more, it conveys feelings below the level of words. Tightness in my core throbs with sudden, unexpected need.

Rising on my toes, seeking his lips. I find them and we kiss, causing exploding fireworks through my thoughts, blasting away trepidation. His lips move against mine, devouring doubts, reservation, and worries. Through his lips, he gives himself to me and I cannot but respond the same.

Wrapping my arms around his neck, I lift myself into his kiss, and then he lifts me off my feet, matching our heights. When I lock my legs around his hips, the bulge in his pants presses hard into my core, fanning the flames higher. Desire runs through me with a wracking shudder.

His tongue drives past my lips, claiming my mouth as his. Giving myself to him in ways I've never opened to another, I am his. This moment, right now, nothing else matters.

Disagreements, worries, duty, all crumble before the assault of his lips on mine.

My hips grind instinctively, seeking relief for the pounding need in my pussy. A deep, empty ache that calls to be filled. Never in my life have I felt such burning desire.

Keeping an arm hooked behind his neck, I force my other hand between us, into the tiny gap between my hips and him, sliding it under the binding of his pants. I touch his cock for the first time. A sigh bursts from my lips when it jumps under my touch. He hisses pleasure, and I push my hand further between us without easing the grinding of my hips against him. I encircle his dick with my hand —there are the ridges I've only heard about. I find its soft underside and stroke it lightly.

He groans into our kiss, thrusting his hips forward hard, pinching my arm between us. His tongue, more insistent, drives in and out of my mouth. One hand curls in my hair, tugging, and I stroke his cock faster, responding to his desire.

His hips thrust faster, harder in response. The pounding deep in my core consumes me.

"You there!" an outside voice intrudes, jerking my awareness back to our surroundings.

Visidion hisses, loud and angry. He sets me on the ground and steps in front of me, facing the intruder.

"Back in your hut," a guard says.

There are four of them, part of the nightly patrols.

Stupid, how did I let this go so far? I should have known this would happen. Visidion tenses, hands balling into fists, tail rising.

Stepping around him, I place a hand on his bicep, hoping to calm him.

"Sure," I say, eyes downcast but keeping the patrol in my gaze. "Right away."

"Good," the guard says, hand on his sword.

Unlike the weapons we're issued as gladiators, the guards have steel with sharp edges. Our wooden, blunt weapons wouldn't stand much of a chance against them. Even if we did, it's not these four I'd be worried about, it's the dozens more on the walls and scattered throughout the compound, ready to come at a moment's notice. We're outnumbered. Visidion tenses, leaning forward. Tightening my grip on his arm, I will him to stand down.

The tension drains from his muscles at last. I open the door to our hut and let him walk in first. The guards stand staring at us until the door closes on their gazes. The common room of our hut is empty—everyone has retired to their own spaces. Visidion takes my hand and leads the way to our room.

He settles on our bedrolls on his side, head propped on an arm gazing at me.

"What is it that's wrong?" he asks at last.

Swallowing hard, an urge to lie races through my thoughts. Almost, I do. Something stops me. I can't do it. Having come this far, there's no point in holding back now.

"Cancer," I answer.

"What is cancer?" he asks.

"Mutation in my cells that causes them to grow too much," I answer. "It creates growths, called tumors, that destroy the cells around them."

Slowly he nods, pursing his lips.

"Epis," he says at last.

"What about it?" I ask.

"Epis has healing properties," he says. "You said you wondered every day if that would be the last."

"Yeah," I agree, not grasping his point.

"How long ago did the doctor tell you that you would die soon?"

How long had it been? I've lived with this so long now without examining it that I don't know. We've been crashed on Tajss for how long? We've had babies. There has been time for them to grow in the womb and reach walking age, at least. Three Earth years? Five? None of us have adjusted our time sense to Tajss. Since there are no seasons, it's difficult to judge things like that. Over a year... I should be dead.

But the tremors still come, the weakness still hits me.

"It hasn't grown worse," I whisper. Visidion nods but remains silent. "Could it be?"

"Maybe," he says.

A dim light of hope lights inside me, and I grasp to it like a child to its mother. A chance, a last, glimmering chance and I'm not going to let it go.

20

VISIDION

"*A*gain," Thrace barks.

"Ha!"

We attack the dummies as one, all of us bringing the wooden swords down in the new move we are drilling. The burn and ache in my muscles is extreme. Every time I reach a new plateau of skill and strength, Thrace seems to notice and push me harder.

Following the motions through muscle memory, my thoughts are consumed with how to escape. I have to get Rosalind back to Tajss. Right now she's growing weaker, but it won't be long before the other signs of withdrawal set in. It's a long, slow, and painful path to death.

"Again!" Thrace yells.

The sword hits the dummy, and there's a satisfying vibration that runs up my arm. I repeat the move until it's second nature, done with no thought, in an instant.

"Enough," Thrace says. "Line up."

We shuffle into a line at his command. He walks the line of us, looking at each one of us, nodding as if self-satisfied.

"Will they make good?" the master asks, his voice drifting down from the balcony that he watches us from on occasion.

He's standing there on the shoulder of the purple monstrosity he rides. It would be so easy to crush him—there's nothing to him. The monstrosity and the armed guards with him are the problem. I can't get to him without going through them.

Every night in our hut since Rosalind's speech, we've looked at ways to escape. So far nothing has come close to a viable plan.

"Yes, sir," Thrace says, turning to face the balcony. He stands with his arms crossed behind his back, one hand clasping the other.

"Good," Master says. "There is heavy betting this turn. If I win there will be rewards."

"Very good," Thrace says, bowing his head.

The master pulls on the ear of his ride, turning it, and then he and it shuffle out of sight. The guards leaning against the walls of the practice area shift. Two of them are in my line of sight, standing below the balcony where the master was.

"Rewards," one of them says, spitting on the ground. "Right."

"An extra slice of bread," the other snarls.

It's become obvious that our new master is not well-off, though I would guess he once was. The guards' armor is ill fitting and shows signs of heavy wear along with lack of proper care. Many walls have cracks or are crumbling. We are surrounded by signs of neglect and decay. The guards' comments underscore my observations.

"Again," Thrace barks, pushing us back into our training routines.

Muscle memory carries me through the stances, allowing

me time to think. We came a long way from the spaceport. I'm not sure how far, but Rosalind says it was almost a day's journey. Even if we escape this place, we're a still long way from getting off the planet.

"Tell you what reward I'd want," I overhear a guard say.

"A face that isn't so damn ugly?" the other asks.

"That white-lady," he responds, ignoring the jab. The guard grabs his crotch and thrusts his hips. "I'd show her a good time for a reward."

The bijass grabs me and I rush him, wooden sword in hand.

The two guards turn, surprise obvious, reaching for their swords, but too slow. The wooden sword in my hands blurs, striking the speaker about his head and shoulders multiple times. He drops to the ground in a heap.

"Visidion!" Rosalind yells.

Ignoring her, I face the other guard. He has his sword drawn and held ready before him. Weaving my own wooden sword in front of me, I establish a defense.

"I'm going to cut you to pieces," he says.

I don't answer his words. They're meaningless. Actions are all that matter.

We circle, the tips of our swords dancing, each probing for an opening. His guard drops slightly and I'm ready. Lunging forward, inside his reach, I swing my wooden sword towards his neck. It hits with a loud crack, and he drops.

Spinning on my heel I turn, sword held across my middle, back to the wall, ready for anything.

The other gladiators stare but don't move. Rosalind is a few steps away, eyes and mouth wide. Thrace stands next to her, arms crossed over his chest. Slowly his arms part and he claps. The sound of his hands coming together is loud in the silence of the training grounds.

"Done?" he asks, as if what I've done is the most normal thing in the world.

"Yes," I say, not lowering the sword from ready.

Other guards are not far away, hands on swords, but none look eager to come forward.

"Good," Thrace says. "Back to practice."

He turns towards the others and barks out a series of orders. Everyone except Rosalind complies. Her eyes bore into me, then she looks around the area, pursing her lips. Gaze returning to me, she nods, then lifts her own sword and returns to the training dummies.

Those guards still standing continue staring at me but not moving. I lower my sword and walk back to my position in front of a training dummy. The scales on the back of my neck itch, waiting for an attack, but none comes. Everyone resumes the day's routine. The other guards go to the two I dropped, gather them up, and carry them off somewhere. Life continues as if nothing happened. The hours pass, and at last it's time for lunch.

Two servants set out pots of mush on a rough wooden table. Thrace keeps us going through routines until they are done, then calls a break. Stomach grumbling, I walk beside Rosalind to the table. No one speaks as they each take a bowl and spoon the slop into it. Rosalind and I get our bowls and join the circle of the others in the middle of the dirt training area. The mush has bits of meat mixed into it, but overall has no flavor. The silence continues as we eat.

Usually there is conversation, but today no one speaks. There are some furtive glances at me then at Thrace, who stands next to the table of food, eating. The silence is uncomfortable. I'm waiting for something to happen with no clue what it might be. There must be some repercussions for my actions. Out of the corner of my eye, I notice Thrace set his bowl down, and then he walks towards our circle. An itch between my shoulder blades begs to be scratched, and I can barely swallow the food in my mouth as he approaches.

"Scrub," Thrace says, stopping next to me and staring down.

"Yes?" I ask.

"Yes, what?"

"Yes, sir," I say, swallowing hard, muscles tensing.

"Your form was sloppy. Attacking two opponents is foolish, but if you must, work faster. The last four blows on your first opponent were unnecessary and left you open to the second. He was out after your second hit."

Everyone's eyes are darting between the two of us.

"Yes, sir," I answer, nodding.

"Good," Thrace says, spinning on a heel and marching away. He stops after four steps. "Everyone will work an extra hour tonight, multiple-opponent routines need to be drilled."

Groans greet his pronouncement and he turns back to our group.

"You scrubs think I can let something like that slide?" he barks.

A chorus of "No, sir" rises from all throats, and all are eyes focused on me.

"Good," Thrace says. "Now up and at it. Lunch is over."

"Ha! Not done," Mesto says.

"Did I ask?" Thrace barks, hand drifting to the sticks at his sides that we all know he can wield with painful force.

Mesto shakes his head and climbs to his feet.

"In line, scrubs," Thrace barks. "Todd, Cenar, you're against Visidion. Rosalind, K'sara, you're against Mesto. Go!"

The afternoon passes until at last it's evening. Sore muscles and bruises throb from the day's training. As we head to our hut, I notice more guards around the estate, but the two I took out are nowhere to be seen. If nothing else, I established one thing—no one should comment on Rosalind.

"Whose turn for dinner?" Todd grumbles.

While lunch is served to us, we're on our own for dinner. We'd agreed on a rotation for cooking but no one kept close track of it.

"It's mine," Rosalind says, stepping forward.

She sorts through the pile of supplies that are left in our hut each day. It's thin pickings, further proof that our owner isn't well-off. I help her as she makes a stew, which is what we have most nights because there's little else to do with the odds and ends of food given to us.

It's not long before the pot is simmering over our communal fire. Rosalind catches my eye and motions towards the door. I follow her out into the cool night air. It's so much colder here than Tajss, and the nights are the worst. It makes my muscles ache more once the sun goes down and leaves me feeling lethargic.

"That was stupid," Rosalind says as soon as we're outside.

"He threatened you," I answer.

"No, he didn't," she shakes her head. "He made a stupid comment. It was nothing."

"It was something to me," I answer. "No one can threaten you."

"It wasn't a threat, damn it, Visidion, you can't do this!" her voice rises.

Her left arm trembles and she crosses her arms over her chest trying to hide it.

"It's getting worse," I call her out.

"I'm fine," she says but I stare at her until at last she crumbles. "It's probably withdrawal."

Swallowing hard, I nod. Withdrawal. She's holding up well, but she needs epis. The humans haven't been taking it all their lives. Zmaj can go weeks or months without feeling the effects of not having epis, but the humans need it. Their bodies are still adjusting.

"We need a plan," I say.

"You think?" she snaps, but then her arms quiver and she grits her teeth.

I draw her into my arms and hold her tight to me. The ache in my chest pulses with each beat of my hearts. Give me an enemy, any enemy, that I can face and defeat. Losing her, when we only now are coming into our own, is not something I can permit. I'll find a way. I will save her.

Her body melds against me, fitting into my arms as if she was made for me. Stroking her hair with light touches, keeping her pulled tight, I listen to the rhythm all of our hearts make, beating so close together. Tremors pass through her, and when at last they pass, she wraps her arms around my waist. This moment could last forever, and I'd be happy for all of it.

A loud bang echoes across the training grounds. Rosalind jumps, pushing away from me. The sound repeats, coming from the wooden double doors that lead into the grounds. Two guards walk out of the small building by the gates, muttering loudly. They're both weaving, probably drunk. One opens a small panel in the door and looks out.

"Shit," he exclaims, stumbling back.

The other guard looks out, then moving quickly unlocks the doors and pulls one side open. A hooded figure cloaked in shadows walks through. The guard swings the door shut behind him and slides the locks back into place.

"I'll get the master," the guard who had exclaimed says, stumbling over his words.

"No," the figure says. "I'm not here for him."

"Oh," the guard says, and his hands flap uselessly to his sides.

"Go about your duties, I'll see myself out shortly," the figure says.

It's impossible to see where he's looking between the shadows and the hood, but it seems his attention is on Rosalind and me. I move to protect her, putting my body between her and the stranger.

"Uh, we shouldn't—" the guard starts.

"Are you questioning me?" the figure asks without so much as a glance toward the guard.

"No, uh, sir, no, back to our duties, right," the guard answers.

The two guards walk backwards, keeping each other upright, into their hut. The hooded figure walks across the open area towards us. My tail swishes through the dirt, my scales tingle, and my hands close into fists, ready for anything. He stops a few feet away. Just then, as if the stranger has planned it, the moon comes out from behind a cloud, shining bright, silver light down on him. Moving slowly, he takes the sides of his hood and lowers it. As the hood drops, moonlight gleams on tan scales and reveals the Zmaj from the arena.

"Sorry for the subterfuge," he says. "Unfortunately, it's necessary."

My throat tight, tension in all my muscles, and expecting an attack at any moment, I swallow before speaking.

"Who are you?" I ask the most obvious question.

"My name is Arcan and I know you're Visidion and Rosalind," he nods to each of us as he says our names. "When I saw you in the arena…"

He trails off not finishing his thought. We stare at each other for a long moment until clouds cover the moon again and cast us back into darkness.

"I was surprised to see a Zmaj," I say, filling the void.

"You were!" he snorts, shaking his head. "How did you escape the Devastation?"

"I didn't," I say.

"You didn't?" he shakes his head side to side. "But... the planet was destroyed. There's no life left on Tajss."

Instead of answering him, I meet his gaze with a stare, schooling my face to reveal nothing. I don't know if he's an ally or not, but something tells me we're on dangerous ground.

"How did you come to be here?" Rosalind asks, redirecting the question to him.

He sighs, shoulders slumping, and gazes into the darkness.

"I thought I was the only one," he says, voice heavy with despair. "No one could have survived. The entire galaxy thinks Tajss is gone."

Fear, cold and creeping, seeps out of my core at his words, but I don't know why. The words call something, vague and uncertain, in the bijass. Memories I once had but are now lost to the fog of the bijass.

"It should stay that way," I say.

He turns his attention back to me, then shakes his head. "It's too late for that," he says. "I think."

"Why are you here?" Rosalind asks.

He straightens, clears his throat, and then rolls his shoulders. "Right," he says. "You're in danger."

"Of course we are, we're slaves sold to be gladiators," I snap.

"No, worse," he says, ignoring me. "The situation here is not stable. The 'king' is a crime lord who holds his position through fear. He claims he's descended from Prince Astirian but everyone knows that's a lie."

"What does any of that have to do with us?" Rosalind asks.

"Not you, him," Arcan says. "Tajss was believed dead. The Zzlo aren't hiding the fact they captured you there. That means there's life on Tajss."

"And they want the epis," I say, the cold chill in my guts finding its form and spreading across my limbs.

"Yes," he says.

"Rumors are all there are right now," Arcan says. "But they will be coming after you. Some want you dead, so they can bury the secret and use it for their own ends. Others want you to lose, so they can steal you. There are many plans for you. But it's enough to say you have changed the land-scape of Krik and thereby the galaxy."

My thoughts race as dim memory struggles to emerge from the fog of the past.

"Will you help?" I ask.

Arcan stiffens, his tail stops moving. My hearts beat loud in my ears, counting the passing moments. Thoughts play behind his eyes, and I have to wonder what it is he's really after.

"I'll do what I can," he says.

"We need a plan," Rosalind says. "A way off this planet."

Arcan nods as he starts to go. "Yes, you do," he says over his shoulder.

"How are you going to help?" I ask, as he reaches the door.

He stops, one hand on the door, head bowed. "I don't know," he says. "I'll be in touch."

The door closes behind him, and one of the guards comes stumbling out to replace the locks. When he turns and sees Rosalind and me, he steps towards us.

"Get in," he barks, pointing at our hut.

Silent, we go back in to our dinner. Everything has changed. It's changed in ways I can't foresee yet. Rosalind and I eat in silence, getting through the dinner. When we're

177

finally lying beside each other in our small room, she rests her head on my shoulder, an arm draped across my chest.

"What does it mean?" she whispers.

"I don't know," I say, honesty pouring out in those three words. There's a cold, hard ball in my guts.

"I'm trying to decide if this is a good thing or a bad thing," she says.

"So am I," I answer, squeezing her tighter to me.

21

ROSALIND

*W*e've had three arena fights since Arcan came to visit and no word.

The effects of withdrawal are increasing, becoming harder to hide. Visidion covers for me, but our team knows what's happening. I can't hide it from them, and soon I won't be able to hide it from our opponents. I'm slowing down. My muscles aren't responding as quickly. Spasms and weakness come and go as well. My body is declining, betraying me. I don't know if it's the lack of epis, or if the cancer, which I'd thought to be in remission, is advancing.

Dirt falls from the ceiling as the crowd erupts into a new round of cheers and stomping. Mesto and K'sara are fighting in the arena. I can only hope the cheers are for them doing well. We are all climbing the ranking ladders in the arena and are known forces to watch. Thrace is a good trainer, one of the best, if the rumors through the pit are to be believed. The other gladiators show him respect they don't give to anyone else. All of them except Brisong and his partner Rikon. They're dominating the ladder with a long winning streak. Fifteen wins with no losses.

Soon Visidion and I will challenge their position at the top, and they know it. We avoid each other for now. Dirty looks across the pit, glares and murmurs from them, while Visidion and I ignore them. This pisses Brisong off, which is what I want. It always makes me smile.

"You two are up next," Thrace says. "Come here."

He motions with his head towards a far corner of our prep area. It's not exactly private but it's far enough away from the others, and with the noise of the crowd over our heads, it would be difficult to eavesdrop. When we stand before Thrace, he stares at us with his fiery, unblinking eyes.

"Yes, sir?" I ask, prompting him to speak.

"You two are fools," he says, shaking his head.

Visidion and I exchange looks of confusion.

"What do you mean?" Visidion asks.

"You," Thrace says, pointing at Visidion. "Being here, being what you are, has set things in motion. You think I don't know about your meeting with Arcan? Do either of you know the absolute shitstorm you've started?"

"Thrace—" Visidion says, but Thrace cuts him off with a sharp motion of his hand cutting through the air.

"No," he says. "You don't. There is no getting off this planet. Accept your fate, shut your mouths, and pretend that you didn't come from Tajss. Anything else and you two are stupider than a mokul pack in heat."

"We have to get back," Visidion says.

"No, you don't," Thrace says. "You can have a good life here. What is back there for you? You can have it all here."

"No, I can't," Visidion hisses. "You've seen it, don't try to tell me you haven't. Rosalind is sick, she's getting worse. She has to have epis—"

"No!" Thrace barks. "Don't you say it. Don't say that burnt word, by the Seven Widows."

The edges of Visidion's scales tint red, and his tail stops

moving, rising up. Anger is getting the best of him. I have to stop this. I run my hand along his upper arm to his shoulder. He doesn't turn to look, eyes locked on Thrace.

"Visidion, let's hear what he has to say," I say. Visidion doesn't say anything or move except to nod. "Thrace, continue, please."

Thrace's eyes dart to me before he speaks.

"That burnt plant lies behind everything that's wrong with the entire galaxy. Entire planets laid waste in the quest to control who gets it. Right now there are rumors, but that's it. No one believes the Zzlo, they're the biggest liars in the universe and will say anything for a credit. If you let them know that Tajss isn't laid waste, if they figure out the epis is still there, it will all start again."

"Help us," I say. "Haven't you trained us that the best way to avoid being hit is to not be there when the blow lands?"

Something flickers in his eyes, his lips tighten, but then he shakes his head.

"Using my own words against me," he says.

"NEXT!" a booming voice echoes down into the pit.

"Go," Thrace says.

I can't get a read when I meet his eyes. I don't know if I'm getting through to him or not. Will he help us or betray us? Walking up the ramp to the gates, cold sweat drips down my back, and my breath comes in short hitches.

"Are you okay?" Visidion asks, worry in his voice.

"I'm fine," I answer, shifting my grip on my wooden sword.

Visidion nods, any words he would say cut off by the clank of the gate being raised.

"PEOPLE OF KRIK!" the announcer's voice booms through the wooden doors. "For your amusement and betting pleasure, the terror of Tajss and his female will face off against Anaseien Exiled Prince of Alva and his Pari!"

The crowd gasps and oohs their pleasure, and the gates swing open before us. We march out of our tunnel, timing it so our opponents emerge from theirs at the same time. I'm shocked to see a human female marching next to a tall, purple alien. The alien is as tall as Visidion but more human in build, though he has long pointed ears, and fangs show in his mouth along with the purple skin. He has two wooden swords and she has a wooden staff.

Stopping ten feet apart, we face each other, waiting for the signal to begin.

To their credit, our opponents show no signs of fear. It has been common for the others when they see Visidion because of his size and reputation as a fighter. The crowd quiets until the only sound is a light breeze flapping the banners in the wind.

My heart rate slows and the calm centering takes over. The female I'm facing is about the same size as I am, but slightly bigger in build. She holds her staff competently and stands prepared, making it clear she knows what she's doing. She has bright green eyes that are alight with intelligence. This is a rank fight—they're two rungs over us, second place. If we win this, our next match will be against Brisong and Rikon. Tension builds in the air around us. Someone is playing to the crowd as they murmur and shift in their seats. Anticipation becomes palpable then, right when it feels it must burst, the bell sounds.

The female flips backwards, landing neatly with staff at the ready. Her partner moves in to attack Visidion, but that's not the way we're playing the game. As the prince attacks, Visidion steps to the side towards me, and I step in front of him, blocking the prince's attacks. The loud clang of wood on wood echoes. He hits so hard my hands go numb. His eyes widen in surprise at the move, but then it dawns on him what we're doing, and he whirls towards the girl.

Visidion is flying through the air, wings spread wide, gliding down towards her, his swords a blur before him creating confusion about where she should place her defense. She backs up, moving fast. Too fast. She stumbles then is flailing to keep herself upright. Visidion lands, swords swinging in.

"NO!" the prince screams, running towards his female.

EXACTLY AS WE PLANNED. HE TURNS, GIVING ME HIS BACK, concern for his partner overriding his self-preservation instincts. Aiming for the base of his neck, I swing. The ground next to Visidion shifts as my sword swings. A dark hole opens, and then something leaps out with a screeching sound. Visidion turns his blow from the girl to the new threat, barely bringing it up in time to defend himself.

The thing hits Visidion straight on, knocking him to the ground. It looks like some kind of cross between a gorilla and a bat mutated into a nightmare. Black fur covers its massive, heavily muscled body, while large, leathery wings flap from its back. Its face is humanoid but filled with rows of sharp teeth and two large fangs that rise from its lower jaw. Huge fists slam down on Visidion with bone-crushing force. The girl screams and backs away, so the Prince circles the monster, heading for her.

Fear pulses in time with my heart, but I race forward, pushing past it, sword held ready. As I approach, the creature looks up and roars, baring its fangs. It hits the ground on either side of Visidion, and the vibration of it runs up my legs.

Cutting to my left, I force it to turn to keep me in its sights. Visidion struggles beneath it and tries to slide free, but the thing grabs him with a hand that's big enough to grip him by his chest and casually slams him into the ground. Visidion grunts. I have to do something.

Breaking into a run, I circle the monster, making it turn faster, focusing its attention on me. On the other side of the creature, the prince has his female in his arms, but seeing my approach, he pushes her behind him, bringing his swords to bear.

Rather than risk facing him as well, I sidestep, moving to the beast. It swings. Ducking backwards, I bend in half, swinging my sword into its bicep, landing four blows on either side of its arm while sliding across the dirt on my knees. It screams in pain and surprise, pulling its arm back, but then it lowers its head towards me. Foul breath washes over me as it roars, leaving my ears ringing. Visidion slides out from under it, forgotten by the creature.

Gnashing its teeth over my head, it lifts a massive fist above me. I slide my feet out from underneath me and roll to the side as the fist slams the ground. I'm bounced up into the air as the ground jumps.

"Rosalind!" Visidion yells.

Continuing my roll to the side, I catch glimpses of Visidion landing on the creature's back, attacking with his swords.

I get to my feet. My thighs are trembling, signs of the growing weakness. Taking a deep breath, I raise my sword and step forward to help Visidion when a warrior's tingling sense tells me to duck.

A wooden swords cuts through the air just over my head. Spinning on my heel, I meet the prince's next blow, stopping it an inch from my face. He grins, showing his fangs, nodding respect.

The girl circles around the two of us, the staff in her hands twirling a slow circle.

The thing roars behind me and Visidion grunts in pain,

but I don't have time to see if he's okay. The prince and I circle, testing each other with series of quick jabs and feints. Dancing out of his reach, I come too close to the girl. She lands a solid blow on the left of my chest. At least one rib cracks, the pain blinding me for an instant.

Prince doesn't hesitate, attacking with a fast flurry of strikes, mid to high then back and suddenly shifting and swinging low, finally landing a blow on my right thigh.

The leg goes numb and tries to give way. My only option is retreat. I hop backwards and try to keep both opponents in view.

Someone planned this. The crowd is screaming and pounding their feet. This isn't a blood match, but whoever added that monster wants it to be. Knowing it's true does nothing to help us survive.

My thigh tingles as blood flows back into the painful place, and I test it before trusting it with my weight. It hurts, but no longer seems inclined to give way. The wall of the arena is coming up behind me. The prince and his girl are herding me back towards it. This isn't good.

When I turn slightly to work my way back towards the center, they shift positions to block me.

Now I see Visidion, locked in combat with the monster. He leaps high, bringing his sword down on the creature's head while his tail swings and slams into its chest. The creature is bowled over, dropping onto its back, and then it shudders and lies still. Visidion stumbles over it and lands in a heap beside it.

Prince moves in to my right, his sword a blinding blur, so I turn to meet his assault. Our swords clack together with the staccato beat of a deadly dance. Because of his longer reach, I retreat, pulling him in, but I have to keep my attention split. I keep one eye out for the girl, ready for her to join his attack.

185

I'm trying to move closer to Visidion, but the prince anticipates my goal and jumps to the side, blocking me.

Somehow, I lose track of the girl when he moves. She appears behind me and to my left, jabbing her staff into my kidney. An instant of blinding pain causes me to drop my guard. The prince makes his move. Grabbing me and spinning me around with an arm over my throat, his sword held across my chest, he turns us.

Visidion stands there with both swords held ready. Dark bruises show on his scales, but the rage dancing in his eyes tells me he isn't feeling the pain.

"Let her go," he hisses, swords making slow circles in the air between us.

"Only one of us can win," Prince says.

"Win or lose, if you harm her, I will destroy you," Visidion says, his voice low and dangerous.

"You love her," Prince says.

Visidion doesn't answer with words. Stepping forward, swords circling faster, he feints. Prince pulls back, dragging me with him. Pain shoots through me with every breath, growing worse as he drags me back. Visidion marches forward, relentless.

I drop, letting my full weight come down on my captors arm, forcing him to hold me up or drop me. His arm tightens on my throat, cutting off my air. Blood pounds in my ears and my vision darkens as he continues to back away from Visidion.

Visidion roars, charging.

Prince drops me so he can meet the charging mad Zmaj. Visidion attacks with a flurry of blows so fast that I can't follow them. Rolling to my knees, I gasp, desperate for the air but each breath comes with a sharp stabbing pain that cuts it short. Slowly my vision clears as oxygen refills my lungs.

"No!" the female screams.

Visidion has landed at least one solid blow and the Prince is on the ground. The girl rushes to his side, dropping her weapon. Visidion stares at her, wary, until she's on her knees next to the prince with tears streaming down her face. Not taking his eyes off her he backs his way to my side and kneels.

"Are you okay?" he asks, swords still ready and pointed at the girl.

"I'll be fine," I say, wincing with pain, wheezing as I struggle to catch my breath.

The crowd chants as Visidion helps me to my feet. Standing, arms waving, stomping their feet the noise is so cacophonous it takes me a moment to realize what they're saying.

"Kill! Kill! Kill! Kill!" they chant.

An empty pit opens in my core, swallowing the warmth of my body, leaving me cold. Turning away from the girl, I look at the balcony where the king sits. This isn't the way it's supposed to be. Blood games are rare. They're not done on a whim.

That's what we were told, but then adding a vicious creature to a fight isn't within the rules we were told either. Yet there lies one in the middle of the arena. Dead or stunned, I don't know which.

The king rises to his feet, helped to his feet by two servants on either side who strain to lift his bulk. In a slow shuffle, he moves to the edge of the balcony to stare down. His bulbous head turns to each side, taking in the crowd. He holds one, short, fat arm out in front of him, palm down. The crowd cries out louder, demanding death.

The king smiles, and it seems our eyes meet across the arena. His hand closes into a fist, thumb sticking out, parallel to the ground. My heart pounds in anticipation. If he orders the kill, I can't do it, and I don't think Visidion will either. If we don't, what happens next? Located at regular intervals are well-armored guards who have real weapons, not wooden ones.

The king's hand wavers, thumb moving down then up. Down is the order for death, up means it's over.

Closing my eyes, I will him to move his hand up. Do not do this. Don't break your own rules any further.

When I open them, his hand moves.

Up.

It's over. Thank all the stars it's over. I even send a thank-you to the Seven Widows, not that I know anything about them, but if they do exist and had something to do with this, I'll praise them.

Visidion exhales sharply then slumps next to me. Arms around one another's waists, we aid each other back to our tunnel and down to the rest of our team. Guards come into the arena to take the prince away and his girl with him.

"Curse the Widows' will," Thrace growls as we emerge from the tunnel.

Medics come over and assist both of us to the tables where they start tending our wounds. The medics are short, gaunt, gray men with three long fingers and a thumb on each hand. The one tending me pokes at my side and stars explode, blasting away thought until it passes. He mutters something then starts making a mix.

"What in the hell was that?" I ask.

"Someone is messing with the rules," Thrace says. "We've got enemies."

"You think?" Visidion hisses sharply as the medic prods.

"Keep your mouths shut," Thrace says, eyes darting around to all the gladiators listening in on our conversation.

The skin on back of my neck crawls as the hair stands on end. The waters are getting deeper and we don't have a life raft.

VISIDION

*T*he sound of Thrace barking orders echoes through our hut. Rosalind and I are still recovering from our last fight, so Thrace has given us time to heal. Medics come once a day, examine us, then leave. Along with the sound of our fellow gladiators' training comes the noise of construction. We've won enough fights now that repairs are being done to the villa.

"There has to be some way to get a message to Arcan," Rosalind says.

"I can't think of one," I say. "He is probably being watched. We'll have to wait for him to contact us."

"I don't think we have that kind of time," she says, hunching over, her brow furrowing with worry.

Outside there's a roaring sound, growing louder. Frowning, we both stand and walk out of the hut. The sound is close now, echoing off the stone walls. It pulls up outside the gates to the villa, and guards rush around in a flurry until at last one of them opens the door.

An entourage walks in, dressed in the green and gold

colors of the king. A door into the main house slams open and the master rides out on his purple monstrosity.

"Welcome!" he says, walking up to the delegation. "May I offer you... anything?"

"No," a man in the middle of the group says, looking around with disdain. "I have a message from the king. Accept it so I can be on my way."

"Of course, what an honor," Master says, forcing his ride to bend at the waist then holding his hands out to take the message.

The messenger hands a paper to him, then turns and walks out the door without another word. The guards swing it shut as the roaring sound comes back to life, and yellow dirt is thrown through the opening. The machine he rode here in leaps into motion and speeds away.

The master tears open the letter, paper dropping away. All of us, gladiators and guards, watch in anticipation. I watch his eyes widen, his head shake and then tilt to one side. A slow smile spreads across his face. He walks his ride up to Thrace, who is standing with his arms crossed over his chest.

"Thrace!" he exclaims, waving the paper. "Good news!"

The paper flutters towards Thrace, who plucks it out of the air then reads it. His eyes narrow and his mouth hardens into a tight line.

"No," he says, shaking his head. "This throws out all the rules."

"Look! Look at the rewards!"

Thrace reads it again and shakes his head negative. "Not worth it," he says.

"You don't get to choose!"

Thrace straightens, glowering, and for a moment it's about to happen. Thrace could take out the master. We all know it, and so does the master. Metal on metal echoes as the guards shift, leaning forward, hands on weapons. They're ready to go if Thrace makes a move.

Thrace blinks and seems to cave in on himself. He sighs and turns away.

"Ha! What is it?" Mesto asks the question on all of our minds.

Thrace looks at me then Rosalind. "You two will fight in the next arena for top ranking," he says.

A sigh of relief slips out. I'd expected much worse, fighting Brisong is a welcome opportunity. I've wanted to put him in his place for a while now.

"Okay," Rosalind says. "So why the long faces?"

"I don't know what you mean 'long faces'," Thrace says. "But it's not a normal fight. It's a Blood Game."

A collective gasp fills the silence that falls.

"No, that can't be," Todd says.

"Not fair," Cenar adds.

"That isn't all," Thrace says, glaring at the master. Chills race along my scales while waiting for him to say what else there is. "Everything is on the line. If you lose, the master loses everything."

"Why do we care?" Rosalind asks.

"He loses us," Thrace answers. "All properties of the loser become property of the king."

The chill turns so cold my body slows, aching muscles tremble, but deep in my core a fire burns.

"Ha!" Mesto says.

"It doesn't matter, the Zmaj will win," the master says, bouncing with excitement.

"What do you get out of this?" I ask.

"Ha, ha, ha!" he laughs, a screeching sound that tears at my ears. "Fame! Fortune! King will give me the pick of the surviving gladiators and one million credits!"

Of course the stakes had to be high, otherwise why post them.

The master turns his ride and goes back into the house, his laughter echoing in my ears long after he's gone. Thrace stands still as a stone, saying nothing, staring ahead. A Blood Game, Rosalind at my side. No wooden weapons this time. They'll be real, edged, and deadly. How can I protect her?

The weakness is growing worse. If she wasn't in epis withdrawal, maybe she would be competitive, but the fight isn't for days and each one she weakens. Time slips away like the sands of Tajss blowing in the breeze.

"Enough, begin training!" Thrace barks, cutting through the gloom of my thoughts.

No one moves, staring at Thrace as if waiting for a new order or a change of heart. Shaking my head to clear it of the cold and building anger, I move to the weapons rack, picking up my wooden swords.

"Wait," Thrace barks, jerking all of our attention back to him. "Blood games require a new strategy."

He turns and walks over to a door that is always locked. No one has ever opened it or entered it since we've been here. He pulls a key from his pocket, opens the door, and steps into the shadows. When he comes out again, his arms are loaded with weapons. Real weapons.

The guards shift, shiny new armor rattling as they do. Thrace ignores them as he walks to the middle of our semi-circle and dumps his load on the ground. The metal weapons clatter and spread out before us. Looking from the weapons to Thrace, a fresh glimmer of hope awakens in my core.

Crouching, I sort through the pile first, picking out two large swords, big enough that a smaller person would need two hands for each of them. Setting those aside, I spot a trident and an idea crystallizes. I stand up and hand it to

Rosalind. She frowns, staring at it, then her eyes light up and she takes it.

The others pick out weapons, each to their liking, then we're standing circled around Thrace.

"Someone is manipulating the games," he says. "It was obvious after the last bout, but now it's clear. The rules are gone. This is no longer a game of rank and prestige. It's survival. The only question is, will you?"

"Sir, yes, sir!" we answer, speaking in unison.

"Good. Pair off," he barks.

We set to work, rotating teams and training harder than we ever have. Thrace is right. We're fighting for survival.

THE SUN'S LAST RAYS SLIP ACROSS THE TRAINING GROUNDS. Aches and pains plus my muscle-deep exhaustion blot out my thoughts. Rosalind is leaning on the trident, breathing heavily. Cenar sits on the ground with Todd next to him lying on his back wheezing. Only Mesto seems as fresh as when we started, his apparently inexhaustible supply of energy not yet tapped out.

"Good," Thrace says. "You might survive. Your dinner is ready, eat."

I offer my arm to Rosalind and she leans on it, giving me a brief smile. A long table has been set out laden with food. Whether this is Thrace's doing or the master splurging on us, I don't know or care. The food is good, rich, and flavorful, the best we've had since arriving. Eating with the gusto of a starved body, I down several helpings before finally feeling full. Thrace joins our circle and eats with us, another new thing.

"Thrace, what is going on?" Rosalind asks.

Thrace chews slowly, staring at the plate before him.

"I don't know," he answers, after swallowing. "I've been here a long time. This doesn't happen. Blood games are for criminals or retirement. They're rare, and never for someone climbing the ladders. A gladiator's value is in long-term entertainment. A bet of this size, by the king himself?"

Arcan's words come back to me. Epis. It has to be about epis and Tajss. When we were captured, I'd resigned myself to never seeing Tajss again. That brought with it a certain appeal. On Tajss, Rosalind and I were prevented from being together by duty and the demands of our positions. All of that was behind us, but it turns out there's no escaping responsibility.

My presence here has set things in motion. Unwelcome things are coming for Tajss, and they're not ready. Closing my eyes, the weight settles on my shoulders. My plans to escape had been to save Rosalind, but this makes it about more than our personal concerns.

"Who gains what?" Rosalind asks. "What are the politics of the situation?"

Thrace shakes his head. "I don't know. Too many, too varied, but there's only one thing that ever stirred up the galaxy this much."

He stares at me, not saying what he's thinking, but I know. Rosalind does as well. His suspicions are the same as mine. The king wants to know if Tajss is still viable. He wants epis and control of its distribution. Power in this galaxy was and could be again defined by the one who controls epis.

Tajss needs to fade back into obscurity. There are only two ways for that to happen. The knowledge they want is in Rosalind and me. Either we escape or . . . The other alternative isn't an option.

"All right scrubs, sleep," Thrace says, rising to his feet. "There will be new strategies to drill tomorrow."

He walks away, fading into the black of the night, leaving us sitting in the dark. Todd and Cenar climb to their feet, Cenar's body making loud grinding noises as the rocks that serve as his skin rub together. The two of them walk into our hut followed by Mesto and K'sara. Rosalind and I sit alone in the dark. She lays her hand over mine.

"We have to get back," she whispers.

"Yes," I agree. "It's bad. Worse than I could have expected."

Putting an arm around her shoulders, I pull her into a kiss. Her soft, delicate lips ignite the fire, and my first cock is instantly hard, throbbing with need and desire. She is all I want, all I need, and what I would give to be able to push aside everything else and have her.

She presses against me, the soft mounds of her chest smashing between us, making my core a raging inferno. My cock pounds with need, and blood drains from my head to fill the demands of my dick. Leaning further into her, I bend her before me until she's on the ground and I'm over her. My massive erection tenting out my pants, I press my hips down, grinding against her. She groans, hands running along my arms and up across my back, lightly stroking my wings.

Her tongue presses into my mouth, seeking mine, as our lips move against each other. Reason leaves. I have to have her.

Sliding a hand between us until I find the fastening of her pants, fumbling at it until it springs free. She lifts her hips, letting me slide them down. My fingers run through soft fur, seeking the object of my craving. Moisture greets my fingertips and a sigh whispers past my ear. Rosalind groans into my mouth, thrusting her hips up, driving my finger down along her wet slit. Nothing has ever felt this good. Sliding into her dripping tunnel, folds of her sweetness clamping on my finger as I push deep inside her.

My cock spasms hard, the first hints of my need dampening my pants. She moves against me, pushing onto and off my finger, which slips in and out of her easily. Shoving my tongue into her mouth, I push a second finger into her wetness, claiming her body. She melts against me, but then she's thrusting with wild abandon. Responding in kind, I shove my two fingers in and out of her while driving my tongue around hers. She breaks the kiss, gasping for air, huffing with each thrust I make into her body.

Her eyes bore into me and mine into her as I find the points of her pleasure and tease them with fingers. She stiffens under me, nails digging into my back, while her eyes roll up and she moans a long, low sound. Her body spasms as I drive my fingers deep and hold them inside her. Her muscles clench my fingers tight, releasing then clamping down again. Over and over again while her beautiful voice gives sound to her pleasure. The moon peeks out, and soft silver light illuminates her in this most sacred moment of pleasure. She's so beautiful an ache forms in my chest.

Nothing can happen to her. She is my treasure. She's all I've lived my long life to have. The person who completes the universe, makes it all worth it. All the pain, all the loss, was only to prepare me for her. The arch in her back eases, and she lowers herself to the ground beneath me. As her muscles relax my fingers are freed, and I slide them out, loving the scent of her as I do. My throbbing cock, pounding between my legs, begs for relief. As I reach for the tie of my pants, armored boots appear in the edge of my vision.

"Uhm-hm," the guard clears his throat.

Before thought I'm moving, tackling the guard and taking him to the ground. Everything is red, rage claims control, rearing an arm back with balled fist, I swing at the downed guard.

"Visidion, no!" Rosalind screams, cutting through the red.

I stop my fist an inch from the guard's head. He's struggling to cover his face and protect himself, moisture falling from his eyes, broken teeth mouthing words that don't make sense. Tension drains from my muscles when Rosalind places a hand on my shoulders. The other guards are a few feet away, swords drawn, forming a circle around me. I might be able to take them all, and if I was alone, I'd try. Rosalind is here though, and it would put her in too much danger.

Dropping my fist, I climb off the guard, then offer him a hand up. He takes it, shaking his head. Surprisingly, the guards around us sheathe their swords. Rosalind's and my value must be so much now that the repercussions of harming us outweigh their sense of pride about one of them having his ass handed to him.

The guard shuffles his feet, glances around at the others, and only then meets my eyes.

"I have a message," he says.

"Okay?" I ask, exchanging a confused look with Rosalind.

"The arena is rigged. Be ready. When chaos erupts, move," he says.

"That's it?" Rosalind asks.

"Yeah," he answers, shrugging.

"What does that mean? Who is it from?" I ask.

His eyes move furtively to one other guard in particular, so I turn my attention to him.

"Arcan," he says, speaking at last.

Rosalind and I look at each other.

"And that's it?" I ask.

Something passes behind the eyes of the guard. He knows something more, but will he tell me?

"Yeah," he says. "Be ready. That's all any of you need to know."

The guards walk away. Rosalind takes my hand, and together we walk into our hut. We're in deep sand, and the longer we're here the more it feels we're being swallowed.

There is a lot going on here that is unclear. Inside, the others sit in a circle around the common-room fire. They look up as we enter as if they were waiting for us.

"What did they want?" K'sara asks, making it obvious they were watching what happened.

"A message from Arcan," I say.

They all look at each other.

"Seven Widows' sweat, what have you two gotten us into?" Todd curses.

"It's coming together. We have to escape, and now we have outside help," Rosalind says.

"Maybe, or maybe it's all a trap," K'sara says.

"It could be," I admit. "But do we really have a choice?"

"I do," Todd says.

"We don't," I say, anger flashing hot. "If you're not in, then say so. I'm fine to leave you behind if that's what you want."

Todd shrugs.

"Ha! He's right," Mesto says.

"Cenar stands with you," he throws into the ring. "I want to be free."

"Fine," K'sara says, sounding more resigned than agreed.

"Mesto?" I ask.

"Ha! Mesto behind is not. Adventure I like."

"Todd, please," Rosalind speaks softly, imploring Todd. "We need you."

Todd looks at her, scratching his belly.

"Fine," he shrugs. "Todd will help where Todd can. You don't leave me behind."

"Agreed," I say.

"So what is the plan?" K'sara asks, cutting to the heart of the matter.

"Be ready," I say, wishing I had something more to give.

"Ha! Be ready," Mesto exclaims.

"Sure, but what's the message from Arcan? He's the

blasted adviser to the king, Widows' random hairs, how you got him involved I'll never know. Is it some kind of Zmaj telepathy?" K'sara asks.

"There is no Zmaj telepathy," I say.

"The message was to be ready, and that the games are going to be rigged," Rosalind says.

"Rigged? Rigged how? In our favor, against us, what?"

"We don't know. Something's going to happen, and when it does there will be chaos. That's our sign to move."

"Great, be ready," Todd snorts. "Beautiful plan. Widows' sweat, we are in for it."

"It's more than we had," I say, standing and offering Rosalind my hand. "Until tomorrow."

I pull Rosalind to her feet and lead her to our space. The others sit up talking in muffled sounds. Lying next to Rosalind makes my cock stiffen at her closeness, but there is no privacy, and now is not the time to give in to base desires. She lays her head on my chest and in moments her breathing is soft and even, letting me know she's asleep. Lightly stroking her hair, I stare at the ceiling trying to find sleep myself. All I can think about is how to protect her. How do I save her when it seems the entire planet is working against me?

Somehow I have to. I will. She is my treasure. I will destroy them all to save her.

23

ROSALIND

*M*y head pounds in time with every beating of my heart. Chills run up and down my spine, my mouth is dry, and my vision blurs at random. My withdrawal symptoms are becoming worse. I focus on each breath, inhaling deeply, then letting it out in a long slow exhale. It helps my focus.

"This is it," Thrace is saying, his words coming through the fog of pain. "I've given you all I can. I hope it's enough."

"We will win," Visidion says.

The crowd cheers above us and dirt sifts from the ceiling. As Second Tier of the arena competition's ladder, we now have a private area to wait our turn. Winning has its perks. Visidion keeps an arm hooked under my shoulders. Outwardly it looks friendly, but he and I both know I need it to stay upright. How I'm going to fight today I don't know. Right now, I'm taking each moment as it comes.

"You'd better," Thrace says. "One more thing. Don't trust Arcan."

My heart stops, surely I didn't hear him right. The pain

must have made me confuse his words, he had to have said something else. We haven't talked to him about Arcan.

"I don't understand what you are saying," Visidion says stiffly. He's a terrible liar.

"Don't play me for a fool," Thrace snaps. "Nothing happens with my gladiators I don't know about."

No one meets his gaze as he looks at each of us in turn.

"Look—" Visidion says.

"No, you look," Thrace cuts him off. "I get it and maybe, just maybe, it might work. More likely it won't. You're a cog in a very big game that you don't even begin to understand. No one on this planet is your friend. Everyone wants something, either from you, or because of you. We both know what the hell it is you represent. The way I see it, there's only two ways you're good for the future of this galaxy. Gone or dead. Today is going to see which way that plays out."

"Thrace, come with us," Visidion says.

"Ha!" Mesto exclaims, and Todd gasps.

"Don't be a fool," Thrace says. "You can't go around inviting half the damn planet to escape with you. Didn't I just say trust no one?"

The crowd gasps loud enough that it echoes through the pit. Someone knocks on the door to our area.

"You're next," a voice calls through the door.

Visidion and Thrace stare at each other, neither appearing willing to bend.

"Fine," I say, pushing off of Visidion. "We'll be careful."

"Good," Thrace says, turning away from Visidion. "Now go out there and win this damn thing."

"Good luck," Todd says, shaking his head.

I grab the trident I've been training with. The hardened steel has three sharp prongs that catch the torchlight and gleam. Visidion slides his swords into their sheaths on his back. He goes to each of the other gladiators and clasps hands with them. It's an effort of will to not only stand up straight, but to not weave. Dizziness comes and goes.

We step out at the base of the ramp to the arena. Side by side, we walk to the gate and wait. Visidion wraps an arm around my shoulders.

"Rosalind," he says, voice so soft it's hard to hear him.

"Yes?" I ask.

"All my life I've waited for one thing," he says. "The thing that makes the universe make sense. That completes me."

He stares straight ahead, hand gripping my shoulder tight. He swallows, and a subtle shudder runs down his spine.

"Yeah?" I ask, prompting him to finish his thought.

"You're it," he says, looking into my eyes.

My heart jumps into my throat, making it impossible for me to say anything in return. Unable to speak, I rise on my toes until we're kissing. He turns into the kiss and returns it with a burning passion that absorbs and consumes me, pulling me fully into him and making us one. Dimly I hear a metal clank, but it doesn't matter. This kiss, this moment, I give myself to him. All the reasons that I can't don't matter. He's right, he makes my world better. Giving myself to him is all I want, all I need.

Sunlight stabs into my eyes, and the roar of the crowd washes over us. Only then am I aware that the gates have swung open. The arena waits before us, ready for our grand entrance. Our final entrance, one way or another, for after today we will no longer be gladiators. We'll be free, in death or on our way home. Either way, this ends.

As we break our kiss, acceptance comes, bringing peace along with it. We hold hands as we walk into the arena, and in a strange display of bravado, Visidion raises his free hand into the air, pumping his fist up and down. I follow suit and the crowd responds, screaming and stomping as they mimic the gesture.

There are more guards around the arena today than I've seen before. Gleaming in gold- and red-tinted armor, there's one every twenty feet, and today they have guns instead of their normal swords and staves. There are also guards on the stairs that lead up between sections of the bleachers. Strange. Do they do this for all Blood Games?

Stopping a few feet from the center, we await our opponents. Their gate swings open, and the crowd gasps as they storm into the arena. Brisong and his red-skinned partner, Rikon, are armored head to toe in gleaming steel. Visidion and I look naked in comparison. They're ready for a death match, and we have come woefully under-dressed for the occasion.

They stop a few feet away. Brisong raises his fist in the air, slowly lowering it then pointing at Visidion. The crowd explodes with excitement and loud calls for death.

Brisong draws a sword that looks as big as me and half as wide. His red partner is wielding a club the size of a small tree, swinging it one-handed as if it weighs nothing. My thighs tremble, a bout of weakness threatening, but it subsides. Along with my trident I have a net, which will be my best bet against whichever of them comes after me.

"Begin!" a booming voice echoes, and it's on.

Brisong roars, throwing his arms wide then leaning in and charging. His partner mimics him, almost as if he's an extension of Brisong. Surprisingly, they both charge at Visidion, ignoring me. Visidion hisses, drawing both of his blades in a single smooth motion and whirling them in front of him. Dancing to one side, since they've chosen to ignore me I circle behind Rikon.

He gives me his back, but it's fully armored as well, overlapping plates of shiny steel. Running after him in the wake

MIRANDA MARTIN

of their charge, I stab with my trident, hoping to slide it between the plates of armor, but it deflects, skidding across the steel.

Damn it. Bringing the net to bear, I whirl it once then, holding onto one corner, let it fly towards his rushing feet. It wraps around his right leg, entangling him, and he trips, falling forward and landing with a loud thump a couple of feet short of Visidion. His massive club swings down, trailing his fall, and scores a glancing blow on Visidion, who fails to dodge it while also avoiding Brisong's massive sword.

Visidion pops his wings out wide as he leaps backwards, using them to gain room between him and Brisong.

Brisong roars seeing his partner down, but it's not for long. The red monster is pushing himself to his feet. Racing forward, I jump onto his back and slam the butt of my trident on either side of his helmeted head, hoping to disorient him. Rikon pushes up hard, and I lose my balance, flying back through the air. When I hit the ground, my breath is knocked out of me. I roll away. As long as I'm unsure where my opponent is, I don't want to be a sitting target.

The ground jumps under me, and I'm thrown into the air only to slam back down again. I try to rise to my feet, but my left leg spasms, jerking out from under me, and I plant into the dirt face first. Rikon bears down on me, club raised over his head, ready to crush me in a single blow. I take a deep breath in—my timing has to be right—he swings, and the club casts shade on me as it passes over his head and descends to me.

I roll towards him, not away. He tries to shift his club but he's committed to the move, and it has too much mass and inertia for him to affect its swing enough. Springing to my feet inside his reach, I drive my trident up into his face. The

204

helmet he wears protects him from all but one tine of my trident, but that one draws first blood.

He screams in pain as I jerk the trident free, but only a trickle of blood rewards my effort. Arms spread wide, he whirls towards me, stomping the ground with his massive legs. Ducking, I dodge to the left, but it stomps again. A spasm hits my right thigh. I stumble, then fall, thrusting my shoulder forward and tucking my head as I perform a less-than-graceful roll.

Visidion and Brisong circle each other a few yards away. Rikon roars in my direction then turns away, heading for Visidion. Damn it.

My net drags along with him, stuck to his leg, no use to me.

Running forward, desperate to think of a plan, anything to help Visidion. He's in trouble. I have to get one of them distracted, give him an opening. One desperate idea comes to me. Committing myself to it while knowing it's insane, I run faster. My muscles tremble but I push them harder, willing them to do their job. Five feet behind Rikon, I kick my feet forward, dropping into a slide. Holding the trident at an angle in front of me, I skid between his legs.

I thrust the trident into its crotch. The armor covers this sensitive area too. I'm jerked to a stop when the tines catch on a seam. Then momentum drives them in, piercing his protection. He roars and leaps into the air.

Shit!

Two massive, armored legs drop towards me out of the sky. My heart leaps into my throat. They're coming fast, too fast. I can't get clear.

"Rosalind!" Visidion screams, the syllables of my name sounding drawn out into a long, drawling battle cry as time slows.

Bracing myself for the impact, I throw my arms up, flimsy protection for my head, and wait for him to land.

A massive crash, but no pain. I open my eyes to see the sky. Instinct kicks in, and I roll to the side, coming to my knees. Visidion is on top of Rikon, pounding his helmeted head with his fists. Blood is flying, but not from our opponent. Visidion's fists are bleeding profusely, and he's fighting in a rage. Brisong runs at him and again time slows.

Brisong raises his massive sword over his head, two handed, aiming as he runs. If his blow lands, it will likely split Visidion in half. Brisong is grinning, his helmet lost at some point. Cold ice forms in my stomach. Gripping the trident as I leap to my feet, I aim and throw in a single motion.

The trident flies through the air. My aim is true. It's heading for Brisong's head. This is it, I can end this, now. Hit, damn it, hit that bastard!

Brisong's smile falters as his eyes dart to the side. He turns at the last possible instant and knocks the trident out of the air with a swing of his huge sword. Rage burns in his eyes, focused on me now. Turning his charge, he comes at me.

My knees tremble, and my heart is racing from more than exertion. Brisong bears down on me like a freight train coming. I have to time this just right. The ground vibrates beneath my feet. Closer . . . come on, you son of a bitch.

I dig my foot into the dirt, waiting. He leans into his charge, sword in right hand held out, ready to swing it. If my timing is off even a split second, I'll lose my head.

His arm moves, swinging before I expect. I didn't factor enough for his reach.

Abandoning my plan, I push off, flipping backwards. I do handsprings over and over, trying to get distance between us, but with each rotation he's coming closer. My heart pounds, loud in my ears. My arms tremble with exertion, aches and pains forgotten in the adrenaline rush fueling me.

I'm running out of room and he's closing. Flipping again, my feet hit the wall of the arena. Brisong rages forward, mighty sword swinging back and forth in front of him. I'm out of options. Something moves behind Brisong, pulling my attention.

Visidion is a few feet behind Brisong, too far to help, but my eyes widen and my mouth drops open. The red monster is in his arms. Screaming, he lifts Rikon, who has to be three times his size, over his head. Rikon struggles, roaring, but Visidion roars louder. Muscles rippling across his chest, he throws the beast at Brisong.

"ROSALIND!" Visidion screams, and Rikon screams too as he flies, helpless, through the air.

Brisong ignores the screams behind him, focused on my destruction. His hand pulls back and the sword swings, cutting towards me with a whistle through the air. I'm ducking low and dodging to my left when a tremor starts in both thighs. My legs give out and I collapse again to the dirt.

Rikon slams into Brisong with the loud clang of metal on metal. Brisong is knocked into the dirt too, his sword skittering away. Crawling, desperate to get out of his reach, I claw at the dirt, pulling myself forward, my legs suddenly useless. Pins and needles stab through them, life returning, but slow, too slow.

Something grabs my feet, and I'm sliding backwards. Digging at the dirt, seeking any purchase to stop myself, my hands claw furrows as I'm dragged. I give that up and twist to face my opponent.

Brisong is on his knees, pulling me to him by my left ankle. I'm only dimly aware of the pressure of his grip. Both legs have lost most of their feeling and neither is doing what I want.

"Got you," he laughs, foul breath assaulting my senses.

He has gross yellow eyes that look evil. His smile broadens as he lifts me off the ground, dangling me by my foot.

"You'll regret this," I say.

"Bring it, little female," he laughs. "Maybe I'll bite your tiny head off. You're too little to be of any use for anything else."

I'm struggling with all I've got, and my legs are coming back to life with prickling pain of their own. I swing my body and bend upwards, grabbing onto his hand. Striking at his hard muscles, I hope to make him drop me. He laughs at my efforts, turning around to face Visidion.

"Lose something?" he laughs, shaking me back and forth until I lose my grip on his hand, leaving me dangling again.

Visidion is hunched over, wings spread wide, tail straight up. In one hand he has my forgotten trident.

"Let her go," he says, voice soft.

The arena is quiet. No one dares to breathe.

"And if I don't?" Brisong says.

Visidion doesn't answer him. I see his grip tighten on the haft of the trident. It won't do any good, even with the missing helmet. I don't think it will pierce his thick hide.

Visidion shakes his head, lowering it. The crowd gasps in shock as the trident lowers to the ground. Visidion looks to his right, turning his head away, submitting.

Cold rushes through my limbs.

"HA! HA! HA!" Brisong's laughter is deep and booming.

The red monster, Rikon, rises to his feet next to us, shaking all over. Moving faster than it should be able to, he grabs my arms, pulling me taut between him and Brisong. Pain explodes through my body. Distantly I hear myself screaming as my limbs are strained to their limit. My shoulder pops out of its socket, and everything turns white and hot.

"Mine!" Rikon roars.

"Let her go," Brisong growls.

I look at Visidion, desperate.

The look on his face is unlike anything I've ever seen. My heart swells and chills run through my limbs. His rage is pure burning hot with his love of me. He takes a step, then another, trident rising, arm cocking back. He's going to destroy Brisong.

I'm jerking back and forth. Brisong turns his head.

"Don't try it," Brisong barks.

Visidion runs, arm swinging through the air. The trident is going to fly at any moment but it won't be enough. Closing my eyes, I say a fast prayer, then open them and prepare for the worst. I want to die looking at Visidion. It's the only comfort to be had.

Visidion plants his foot but doesn't release the trident. He spins, a half turn, then the trident flies.

Confusion rocks through me. What did he just do? Brisong's head turns, following the trident's path through the air. Sunlight glints off the sharp metal tines as it flies in a rising arc, reaching its zenith and coming down. It drives through the king's throat, pinning him to his chair.

24

VISIDION

*T*ime stops.

No one makes a sound, for a long, drawn-out moment of shock and fear nothing happens.

Then everything happens at once.

Bursting into motion I run for Brisong. Rosalind dangles between him and his partner, and I must save her. I have to reach her before the guards can fire down on me, must get her to safety.

The crowd screams as gunfire echoes through the arena. Screams of fear now, not screams for blood. Whatever is happening doesn't matter. My feet pounding the dirt, pushing off with each step, leaping forward, flapping my wings to cover the ground faster.

Reaching Brisong, I hit him with a wild swing, coming up under his jaw. His head snaps back, and my other fist crashes across his jaw, cracking him the other way. No retreat, no quarter. Pounding him, hitting him with everything I have as fast and as hard as I can. His yellow eyes roll up into his head with my last hit and he falls backwards, dropping Rosalind who cries out as her top half drops to the ground.

Rikon drops her, looking around as if confused. He cocks his head at me, shakes it, then stares at me again. He seems lost and presents no immediate threat. Dropping to my knees, I gather Rosalind into my arms and run across the arena.

Only now do I glance into the stands. It almost brings me to a stop. The guards are shooting the crowd. They're using electrical guns, like the ones the Zzlo use that stun instead of kill, but they're not shooting me. The crowd is stampeding, trampling over each other in desperation to get out.

"Visidion," Rosalind says.

I can hear the pain in her voice.

"Come on, you damn fool!" Thrace yells, jerking my attention ahead.

He's standing at the opening to our tunnel, waving me forward. Behind him I see our friends and other gladiators. Digging deep I rush forward, pouring everything I have into moving faster.

"Ha!" Mesto exclaims as I burst into the tunnel.

"Curse the Seven Widows," Thrace exclaims. "Can't be satisfied can you, always stirring the cursed pot!"

"We have to move," I say.

"We need to get to the spaceport. This is our one chance, we can't let it slip away," Rosalind says. "Put me down Visidion."

"I've got you," I say.

"Yes, you do, but you can't fight with me in your arms like some kind of damn invalid," she retorts. "Now put me down."

Unable to argue with her logic, I set her on her feet, but keep an arm around her until I'm sure she can stand on her own.

"There's no way we can make it to the spaceport," Thrace says. "This entire place is going to be a war zone."

"When you have no options, you do what you have to do," Rosalind says grimly.

"Curse the Widows," Thrace mutters, nodding.

"Curse whoever you like, but move your ass," Rosalind says. "Do you know the way?"

"Yes," Thrace answers. "Grab gear, this is going to be messy."

We force our way through the other gladiators choking the tunnel and make it to our prep room where everyone grabs weapons. Yelling and the sounds of fighting drift in.

"This is it," I say. "Rosalind and I are getting off this planet. If you want to come with us, we're glad to have you. We'll make you a home on Tajss with us. If you want something else or you want to stay, we wish you the best. You have to decide, now."

They exchange looks with each other. Cenar shrugs.

"I'm not staying here," K'sara says.

"Ha! Stay not," Mesto adds.

All of us turn and look at Todd.

"What?" he asks.

"Are you in?" I ask.

"How could I pass up seeing the next stupid thing you do?" he asks, shrugging.

"Thrace?" I ask.

"You've shoved my entire life into a cursed pot filled with dung and pissed in by all Seven Widows, what am I supposed to stay here for?"

"Colorful," I say.

"Stow it, scrub," he says. "There's plenty more to go."

Nodding, I raise my swords and pace to the door out of our area. Sounds of struggle come through the thin wood, arguing and cries of pain. When I kick the door open, the pit is in chaos. Gladiators are fighting each other, beating one another with no rhyme or reason. Even teams are tearing each other apart.

Sticking to the wall, I lead our team past the worst of the fighting, making the exit with a minimum of conflict. Thrace steps past me and takes the lead. Following him out, we emerge into the dirty, choked streets of Krik. Makeshift stalls of rickety wood line the street. A mob is raging through, looting, overturning the stalls, destroying everything in their path.

"Damn," Rosalind exhales.

"Roofs," Thrace barks, pointing as he runs for the building across the street.

Following, Rosalind stumbles halfway across the street. I hook an arm under hers and lift her up, sweeping her off her feet. Someone at the head of the crowd points and screams something unintelligible. It galvanizes the mob and they scream, racing towards us in a mass.

Todd is struggling to get his bulk up the side of the stall when I get there. K'sara is reaching down from the roof of the building, trying to help Todd. The mob is coming fast.

"Sorry, Todd," I say, placing my hand on his ass, bending my knees, and thrusting up.

Todd flops up onto the roof of the stall. It creaks and buckles, but holds as he stands up and climbs on to the roof. Something hits me in the head. Pain explodes, and the red rage of bijass leaps forward. Roaring in anger, I toss Rosalind up onto the roof and turn to face the crowd. Those in front stop, leaning back in fright. Spreading my wings and arms wide I roar again, and this time I push air from deep in my throat, releasing firein their faces. The mob entangles with itself as those in front turn and race back into the ones pushing them forward.

Pushing the bijass down, I leap onto the stall then onto the roof with the others.

"Impressive trick," Thrace says.

"Right," I agree. "Which way?"

Thrace runs and we follow, leaping from roof to roof, moving deeper into the city. Rosalind stumbles as we reach the third roof. Taking her in my arms, I run for the ledge.

"Visidion, you—" she says, cutting off as I leap, spreading my wings, swinging my tail to keep us upright as we glide between the buildings.

Landing with a crunch on the stone and gravel roof of the next building, I bend my knees to absorb the impact.

"I can do anything... for you."

She smiles. My chest expands, swelling, and a lightness spreads.

"Come on, you two!" Thrace yells.

"Ha! No love time! Run time!" Mesto adds.

Rosalind pushes to be let down, but there's no time. Tightening my grip around her, pressing her close to my chest, I run and leap, run and leap again. The distance between the buildings is getting wider as we head away from the heart of the city. When we slide to a stop, everyone, even Thrace, is panting. The streets are mostly empty now. The chaos hasn't reached this far out yet. Ahead is the spaceport. Gleaming ships thrust into the sky over the low stone buildings. We're almost there.

"Drop down," Thrace orders.

Everyone climbs over the side, I spread my wings and drift down with Rosalind in my arms. We walk down the street as if we have every right to be there. The few people out take note of our weapons and give us a wide berth. The street widens, emptying out, then we turn the corner.

"On the ground!"

The voice booms, echoing off the nearby stone structures. A contingent of armored guards, four kneeling with four behind them, guns cocked and loaded, block our path forward. They're fifty feet ahead, too far to close the distance before they drop all of us.

My stomach sinks and despair threatens to swallow me. My eyes are darting around to find an escape.

"We can dodge back," Rosalind whispers. "Use the buildings for cover."

"We're going to die either way, might as well go out fighting," Thrace says.

"NOW!" one of the guards yells, and their guns whine as they pull the triggers partway, charging up.

Without speaking we move as a unit, splitting in either direction and dodging behind the buildings. When I turn my back to protect Rosalind, the first shots fire, sizzling through the air. My muscles tense, preparing to take the hit. It crackles over my right shoulder as I leap to the side and press myself flat against the building. I peek around the corner to see their position and jerk back just in time to avoid another shot that slams into the wall, sparking dust and crumbling stone.

"Other side!" Thrace yells from across the street.

He's pointing down the street in the other direction. I risk one more quick glance. Another contingent of guards is set up in the same formation there. We're pinned down with no way to reach our destination.

"We can't lose now," Rosalind exhales.

Tremors wrack her and she groans in pain. Pulling her tighter to me, I forge my resolve and temper it with fire. I will not fail. I set her on her feet and cup her face between my hands. She gazes into my eyes.

"You are my treasure," I say.

"Don't do something stupid," she says, trembling.

Kissing her soft, sweet lips, I smile. "Never," I say, whirling away before she can stop me.

When I step into the middle of the crossroads, the guards

shift their attention to me. Raising my hands over my head I walk towards the spaceport.

"Down!" comes the order again.

The air feels electric, dancing across my scales. The guns whine as they charge and any moment now they'll fire. A little closer—it's all I need to be. Eight guards in front, eight behind me. One step, then another, moving slowly, I keep them confused.

"What in the Seven Widows' heart is that fool doing?" Thrace exclaims.

Giving us a chance, I think, but I don't say that out loud.

The guards focus on me which is exactly what I want. I don't have a plan, not a real one. I'm buying time. Time for something to break our way, anything.

"GET DOWN NOW!" the lead guard screams, his voice cracking.

"Excuse me? I don't understand," I say, smiling broadly, hands clasped behind my head.

A few more steps. I'm almost close enough. The ones kneeling in the front row glance at each other, their guns wavering. The back row shifts from foot to foot. Another step, one more, closer. Tensing the muscles in my legs, preparing, one more step.

The air crackles loudly as one guard pulls the trigger. Blue-white lightning forms at the end of the gun, a crackling ball of pain, exploding from the barrel coming for me. I leap, wings spreading, hoping to reach them before I'm hit. The only play I have. The air comes alive as all the guards fire, making the air electric. Multiple balls move towards me in slow motion. This is going to hurt.

A shadow crosses over me. The guards look up, as do I. Wide wings block the sun. My outer lenses snap shut, clearing my vision, and I see a Zmaj floating down from a nearby roof.

Arcan?

It has to be, there is no other Zmaj here, is there?

He lands as the first bolt hits me. My body jerks and spasms as electricity drives through my nervous system, usurping control of my muscles, spinning me in the air.

Arcan raises his right hand, which holds a copper ball. His hand clenches and a pulsing wave explodes out of the ball. A shock wave moves out in a concentric circle with Arcan at its center. The guards are bowled over by the force, but what's more, the incoming bolts of electricity fizzle and disappear before hitting me.

I hit the dirt with bruising force. I skid to a stop, leap to my feet and turn a circle ready for an attack. The guards are in a heap, working to untangle themselves. One of them jumps up and brings his gun to bear, pulling the trigger without hesitation.

I brace for the pain but nothing happens. It doesn't fire. The guard looks down at his gun and then up at me, eyes wide with fear. Grinning, I rush, grabbing him by the waist and lifting him over my head. Spinning him around once to get a better grip I throw him into a nearby wall. He slams into it, a loud clang denting his armor with the force, then he slumps to the ground lying still. The remaining guards scramble backwards, trying to put distance between me and them.

"Enough!" Arcan yells, cutting through the clattering noise of their retreat.

Everyone stops and turns. Arcan stands tall in the middle of the street, copper ball in his fist at his side.

"Sir, they're fugitives," a guard behind me says, the same one who was ordering us down.

"No, they're not here," Arcan says.

"Sir—"

Arcan moves in a rush, passing by me and grabbing the speaker, lifting him up in one hand and shaking him.

"Do you see them?" he hisses.

"N-n-no," the guard stutters.

"Good," Arcan says.

"The king wants—" one of the men from behind me says.

"The king is dead," Arcan cuts him off. "I'm in control now."

Rosalind steps into view as does Thrace and the others. Rosalind is frowning. We've been played, yes, used even, but if we get what we want, does it matter?

"Yes sir," the speaker says.

The guards slam their closed, gauntleted fists over their hearts, bowing their heads to Arcan.

"These people were not here. You did not find them," he says. "Do you all understand?"

"Sir, yes, sir!" the guards bark in unison.

"Good, now order needs to be restored. Go, stop the rioters. Use whatever force is necessary," Arcan orders.

The guards form into a single unit and march off, armor rattling as they move. I go to Rosalind and hook my arm under hers, taking her weight. Small tremors wrack her body, but she's trying to hide them. Arcan watches the guards go before turning his attention to us.

"What does this mean?" I ask, cutting to the chase.

"You're free to go," he says. "There's an unguarded ship waiting for you in bay fifty-two. The guards and crew have been distracted by the riots."

"Why are you helping us?" Rosalind asks.

Something passes over his face, regret? Sadness? A sympathetic ache pulses in my chest. His lips part as if he's going to speak then snap shut and he shakes his head.

"Isn't it enough I have?" he says.

"Will you replace the King?" Thrace asks.

"It won't be that easy," Arcan says. "We'll see."

"Come with us," I say without thinking about it. "Come home."

The pain is clear on his face. Something in his eyes alights. Say yes, come home, Arcan—the plea in my head is so strong, it's a wonder he can't hear it.

"Yes, come with us," Rosalind says. "We need you."

His eyes shift from her to me. Slowly, he shakes his head.

"No," he says, shoulders slumping. "I have to stay."

"Why?" Rosalind asks, pushing off of me. She moves close to him, staring up into his eyes, pleading. "What is there here for you?"

My chest burns as my stomach hardens. I recognize my irrational jealousy, but can do nothing to stop it. Clenching my jaw tight, instinctively I lean towards Arcan as the anger flashes white hot.

"Nothing," he whispers.

"Then come," Rosalind implores.

Hands balling into fists, my bijass rises, forcing me into a struggle for control. She places a hand on his chest, his hand covers her. I'm breathing in ragged gasps, struggling on the edge.

"I can't," he says.

"Why?" she asks. "Tell us."

Tremors run through my muscles, I'm fighting myself so hard to not attack.

"Tajss must remain forgotten. Even the rumors of its survival must be destroyed," he says. "That is all I can give to it. I couldn't stop the Devastation but I can at least try to save it now."

Rosalind purses her lips and nods, taking her hand off his chest. The bijass retreats a little, easing my struggle for control as the burning in my chest subsides. It becomes even less as she steps away from him.

"I'll help you," Thrace says, stepping forward.

Arcan tilts his head, staring at the trainer.

"Are you sure? Freedom awaits you," he says.

"I've done my job with these scrubs," Thrace says, looking at each of us. "I remember the Galactic War. These young fools, they don't have a clue what will happen if epis flows. If that can be stopped, I'm going to do it."

How old is he? I wonder.

"It won't be easy," Arcan says.

"Nothing ever is," Thrace answers. "Don't try to argue me out of it. I've made up my mind."

"Agreed," Arcan says, turning his attention to me. "Vision, I knew your father, before. Return to our home and prepare. If we fail here, they will be coming."

A cold ball of ice settles into my stomach. Arcan extends his arm to me. I grasp his wrist and he returns it. I increase the pressure until his eyes tighten.

"We'll be ready," I say and he nods.

Shaking our arms up and down once, then twice, and we break.

"How did you stop their guns?" Rosalind asks.

"This?" he asks, lifting the ball in his hand. "It drains their batteries, neutralizing them until they recharge."

Rosalind nods thoughtfully. "What's its range?"

"Few meters," he says.

I see thoughts racing behind her eyes and it hits me what she's thinking. Gershom.

"Have an extra one?" she asks.

Arcan looks at the ball in his hand then up to Rosalind. Silently, he holds it out to her. She takes it, hefting it in her hand, then nods.

"Thank you," Rosalind says.

Putting an arm around her protectively I pull her tight against me. Arcan nods, turns and walks away. Thrace falls into step with him. We stand and watch them go until they turn a corner out of sight.

"Ha! Unexpected that was," Mesto says, breaking the solemn silence.

"Well," K'sara says.

"I'm hungry. Let's go," Todd throws in.

Hope lightening my steps, we head into the spaceport towards the dock that Arcan gave us.

25

ROSALIND

"What a junker," K'sara says, looking at the ship.

I can't disagree. The ship's obviously seen much better days. It's a boxy design that I'm surprised can break escape velocity. The hull is covered with dents and burn marks, indicating it's been in more than one firefight. There are no markings on it, which, combined with its overall appearance, leads me to assume it's a smuggler's vehicle. Probably someone owed Arcan a favor. I can't help a mental comparison to *Star Wars*. All it would take is for some roguishly good-looking character to appear at the top of the open ramp to complete the picture.

Except this ship doesn't look as cool as the Millennium Falcon, not by far.

"Let's go," I say, motioning everyone to get up the ramp.

Cenar, ahead of me on the ramp, whacks his head against the jam of the door.

"Ow," he grunts and steps back.

There's a new dent in the hull where his head hit. Wonderful. I hope it didn't damage the seal of the door. With the adrenaline gone, my headache has taken center stage. My patience is at an end.

"Get out of the damn door, Cenar!" I snap. His look over his shoulder at me is crestfallen. My stomach knots and I sigh. Great, now I feel bad on top of the pounding in my head. "I'm sorry."

"It's okay," he says, shuffling through the door, making sure to duck this time.

Pushing myself up the final steps to enter the ship is an effort of will.

"Tight quarters," K'sara observes.

"It's okay," Todd says.

Pushing past Cenar, I get my first look at the inside of the ship. A hallway that's barely wide enough for Cenar to move through goes left and right. The others have gone left and Cenar is going that way so I follow. It opens into a central room with couches around it and some tables with chairs. The floor and walls are bare metal. Visidion stands in the middle of the room while the others have taken up spots on the couches.

"Right," I say, glancing around.

"Ha! Private rooms, good for no more shows!" Mesto says, appearing through a door on the far side of the room.

"Bummer," Todd throws in.

My cheeks warm but I'm not going to acknowledge their crudeness. Visidion shoots an angry look between Todd and Mesto. This has to be stopped fast.

"Okay, if there are private rooms, great. Pick them out and then set about checking for gear and supplies. Visidion, come to the cockpit with me, we need to get this thing in the air."

"If it even flies," K'sara glooms.

"Let's assume it will do the Kessel run in less than twelve parsecs," I quip.

"What is the Kessel Run and what is a parsec?" K'sara asks.

"Forget it," I sigh.

He climbs off the couch, muttering under his breath, and I head for the cockpit.

Like everything else, it's small, and especially tight because Visidion is so big. I sit and he follows suit, but the he has to sit on the edge of the seat and hunch over the control panel. The chairs aren't designed for people with tails and wings.

"Poor design," I observe.

"It will be fine," he says, staring at the control panels.

"Don't worry, I got this," I say.

As I study the layout of the controls, all the pain, weakness, and worry fades away. Concentrating on one thing feels good. After a few tries and a lot of poking buttons and flipping switches, I get the engines to fire up. A heads-up-display appears, and then the rest is intuitive. It's not long before we're lifting off. A radio crackles to life as we lift.

"You're not authorized for departure," a deep voice says.

"Sure, whatever," I mutter, adjusting the ship's angle.

"Return to your bay."

"This going to be a problem?" Visidion asks.

"No," I say.

"Last warning," the voice says.

The ship tilts up and there are curses from deeper in. Someone lost his footing, but they're all going to have to deal. This is going to be tricky. The front screen flashes with a bright blue-white light. They've fired over our bow. Guess they're serious.

"About that problem?" Visidion asks grinning.

My heart pounds in my chest, hard, feeling like it might jump out at any moment. Hands flying across the controls, I touch a lever that I'm sure is the throttle. I hope. Meeting Visidion's grin with my own, I nod.

"Hang on," I say, pushing it all the way forward.

We're thrown back into the chairs with the sudden force of massive acceleration. G-forces increase until I can't get a full breath and it feels like the skin of my face is peeling off. Echoes sound through the ship and lights flash on the HUD telling me that we're being hit by gunfire. Apparently the tub has shields which are absorbing the impact, but it's still causing the ship to rock wildly. Something splashes deep in the ship.

"GROSS!" Cenar yells.

The yellow sky outside the view screen darkens as we break free of the gravitational pull of the planet. The ship jerks hard and we're free. Inhaling deeply for the first time in long minutes, I rub my face trying to push feeling back into the stretched skin.

"I'm not cleaning that up!" K'sara exclaims.

"What happened?" I ask over my shoulder.

"Todd!" K'sara answers. "Disgusting!"

I'm laughing before I can stop it. Visidion laughs, and then tears are streaming down my face as it hits home that we're free. We've survived and now we're heading home. Home to Tajss, where our people are waiting for us.

The next few hours pass quickly as I figure out the ship. At last I've got the navigation system figured out and have it plotting a course to Tajss. It takes a while since I don't know the coordinates, and we have to work by constellation views. Visidion and I master it, and then it's down to waiting. Visidion climbs out of the seat and steps to the door of the cockpit.

"Shall we pick our quarters?" he asks.

I'm struck silent. I want him.

Pulse-pounding, mind-gripping, body-wracking desire

grips me out of nowhere. The hard muscles of his bare, scale-covered chest, his strong jaw, massive hands. Need. I move through a dream state as I close with him. An inferno burns in my core, and my pussy aches with emptiness. Stopping a few inches in front of him, looking up into his beautiful eyes, I can't resist the call of his soft lips. Slowly, I reach across the tiny space between us and lay my fingertips on his chest.

Tracing along the edges of his scales, across his pecs, then down a layer and back the other direction. His pants bulge out as soon as I touch him and he sighs. The pulsing need in my pussy increases, and my wetness soaks my panties. He traces the line of my jaw with his fingertips, adding a layer of sensation that sends shivers down my body. A soft moan slips out.

I look into his burning eyes.

"Go," I say, voice hoarse.

I don't have to ask twice and I follow him through the tight halls. When we reach the back of the ship there's one door left open and we enter it. The rooms are not bad, and compared to the villa we've been trapped in, they're heavenly. A real bed, big enough for both of us, fills most of the space, and is the only thing I'm interested in.

Visidion turns towards me, and I shut the door behind us with my foot. He moves forward, but I put a hand on his chest as he close the distance between us, stopping him. Surprise widens his eyes, but I put my hand on his mouth before he can speak. My other hand goes to his pants, and I deftly undo the tie keeping them up. They drop off his waist, hanging up on his massive erection. I pull them off, ready to see his cock at long last. I've heard the rumors, but I want—no I need—to see it for myself.

I'm not disappointed. His cock isn't only huge but just as I'd heard, hard ridges flow like cresting waves from the head back towards his groin, where a hard, bony ridge protrudes just over the top of his shaft. Perfectly placed for my pleasure.

"Ribbed for her pleasure," I murmur.

One of the companies on the ship had developed a penis cover that used that as a motto. It was amusing to me when they marketed it back then, but what they had can't compare to this. When I run my hand down his shaft, I find that the top ridges are hard but the underside is soft and delicate, like any cock would be. Visidion groans as I pass my hand down his shaft with a light touch. His cock vibrates, jumping with desire. It's too big for me to grasp fully in one hand, so I put my other hand on it as well. Cupping the shaft between both hands, I press them hard against the soft underside and stroke up and down.

He groans louder, thrusting his hips so his cock slides in and out of my hands. His lips find mine. Our kiss is full of desire, his mouth opening wider than mine and claiming me. His tongue presses against my lips, but I drive it back with my own, taking control while also tightening my grip on his cock.

I guide him by my grip on his cock. When he's backed up to the bed, I guide him to sit on the edge of the bed. When he does, I step away from him. His eyes drink me in, making me feel beautiful.

I pull down the fastener of my suit, cool air assaulting the skin of my chest as my cleavage is revealed. Visidion's breath catches as it comes to view.

"Wait," he says, leaning forward. Stopping, I feel suddenly awkward. His eyes drink me in, roaming over my body, and I feel strangely self-conscious. "Slower, pull it down slower."

I want to tell him no. I'm in control. I'm always in control.

But my hand moves, pulling the fastener down in a slow motion.

"There," he says hoarse. He has one hand on his cock stroking it with long, gentle motions. "Move your hips."

I obey, swaying them. Numb tingling sensations shoot through my limbs. He frowns.

"No, a circle," he orders, twirling one finger in the air.

Resistance to his orders comes out of nowhere, and for an instant I stop, but my pussy aches with need, so I obey. My hips moving in a slow circle makes him groan, and he tightens his grip on his cock.

"More," he grunts.

The zipper slides lower and my stomach is coming into view; my tits are straining towards freedom. My hard nipples pressing against the fabric of my suit send tingling shocks through me. I slide the suit off my left shoulder. My tit bounces free as the suit slips down. Visidion gasps, then groans loudly, seeing my tits for the first time. He strokes his cock faster, and the sound of his skin sliding over skin makes me burn for him even more.

"Uhh," he groans. "The other one."

Grabbing a small bit of control back, I slide my hand under the right side of my suit and slowly, so slowly, push it off my shoulder. As my tit appears, he gasps again, and the speed of his stroking increases. Rotating my hips way back then circling them around and thrusting forward towards him makes him groan again.

"Play with them," he orders.

Grabbing my tits and squeezing them feels good. I drag my fingers down to my nipples, pulling on the hard points of both of them, all while keeping my hips rotating. I hold back my own moans of pleasure until I hear him grunting, and I can't hold back any longer.

"More," he says.

Working my tits and my hips, I'm getting a reaction from

him that trips the pounding of my heart. It's loud in my ears and echoes in my pussy.

"Pants," he barks.

I undo the fastening and open the front of my pants. Sliding a hand under the hem of my panties I push down. Wetness greets my fingers and welcomes them in as my pussy gratefully accepts any relief. He's stroking so hard now it's loud and fast. My pants slip over my hips, sliding down.

"Spread it open," he groans.

I obey, opening my pussy with two fingers so he can see my slick tunnel. He leans in close, standing up and continuing to stroke his cock, now just inches away. My pussy aches more, pulsing, calling for him to bury his hard shaft deep inside me.

"Finger it," he orders.

I do, thrusting my fingers in and out, desperate for release. Sliding two then three fingers in. I'm so wet they go in easy.

"Yes!" he exclaims. Then he grabs me by my hips and lifts me into the air.

I yelp in surprise as he spins and drops me on the bed. My legs hang over the edge and he lowers between them. His mouth closes on my pussy, hot breath then his rough tongue taking me without preamble or warning. Pleasure explodes, lightning bolts racing from my core, taking over thought.

My muscles tense as my hips thrust up into him instinctively, welcoming his tongue. The feeling of his rough tongue driving deep into my soft walls, exploring as my blood rushes down, makes my head spin. Light-headed, on clouds, an intensity is building around my clit until I can't take any more. My toes curl and an explosion tears through me. Blinding, white-hot release rips through my body, leaving me shaken. Falling back to the bed, muscles lax, the aftershocks of the orgasm rock me.

Visidion strokes my hips in long, trailing touches, kissing his way up from my delicate opening, across my stomach, making his way to my mouth. His scales are hot to the touch as I run my fingers down his back and along the huge bulge of his biceps.

His body covers me, so much bigger than I am. His cock hanging between us is huge. A spasm tightens my core and for an instant fear strikes me. Is it too big? Lowering himself onto me, his mouth touches mine with gentle, easy kisses. He's softly pressing his lips to mine, pulling back, then touching again.

His gentleness pushes all my fears aside. Visidion will never hurt me. He is a protector, my protector, strong and bold and everything I could ask for in a mate. Cupping my hands behind his neck, I pull him in for a passionate kiss.

26

VISIDION

*E*very muscle of my body thrums in anticipation. She is more than I've ever dreamed. Her perfection is beyond my ability to form words. Every inch of her is perfect, beautiful, and enticing. She is all I want. A warm, golden glow deep in me pulses. She is mine and I'm going to claim her.

My first cock is at her opening, ready to take what belongs to me, mark her with finality and join us together. She will be my treasure forevermore.

Her soft lips move on mine. In anticipation of penetrating her with my cock I drive my tongue into her mouth, staking my claim here first. Her tongue rises to mine as her mouth opens wider, welcoming my claim. Her hands stroke my back, leaving trails of fire where her fingertips pass. My cock vibrates, jumping and throbbing, pent-up desire almost over-whelming. My balls pull tight against my body, aching, needing release. Instinct rages, pushing me to claim her, thrust my cock into her welcoming pussy and take my relief.

I don't give into it, maintaining my control over base desires.

Taking my cock in my hand, I press into her pussy with just the head, then move it in an up and down motion. As her sweet wetness covers my head, the sensations tighten my balls even more. Pleasure burns through my nerves, and for an instant I slip, pressing in further than I intended. Rosalind groans below me, thrusting her hips up, but I regain control and pull back to keep from penetrating her fully.

Breaking my seal on her lips, I kiss across her cheek while still moving my cock up and down her slit. She so wet it's driving me to the edges of control. I'm not sure how long I can hold off. The ache deep in my stomach pushes, begging me to shove my cock deep into her.

Her hands roam across my back, electric sensations following her touch.

"Visidion," she groans.

Hearts pounding in my chest I slide the tip of my dick into her welcoming warmth. A sigh slides out as I slide into her. The warmth of her delicate walls clasping on my dick transports me. Pushing into the first ridge I stop, letting her body adjust to my girth.

Her body resists, pushing back, and she moans and wriggles her hips. Every nerve in my body is on fire. Tingling, alive, aware of the slightest sensation. Air moving across our bodies, her light touch, the pounding of my heart that echoes in my cock as I wait to push deeper.

Slow, so slow it hurts, I push into her. Wet warmth opens, taking me deeper, expanding to pass over the first rib of my cock. As it passes into her and her pussy closes on me I'm overcome with pleasure. My thoughts go blank. There is nothing but the sensation of her on my dick.

I'm shuddering as it rips through me until my vision clears and awareness comes back.

"Yes, yes, yes," Rosalind pants.

Biting my lower lip, I push forward once more, pressing

the next ridge into her welcoming body. Slowly, letting her body adjust to accommodate me.

"Ahhh," she exhales in pleasure and her eyes bore into me.

Holding my hips still, I lean in and kiss her while moving my free hand to her breast. Squeezing it softly, I work it as I move my hand to capture the hard point between thumb and forefinger. When I roll it between them, she closes her eyes and groans. Her pussy spasms on my cock pushing me to the edge. I struggle to hold off, to maintain control. Her body shudders beneath me. She hisses, then moans as her back arches up, pushing her body past the next ridge on my cock, forcing me back onto the edge I had just backed off.

Clenching my fist next to her and biting my lip, I maintain control, barely.

"Take me," she moans, thrusting her hips up onto me.

My cock slides fully into her as she does. Control disappears as she pushes me into her. Instinct and need take over. I'm in her fully now. With her hips rotating, grinding her hot, wet pussy against me, I give into my basest desires. I pull out to the tip of my cock, and then drive it back into her.

"GOD!" she screams her pleasure, her nails digging into my back.

Thrusting in and out, I claim her. My dick takes her and her body responds.

"Yes!" she screams.

I'm pounding in and out of her, my core tightening. Her moans and wordless screams pull me along. My cock drives into her tight wetness, pulling out, then claiming her again. Her eyes roll up into her head, and then I'm blinded too as my first cock explodes. My seed fills her, my cock pumping out more and more. My muscles are shaking as my release floods my body.

The arch of her back relaxes and she drops fully to the bed below me. My cock softens in her wet warmth. Shudders pass over her and also down my spine as my first cock spreads the last bits of its seed. Only when she's fully relaxed, her eyes open and looking into mine with a warm softness do I slide my first dick out. As it drops, soft and spent, my second cock rises, ready for its release too.

Her face is soft and glowing, somehow even more beautiful. Grabbing my second cock, I shift and hold it directly over her sweet pussy, stroking it. Her hand moves between us and finds it, caressing lightly. A smile spreads across her face.

I rise onto my knees and swing my leg over her. She watches with open curiosity as I grab her hips, lift her up, and turn her over onto her stomach. Positioning myself behind her, I pull her up onto her knees. Cock at her opening, I push forward. A shudder runs through her as my cock enters her again.

"Fuck me," she moans, as the head passes into her from his new position.

Running my hands down her sides, stretching forward, I grab her tits and massage them as I drive my cock slowly deeper.

"Yes!" she screams.

Finding the hard points of her nipples I roll them in my fingers as my cock finds her depths. I hold it there to enjoy her hot pussy clamping my dick.

She rocks forward, pulling part way off my cock, then impales herself on me again. As she pulls forward, I lose my hold on her tits, so I let my fingers trail along her beautiful perfect sides and down across her stunning ass. Grabbing her hips to steady her, I pull out and drive into her again.

Her body and pussy spread to take me. She screams her pleasure as my cock goes deep. When I slap her ass lightly, she groans. Thrusting in and out, taking her, making her mine. She grunts with each thrust in and groans as I pull back. I hiss my own pleasure. My balls are already tight again, ready for release, but I'm not going to give in, not yet.

In and out, I push, driving my cock deep and out again, running my hands over her as I do. I hold as long as I can until the tightness in my core overwhelms me. Losing all semblance of control, I drive into her and then I'm thrusting in and out with abandon.

She screams my name, her hands balling into fists in the sheets. Her wet, warm pussy tight on my dick pushes me past my ability to hold off. Driving fully into her again, hands gripping her ass tight, I hold myself deep inside as my second load explodes. My cock spasms over and over, pumping my hot seed into her. She is mine, now and forever. My treasure, panting beneath me, accepting me. We are as we were meant to be, becoming one together.

As the last of my seed pumps into her, my body shakes and spasms, pushing deeply into her. Holding there, my cock softens, but the warmth of her is too nice to leave. She collapses onto the bed, and I lie on top of her, letting my dick stay inside her.

Lying on top of her, I can feel her heart pounding in her chest, and my own hearts match the rate of hers. As the pace slows and our breathing returns to normal, she sighs, then laughs.

"Amazing," she exhales.

My smile must be covering my whole face. Nibbling on her ear, I push her hair aside and nip her neck, tracing my fingers along her side.

"You are my treasure," I whisper into her ear.

"Yes," she says, wriggling beneath me.

My cock, still deep in her, surprisingly, begins to stiffen. It jumps to life, making me aware it's ready. Rosalind's eyes widen, feeling my cock harden inside her yet again. Biting her lower lip, her eyelids close half-way and she nods, encouraging.

Sliding out until only the head is inside her wet pussy I pause, leaning in for a kiss. She turns her face to me, welcoming, soft lips meeting mine. With sweet kisses, we devour each other as I slide my cock deep into her hot tunnel, burying myself to the hilt. When my ridge finds her clit she screams pleasure into my mouth.

She moves forward and my cock springs free. She crawls away a bit, rises onto her knees, and turns. Hands on my chest, she pushes me backwards until I'm lying on the bed, my stiff cock standing up in the air. Swinging her leg over me, she positions herself over my erection.

She grabs my cock and holds it as she lowers herself slowly down. Somehow this feels completely new. Reaching the first ridge, she pauses until her body adjusts and she slides past it. Excitement fills my core. My balls are so tight, I'm sure they'll explode. Electrical jolts singe their way through my nerves as she continues to lower herself. Passing the next ridge, she moans in a high pitch, throwing her head back. Her breasts hang heavy, calling to me, so I take them in my hands.

She's wet and warm and perfect as she lowers herself, and now I'm fully in her. Shudders run down my spine when she moves her hips back and forth.

"Hmm," she moans, moving.

Massaging her tits, I focus on not losing control. My balls tighten and my dick stiffens more. I don't know how long I can hold off.

"Yes-s-s-s," I hiss, hands moving to her hips.

She moves her hips in a circle, tight tunnel gripping my cock. Suddenly she leans backwards, arms behind her, holding her out, and she moans. Her body is rocked, muscles spasming, hips pushing on and off my cock, fast and hard.

Another load explodes as I give myself over to another orgasm too. Coming together, we're both moaning. Slowly, awareness returns as last shivers run through my body, leaving me exhausted. Rosalind is breathing heavily, holding herself there until her breathing slows. She slides off my softening cock, moving next to me and laying her head on my shoulder. I wrap an arm around her, and we lie quietly together.

As my heart rate slows to normal, I feel a peace I haven't felt in so long it seems unfamiliar and strange. I run my fingers along her body, loving the soft touch of her skin. My thoughts turn to our homecoming and the things we will have to do.

"Now more than ever, we have to bring the City and the Tribe together," I muse out loud.

"They are together," Rosalind says, sighing at the passing of my fingers over her hips. She puts one leg over mine, snuggling closer.

"You don't have the City."

"It doesn't matter," she murmurs, kissing my neck.

"How so?" I ask.

She stops nibbling, pulling her head back.

"Are you serious?" she asks.

"Of course I am," I say, confused.

"Now? Of all times now is when you want to bring this up?" she asks, pulling her leg off of me and pushing herself away.

"I don't—"

"Of course you don't," she snaps, climbing off the bed.

Her beautiful breasts bounce as she jumps to her feet. Her ass is exquisite as she bends over and grabs her clothes. My first cock stirs to life, but my thoughts are a raging confusion overriding its baser desire.

"Rosalind I—"

She cuts me off with a look. I sit up on the bed, my first cock rising to attention between my legs as I swing them over the edge of the bed. I'm hoping to somehow understand the shift in her mood.

"Now was *not* the time to bring this up," she says, shaking her head. "All of that is in the future, those are tomorrow's problems, but no, you couldn't just be happy for the moment."

"I didn't mean... we have to make a plan," I say, trying to keep up with her.

"Yes, but not *now*," she barks.

"But—"

"No, no buts, not a damn one. I know where you stand." She's pulling her clothes on violently, talking fast. "You're wrong and that's all there is to it. I can't lose any of them. I need every set of genes in the pool if either of our races are to survive. Nothing you say will change that. All of that was tomorrow's problem, but you couldn't just leave it there!"

She stops, clothes in disarray, shirt barely covering her breasts, armored jacket swinging from a finger. She stares at me, eyes drifting to the erection between my legs.

"God!" she exclaims.

She turns on her heel and storms out the door without another word.

27

ROSALIND

"This could get rough," I call over my shoulder.

"Rougher, you mean?" K'sara asks with a smirk. "Damn it, Todd, get a bucket!"

Todd's retching echoes through the ship. We're entering Tajss's atmosphere. Since I've taken over manual control of the ship, it's been vibrating so roughly I'm worried it will shake apart. The air passing by the front screen dances with flames as I shift the angle. Visidion is having a hard time staying in the co-pilot seat and running the controls on his side, which isn't making this any easier. The turbulence bounces him up and down since he can't strap in.

"Ha!" Mesto exclaims as Todd vomits loudly.

"Gross, Todd, by the Seven Widows, can't you control yourself?" K'sara curses.

The ship bounces again as we pass through the thermosphere. As we slow and level off, the jarring eases up.

"I think we're close," Visidion says, checking the navigation systems.

We haven't spoken much since he put his foot in his

mouth. I'm not ready to forgive him yet. I know I will, eventually, but right now I think he deserves the cold shoulder.

"Rosalind," he says.

"No," I say. "We'll deal with it later."

His shoulders slump but he nods. Of all the moments, the one he chose was the worst. Now it's here. I won't be able to put off a decision much longer and I know it. It doesn't mean I'm looking forward to it though.

As I guide the ship in, we pass over the outcropping that houses the Tribe. We're low enough to see them looking up and pointing. People are rushing, some running into the caves and others grabbing weapons. We must be scaring the hell out of them. A strange ship flying over, they probably think it's the Zzlo.

Choosing a clear area on top of a dune a short distance away, I bring the ship in for a landing. Once we're down, I power everything off, and then we exit as a group. Visidion stays close by my side, but he's smart and doesn't say anything more. Everyone on the ship has picked up on the tension between us, but none of them have broached the subject which is fine with me.

"This is Tajss?" Todd asks, weaving in place and holding his stomach.

"Ha! Sucks this place," Mesto says, shaking his head.

Cenar steps off the ramp, crouches, and runs a handful of sand through his fingers.

"I like it," he pronounces.

K'sara doesn't say anything, quietly observing the surroundings. Across the dunes, I see a group of males approaching, five of them, all armed and ready.

"Ragnar, Sverre, Bashir, Drosdan, and Ladon," Visidion says, his eyesight better than anyone else's in this environment.

Rather than wait for them to get to us, I herd our group

towards them. They're all armed with lochabers held at the ready, eying our new compatriots with suspicion. Ragnar and Ladon are slightly in the lead. Watching them approach, I sense the tension between the two of them. Nothing's changed there. I guess I should be glad they haven't killed each other in our absence.

The Zmaj spread into a semi-circle, lochabers in their hands.

"Rosalind," Ladon says. "Visidion."

"Commander," Ragnar says, ignoring me.

"It's fine," I say. "These are friends of ours. They helped us to escape."

The Zmaj exchange glances before lowering the lochabers but none of them put them away.

"Ha! Too many dragons," Mesto says. "Hot! Too hot, water?"

"We're home," Visidion says. "There is much to talk about but first let's get out of the suns."

Ragnar stares at him for a long moment. Drosdan crosses his massive tree trunk arms over his barrel chest and harumphs.

"What?" I ask, and my left thigh quivers and goes weak. Gritting my teeth, I will it to hold my weight and manage to waver only a little.

"How?" Ladon asks, looking at the ship behind us. "What happened with the Zzlo? Are you here of your own free will?"

Smiling, I shake my head and sigh. My head is pounding, my heart is racing, and a cold sweat is running down my spine. I really don't want to stand here discussing this.

"Like Visidion said, there's a lot to discuss, but we don't need to do it out here in the suns. Suffice it to say that we're home and yes, we're here of our own free will. Do you have any epis?" I ask.

The Zmaj look at each other, then Ladon and Ragnar lock eyes. Ragnar nods and Ladon seem to agree.

"Right," Ragnar says, putting his lochaber away. "Let's go home."

"Epis?" I ask, again desperate for the pounding in my head to stop.

"Not with me," Ladon shakes his head, frowning. "How bad is it?"

"Not bad," I lie, but the look on Ladon's face makes it clear he knows.

"We'll get you some back at camp," Ragnar says.

Visidion helps me across the sand dunes. Ladon is the only one who seems to notice how much I'm leaning on him, more than should be required.

The wall around the Tribe compound is mostly done. Standing ten feet tall with evenly placed slits for lookouts or shooting, it's impressive. There isn't a real gate yet, but the opening is blocked by frames covered with hardened leather. That would be effective to at least slow anything coming through, and enough to keep most wandering animals out. Two Zmaj pull the frames aside, allowing us to pass inside. The garden is in full bloom with colorful plants. Several humans, mostly female, are working their way through the rows weeding or digging at the irrigation channels.

Craftsmen are working at their stalls that circle the open area inside the wall. Long tables are occupied by people working on crafts or preparing foods for storage. Things seem to be going well. Most of them are looking at us, either openly or with quick glances. Something is off but I can't put a finger on it.

"Good work on the wall," Visidion says.

"Yes," Ragnar agrees, stopping and turning to face our group. "We're home."

"Yes, we are," Visidion says, turning a slow circle to look at the Tribe. "It's good."

"Epis?" I ask, once more, forcing a smile my vision is blurring the pain is so great now.

"Samil!" Ragnar barks. "Epis, now."

Samil looks up from the table where he was working on something, nods enthusiastically and runs off. In moments he's back, a soft blue glow in his hand. He holds it out to me and I take the strand, popping it in my mouth. The familiar taste explodes across my taste buds. Warmth spreads through my cheeks, racing along my nerves, growing hotter. It's like swallowing liquid fire that burns through my system. The pain fades, and my weakness is consumed in its flames. Sighing, I nod and swallow the last of it, feeling more like myself than I have in a long time.

Vision clear now, I turn my attention outward. I try to put my finger on what's bothering me, then it hits me.

"You're not getting along," I say, turning to Ragnar and Ladon.

"What do you mean, Rosalind," Ladon asks.

"The Tribe and the City, there's almost no mixing, even doing the same work," I accuse, pointing a finger in a circle around us.

Ladon and Ragnar exchange a look that tells me I'm right. Closing my eyes, I sigh. Damn it, this isn't what I was hoping to come back to.

"You're home!" Olivia exclaims, waddling forward.

She's very pregnant, and it obviously won't be long before she'll be on bed rest. As we found out with Calista, Zmaj babies take longer to come to term and the only way our bodies can manage is to go on bed rest for the last couple of months. She moves to stand next to Ragnar, who puts a protective arm around her shoulders. A movement behind them catches my eye—Mei climbing the ramp up to the caves. She sees me looking and waves, then she produces a key and unlocks the steel gate blocking off the entrance to one of the caves.

"Who's in that cave?" I ask.

Ragnar looks over his shoulder then back. "Ryuth."

"Ah," I say. I'd heard about him, captured by the Zzlo and tortured for who knows how long. He had given himself fully over to his bijass. "Is it safe for Mei to be in there with him?"

Ragnar shrugs. "He likes her."

"She's been working with him, says she's getting through," Olivia adds.

I let it go for now, filing it away for later.

"Ragnar, Ladon, we need to be debriefed," I say. "How's the food? Any word from the City?"

"The City is gone to hell in a hand basket," Amara interjects, walking up with a baby on her hip.

The baby coos, looking around with big, wide eyes. His scales are deep green and his hair is reddish, edging towards brown. He smiles, a toothless showing of his gums. His tiny fingers clench in Amara's shirt as he rocks himself back and forth, tiny tail slashing left-right in time to the rest of his motion.

"What do you mean?" I ask.

"She means they're running out of food," Lana says from behind me. Astarot stands next to her. "Gershom didn't think through the fact that the Zmaj did all the hunting."

"Or he thought his Human First idiots would be able to shoot better than they do," Amara says.

"They need our help," I say.

"No, they don't. They've made their choices," Ragnar says.

"They do, because it's my City!" Ladon says.

Ragnar and he glare at each other like two opposite ends

of a spectrum. Anger flaring makes their scales edging turn red.

"Visidion, now that you're back, can you talk some sense into him?" Ragnar asks.

Visidion gives me a look I can't read.

"This isn't the time," he says instead of answering.

"The prisoners you freed are here too," Amara says. "Thanks for that, by the way," she says with acid in her voice. "All the millions of lives on the ship you could rescue, and you find that batch."

"What do you mean?" I ask.

Amara snorts. "You'll find out."

She spins on her heel and walks off. Good to know she hasn't changed in my absence.

"Okay," I say. "There's a lot to catch up on, and this isn't working. Lana, this is Cenar, Mesto, K'sara, and Todd. Can you help them find quarters and show them around? Ragnar, Ladon, can you two come with Visidion and me and bring us up to speed, please?

Not waiting for a response, I start walking toward Visidion's rooms. I can feel their eyes on me as I climb the ramp. Somehow they all have to come together, get along, and focus on breeding the next generation while also figuring out how to improve our quality of life. A few little things that I wouldn't think would be that hard to get people interested in. Except for the infighting, disagreements on what should be done. All the situation needs is Gershom and his fearmongering about the Zmaj stealing all the human females.

Sitting at the table in Visidion's quarters, Ragnar and Ladon avoid looking at each other. The tension in the room is high.

"Okay," I say. "Who's first?"

"We need—" they both start talking at once, spend a

moment trying to dominate the other one by talking louder, then stop and glare.

I've never seen a more clear-cut case of schoolyard bullies in my life.

"Visi—" Ragnar begins at the same time that Ladon is saying my name. This turns into a fresh shouting match, and then Ladon leaps to his feet, knocking his stool over, and Ragnar is standing on his.

"ENOUGH!" I yell, slamming a fist down on the table. "Sit, both of you."

They turn to me with my shout, shifting their glowers from each other to me.

"Sit," Visidion says.

"Ladon, talk," I say.

Ladon starts telling his thoughts. Ragnar sits and listens then adds his thoughts. The Tribe and the City are doing okay here, but no one is comfortable. The City wants their comforts, and the Tribe wants them to work harder. Nothing that can't be overcome.

"What about over in the City?" I ask. "What do we know about what Lana said?"

"She should learn to obey," Ragnar huffs.

"What do you mean?" I ask.

"I told all the hunters to stay away from the City. They've made their bed; let them lie in it," he says.

"It's not that simple," I say.

"Yes, it is," Ragnar says. "Ladon can get over it. He lost his city. Those who stayed behind will learn to survive, or they will die. It's on them."

"Together we are stronger," Visidion says, quoting the third edict.

"Yes, but we don't coddle the weak!" Ragnar shouts.

"You do what I tell you to do," Visidion says, his voice soft and somehow more dangerous than if he had yelled.

Ragnar's eyes widen, his shoulders hunch, and he leans forward as his tail rises behind him. Visidion doesn't move or even seem to notice. He watches Ragnar, waiting unperturbed, patient. Ragnar hisses, then it's as if he collapses on himself. Leaning back in his seat, tail dropping to the ground with a thud, he shakes his head.

"Yes, Commander," he says.

Visidion nods and makes a motion with his hand that I should continue.

"Here's the hard truth," I say. "We need those in the City. We need every able-bodied person, human, Zmaj, or other that we can get our hands on if we're going to survive. We have an entire planet that needs to be repaired and repopulated. Those too old or young for babies need to help fix things. We don't have a choice if we're going to survive."

"We are surviving just fine," Ragnar grouses.

"Sure, right now, for your lifetime."

Ragnar shakes his head. "What do you mean?"

"Your and Olivia's child," I say, driving my point home. "What kind of world do you want to leave him? This barren, blasted rock or something that is better than what you have?"

Ragnar frowns, crosses his arms over his chest, and doesn't say a word.

"They're running out of food," Ladon says. "Scouts have been watching when they can. There are regular security patrols, armed, along the dome. There's no way to get inside."

"Let me worry about that," I say. "What about here?"

The two men exchange a rare look that doesn't mean they want to kill each other.

"It's fine," Ladon says.

"We're getting along," Ragnar adds.

"And?" I ask.

They look at each other again.

"What is it?" Visidion asks.

"The new people you sent," Ladon says. "They're not fitting in… easily."

"Why not?" I ask.

"Amara," they say in unison, then look at each other in surprise.

"Amara? Why?" I ask.

"Seems there's a rivalry between her and their leader," Ragnar says.

"Something from before your ship crashed," Ladon says. "She's been stirring a lot of sentiment against them. Particularly Stancher."

Stancher, why does that name ring a bell?

"How bad is it? Openly violent or casual disagreement?"

"Disagreements," Ladon answers.

"Fine, we'll get to that later then," I say, shaking my head. "What else?"

They both shrug.

"Good, both of you go and make sure our new friends are comfortable," I say.

"Who are they?" Ladon asks.

Visidion and I share our adventure with them leaving out some bits, mostly about us. I nudge Visidion under the table when he starts to mention the interest in epis out there. That's a problem for later. No need to worry anyone with it now. Once they've heard our story, they leave.

"What now?" Visidion asks, placing his hands on my waist.

"I'm still pissed at you," I say, turning my head to the side as he leans in for a kiss.

He lets me go and steps back.

"Oh," he says, looking crestfallen. "I'm sorry."

"You should be," I say, moving back into his arms and rising onto my toes to kiss him.

His lips are soft and cool. I break the kiss and stare into his eyes.

"This isn't going to be easy," I say.

"Life isn't easy," he says, arms encircling my waist. "That's not the point. If there was no struggle then what triumph would there be? An easy life doesn't change history, it doesn't make a difference."

"True," I sigh, laying my head on the bulging muscles of his chest. "But sometimes it sounds nice."

"It does," he agrees, laughing and running his fingers through my hair.

Pushing aside everything else for the moment I give myself into him, enjoying the strength of his arms, letting the future and all the problems wait.

28

VISIDION

"This is what was in the drop," Lana says, tossing several crumpled pieces of paper on the table.

Rosalind grabs one and straightens it before reading it. Lana shifts from foot to foot while she waits. Rosalind reads each piece of paper before leaning back in her chair, shaking her head as her brow furrows and her mouth turns down.

"It's bad," she says, looking at me.

"How bad?" I ask.

"He's implemented martial law," she says. "Those armed guards aren't to keep us out. They're to keep those who stayed in."

"Why would he do that?" I ask.

"Because he's an asshole," Lana snaps.

"Yes, but it's food that's the problem," Rosalind says. "They've been on short rations for a month, and even that's not enough cuts. They've lost several of those who could hunt, and now the people inside are starving. She says a lot of them aren't showing up for work, as of her last report. They're too weak to get out of bed."

"That should make it easy to take the City back," I observe.

"Maybe," Rosalind says, pursing her lips. "They still have the guns, and I'm betting that the ones who have them are better-fed than the rest."

"And the dome," Lana says.

"And that," Rosalind agrees.

"Thank you, Lana, I appreciate your going out of your way to get this," Rosalind says, motioning at the papers.

"No problem. I can't believe you had a message system worked out ahead of time. Is there anything you're not prepared for?" Lana asks.

Rosalind smiles and says nothing. Lana shakes her head and leaves us alone.

"How is Sarah getting out of the City to the drop?" I ask.

"I'm not sure. She's resourceful," Rosalind answers.

"We need to get them to come out of the dome," I say.

Rosalind nods, rubbing her temples. Suddenly she stops, looks at me and a smile spreads across her face.

"Food!" she exclaims.

"What of it?" I ask.

"They're starving. We bring them food," she says.

"How would it help us to feed them?" I ask.

"Because he has to come out to get it," she grins.

Understanding dawns, and a smile spreads over my face too. "Of course!" I say, jumping up and running outside.

Looking down from the ramp at the Tribe working, I scan them looking for Ragnar. There, he's instructing some humans on how to butcher.

"Ragnar!" I yell.

When he turns to look, I motion for him to come to my quarters. Once he joins us, I lay out our plan. As it becomes clear to him, his grin is ear-to-ear and he nods enthusiastically.

"I'll get Ladon and the others to help," he says.

"How long do you need?" I ask.

"Two days, maybe three," he answers.

"Good," I say. "Get to it."

Ragnar rushes out to gather the others, leaving us alone. Rosalind's smile fades, turning serious again.

"What is it?" I ask.

"Push is coming to shove," she says. "I'll have to deal with Gershom, somehow."

Rather than speaking, I nod. This is her decision, and anything I say will come across wrong. If she had done this when I pushed her to, back when the Tribe arrived at the City, we wouldn't be here now. There is no changing the past. Even if I could, would she be mine now? Besides, I understand her even if I don't agree with it.

She paces the small space of my quarters. I don't know how long she paces back and forth, lost in her thoughts, but eventually it's clear she's not getting anywhere. I step into her path and she bumps into my chest, unaware I was there until then. She looks up, anger flashing in her eyes, but I grab her by her hips, lifting her off her feet to my lips. Taking a kiss whether she wants it or not. She stiffens, pulls back, and I let her. She stares into my eyes, the fire raging in them, then she smashes against me with bruising force.

Her legs wrap around my waist, and before I can move, she's grinding herself against my stiff dick. Her arms are squeezing my neck tight, so that it's hard to breathe, but air doesn't matter. I'm devouring her lips, needing more—I can't get enough of her. Clothes fly off, barely breaking our kiss as we undress. She unhooks her legs from around me to let her pants slide off.

In my arms, she wriggles out of the last of her clothes. Free at last, her legs encircle me. I lift her up, she shifts her hips, and I lower her onto my waiting cock.

"Mmm," she moans as it slides into her wetness.

She takes my full, hard cock, in a single downward motion, not even pausing for the ridges. I'm deep insider her, hitting the bottom. She moves her hips in a small, tight circle, groaning as she does. The hard tips of her breasts move against the scales of my chest, leaving burning trails across me. She's so hot inside, taking me, she's claiming me as hers. I give myself fully to her. She is my treasure.

Moving my hands to her sweet ass, I lift her up, pulling out until the head of my cock is all that's left inside her warmth. She bites her lower lip, eyes half-lidded, anticipating what's to come.

"Yes, yes, yes," she pants.

When I let go, she slams down my shaft until once more my cock finds bottom. She cries out her pleasure as each ridge of my dick passes into her, expanding her soft walls, filling her completely. Her nails dig into my shoulders, she cries out, throws her head back, and moans.

Wrapping one hand in her hair, I lift her with my free hand on her ass, repeating the motion. She gasps loudly. It feels so good, the way her pussy clamps my cock, spasming on it. Her sweet, hot, wet pussy milks my cock, squeezing me, demanding my seed.

Pulling her head back, I kiss the hollow of her neck, along her shoulder, lifting her and slamming her up and down on my dick all the while. Reckless abandon takes over. All control is gone. I have to have more of her. Balls tightening, stomach a hard knot, slamming her on and off my dick, I'm edging closer and closer to an orgasm.

"Visidion," she groans as I slam into her again.

"Rosssss-lind," it comes out in a long hiss, breathing hard, holding the orgasm at bay to enjoy her longer.

"Yes," she grunts, pulling herself up then dropping, over and over.

My entire body stiffens, my cock swells, then explodes inside her. Pumping load after load into her welcoming womb. Giving myself to her fully, her sweet pussy claiming my cock as its own. She is my treasure; I will protect her. She is mine.

29

ROSALIND

"*I*s that all of it?" I ask.

"Yes," Ragnar says, stepping back.

The makeshift sleds are loaded with meat and some vegetables from the gardens. There's enough food to feed everyone left in the city for a month at least. The Tribe and the Exiles look on in a loose group. It's too easy to see the division among them. The Tribe are almost all to the right, the City Exiles to the left, and in the middle of the two groups are those Zmaj and human females who have paired off. If only I could get them all to see that the middle is where our future lies. If only Gershom would see it. Instead, he's too busy scrounging after power and control.

"What now?" Todd asks, scratching his belly. "It's hot."

"Ha!" Mesto exclaims.

Our fellow gladiators stand with Visidion and me next to the sleds. Cenar is the only one who doesn't seem to mind the heat. Is a creature made of rock even aware of the temperature? I should ask him sometime. Everyone is looking at me, including Visidion. We haven't spoken about my plan or what comes next, nor have we decided how to broach the subject of our relationship to those gathered before us. Looking at the divided groups, an impulse takes hold of me.

"Everyone," I say, pitching my voice to carry. The murmur of conversation stops as they all look at me.

"I know this isn't the home we set out for," I say, looking at the humans on the left.

"And I know we aren't the easiest to understand or get along with," I turn my attention to the Zmaj of the Tribe.

There are murmurs of assent on both sides.

"But here is what else I know. We need each other. More than any of you realize, we need each other. Our future, the future of our races depends on us."

"DADDY!" Illadon screams at the top of his lungs, leaping out of Calista's arms, tiny wings flapping hard, arms out stretched as he lunges for Ladon.

The crowd laughs as Calista turns bright red with embarrassment. She looks at me, shrugging, sheepish. I nod to her. The timing couldn't have been better. Ladon lifts Illadon into the air, tossing and catching him, then brings him down into a tight embrace, kissing his head.

"It's up to us," I continue. "What the future of this world looks like. Humans, you followed me into exile. Now I'm leading you home, but it's not going to be the home your families left Earth for, or the home you thought you knew before this happened. It's time for us to all come together, to become one people. No matter if we look different on the outside."

I motion to the Zmaj, then to the gladiators standing in a semi-circle around Visidion and me.

"No matter what form they take, friendship, cooperation, and yes, even love can be had. We have to open our minds and hearts to it. The future, our children, are depending on us. What we do, right now, will determine the future of this planet and both our races."

They look at each other nervously. Soft murmurs between each other. Calista and Ladon, Jolie and Sverre, Amara and Astarot and their children. Lana and Shidan, Olivia and Ragnar look at each other then move together, coming closer, physically showing the bond between them. Padraig steps out of the group of Zmaj and walks over to the humans, and it's like a dam breaks. The two groups mingle together, conversations strike up, and in moments it's a completely different view.

Visidion takes my hand, squeezing it tight. I glance down at it, my heart racing, cold sweat running down my back. The swell of feelings in my chest is too much to be contained. I rise on my toes so that our lips meet. His arms encircle me, welcoming me in, and I melt against him. Distantly at first, then growing, a cheer erupts. Breaking the kiss, I turn, cheeks burning hot, to everyone fist pumping the air and shouting their approval.

"Okay, okay," I say, shushing the crowd. "We have work to do."

The gladiators take up the ropes attached to the sleds. The Zmaj who are coming with us kiss their mates goodbye, then join them on the ropes. Visidion and I lead the way towards the City.

THE GLIMMER OF THE DOME ON THE HORIZON CALLS US HOME. It's been a long time since I've seen it and a lot has happened but still, in my heart, this is home. We pull the sleds into place a hundred yards in front of the airlock to the dome. The armed guards inside stare out at us, rifles held before them.

Now we wait.

The hot suns beat down on us. Gershom makes us wait until they're dipping down to the horizon, but I expected as much. As the day drags on, more and more people appear behind the armed guards. Any fool can see they're malnourished, thin to the point of being gaunt. They look out at us with hungry eyes, so we make a show of eating. Todd enjoys this the most, holding a huge hunk of meat and ripping bites off it. He holds it out towards the dome as if offering it between each bite.

The crowd in the dome parts as an armed escort pushes through them. They open the airlock and march in. In the middle of them is Gershom. Once they exit the dome, they march not quite to the halfway point and stop. Forming a line in front of him, they kneel and bring their rifles to bear on our group.

"Rosalind, what is the meaning of this?" Gershom asks.

"Meaning?" I ask, feigning confusion at his question.

"Yes, this," he glares motioning at the sleds piled with food. "And what have you brought with you? Even more aliens to steal our women from us?"

Glancing at the gladiators I shrug.

"No, they're my friends," I say. "You should try having some. It's nice."

His face turns purple with anger.

"Cut to the chase. What are you doing here? You were exiled, do you not understand what that means?"

"Oh I get it," I say. "But I heard my people were starving. I can't stand by and let that happen, not when I have plenty to share."

The guards kneeling before him look at each other, and I can almost see their mouths watering from here.

"No one in the City is starving," Gershom says. "We're

doing just fine, but since you brought all this here, we'll be happy to relieve you of it."

The whine of guns powering up echoes from behind us. Turning on my heel I'm surprised to see that another line of men, all well-armed and wearing armor, have come up behind us. Visidion's tail straightens as his hands ball into fists. Cenar shifts, rock rubbing rock echoing as he grumbles, turning to the new threat. All of us close into a circle with our backs to each other.

The armed men close around us. Gershom's guard stand and join the group encircling us.

"Rosalind," Visidion hisses.

"Yeah, didn't expect this," I say.

"Have all your aliens stand down," Gershom's voice echoes over the empty dunes. "We want the food. No one needs to get hurt."

The guards stop just out of reach, rifles unwavering, their high-pitched whine letting us know the guns are charged and ready to fire.

"Ha! Plan you have?" Mesto barks.

"Gershom," I shout. "Order your men to lower their weapons. This doesn't have to happen."

"What are you talking about?" he returns. "I'm in control here. How can you be so blind? The City is mine! You and your plans within plans. You didn't see this coming. I'm in charge. I've earned it, damn it. I brought water, I kicked the aliens out. I took what is ours!"

"No," I shake my head. "You didn't."

Gershom rushes forward, beet red, balled fists waving in the air.

"Yes I did! Now I'm taking this too," he screams. "All of it, it all belongs to me. I'm finally getting what I deserve! None of you can stand against me. This is what I was born for. It's my destiny!"

He steps forward, too close. Visidion hisses and leans forward. Gershom stumbles backwards, almost falling over himself in his hurry to get away.

In that moment I see Gershom more clearly than I ever have. I've always known he was power hungry, but I never understood why before. He's scared. Underneath all the bravado and the scheming is a scared little man. If he wasn't so dangerous, it would be sad.

"Get your hands up!" one of the guards screams, thrusting his rifle at Visidion.

We back up further as a group, our backs touching each other now.

"You got a plan here Rosalind?" K'sara asks.

"I can take them," Cenar says.

"Todd will win," Todd adds.

Moving my hand slowly, casually, I touch the sphere attached to my belt. Arcan's ball, my secret weapon. The whine of the guns goes up in pitch. One or more of them are about to fire.

"Do it!" Gershom screams. "Take that monster out!"

I grab the sphere, raise it over my head, and jab my thumb down on the trigger. A pulse blasts out of it, pushing sand ahead of it, and the whining of the guns evaporates. The guards look at their weapons, at each other, then back at their guns. The Zmaj and the gladiators take a step forward, then another. The guards rattle their guns and bring them to bear. The air is filled with the clicking of triggers, but none of them fire.

"Uh," the guard in front of me says, shaking his gun again.

He looks up and up until his eyes meet Visidion towering over him.

"Shit," the guard says, throwing his gun to the ground and falling over onto his ass.

All the guards throw their useless weapons to the ground

and almost as one they drop to their knees, hands behind their heads. Cowering before their opponents, several of them have tears running down their cheeks.

"No!" Gershom screams. "No, no, no!"

He's stomping the ground, fists shaking in the air.

"Enough," I say.

He glares at me. Visidion moves up beside me and Gershom pales.

"What now?" he asks, his voice quavering.

"You've left me no choice," I say.

"So this is it? You're going to kill me?" he asks.

"No," I say. "You'll get a trial."

Shock drops his jaw for a moment, but then a smile spreads across his face. "Fine."

30

VISIDION

"You know how this has to end," Ragnar says.

"If she won't do it, you have to," Drosdan adds. "I'll take care of it. Give me the word."

The sound of running water accents their words. We're standing in front of the fountain, by what used to be City Hall but is now the humans' headquarters. Being here calls through the fog of my memories, trying to pull them into the light. I can't give my attention to reminiscing. There are too many things to consider in the present to have time for the past. Humans eye us as they walk past, talking softly with each other, hurrying their steps if their path leads them close to us.

I turn my back on them and watch the water bubbling in the fountain. Once, I dimly recall, water would have been shooting up and splashing down, creating beautiful rainbows. The octagon base is full of water with bubbles around the base of the statue but no streams shooting up. Touching the stone of the containing wall, smooth and cool, it strikes me that I'm at a crossroads.

Rosalind is my treasure. I will do anything to protect her, but what if it's herself she needs protection from?

Her heart is too big. She loves unconditionally. I don't think anyone else sees that in her, but I do. She talks about survival and the necessity for the gene pool and such but that's her cover. The truth is she loves people and doesn't put a distinction on them. Zmaj to humans, Cenar to Todd, she loves them all.

And it blinds her.

Gershom is a snake, a sismis, hiding in the sand waiting to strike when you least expect. He not only has to be dealt with, it needs to be done with finality. The members of the Tribe see it clearly. Their distrust of him is deep and will keep a wall between them and the City until he is gone.

Rosalind can't do it, and if she did, she wouldn't be able to live with herself.

"We could do it quietly," Ragnar says, his voice barely above a whisper. "She need never know."

Ragnar places a hand on my shoulder, compassionate for my feelings. Feelings a Commander cannot show. Straightening up, I step aside, letting his hand drop off me. Meeting his gaze, then Drosdan's, I make the only decision I can. The one that will protect her from herself.

"No one can ever know," I say. "This must remain our secret, for the good of the Tribe and the humans."

Ragnar nods and Drosdan harumphs his agreement.

"I can do it," Ragnar says.

"Drosdan, you do it," I say walking away.

Tension clamps my shoulder muscles, making my wings ache. If Rosalind ever finds out, she might never forgive me. I don't have a choice. This decision is tearing her apart. I have to make it for her.

Walking the streets of the city, I let myself dream of the future. The buildings are in disrepair, many too damaged for use, and the streets are littered with garbage and debris. If we make a concentrated effort, all of this could be fixed. The City could become what it once was. Draconov used to be a major trade center. One of the biggest cities on Tajss.

Funny how memory works. Dim, hazy, but I recall some facts while others are lost to me. Picking one of the tallest buildings close to the center of town, I climb through a broken wall to the inside. Wreckage is strewn about, but I climb over all of it until I find a stairway leading up. It's difficult to reach my goal. The stairway is collapsed at several points forcing me to leap across gaps. When I reach the roof, there's a sense of accomplishment.

The suns are dropping to the horizon, the final rays twinkling off the dome with dazzling sparkles. Gazing up through the dome, I spot the first visible stars. One of those bright lights is Krik. If Arcan can't squash the rumors of Tajss's survival, invaders from Krik will be here soon. If he does, they'll be here later.

If nothing else, Rosalind is right in worrying about the future, for that reason if no other. We're not ready. We're too few and too divided. It will be the end of both our races if they come. Rosalind and I have to get them ready. Getting Gershom dealt with is the only way forward. I know I did the right thing, for her and for all of us.

Thinking of her makes an ache form deep in my core. I want to be with her. Tearing my eyes away from the stars, I head back to the street.

THE TEMPERATURE DROPS WHEN I STEP INSIDE THE BUILDING, increasing the tension in my muscles. Doubts try to assail me as I climb my way to Rosalind's office, but I push them all aside. When I get to the hall outside the Council meeting room, a young human is emerging from Rosalind's office. Water dripping from her eyes and streaking her cheeks, brow furrowed, frown on her face—something is wrong.

"Hello," I say. "Are you okay?"

She startles, looking up at me and wiping the moisture from her face with two quick swipes.

"Hello, yes, sorry," she says trying to step past me.

Shifting my weight, I block her passage. She looks up, arching an eyebrow.

"What is the matter?" I ask.

"Nothing," she smiles. "Seriously, I have a lot to do—did you need something?"

The pain and upset is gone from her eyes, hidden behind carefully schooled features. It's clear I won't be getting any more information from her, so I step out of her way.

"Good roads," I say.

"Same," she says, hurrying to the stairwell and disappearing into its dimness.

I walk into Rosalind's office. She's sitting behind a large desk from which she looks up and smiles when I enter.

"Visidion," she says.

The bags under her eyes and the weariness in her smile are all signs of what I already know. She's not sleeping well. Last night she woke up in the middle of the night, rising and pacing the floor for hours. Certainty fills me that I've made the right decision. The weight of Gershom will be removed from her shoulders, and then we will find a new normal, a better one.

"Hello," I say. "Who was that?"

She looks past me, smile faltering for an instant before locking firmly in place.

"Oh, she had a problem and wanted my help," she lies.

I see it in her eyes. It crosses her face for an instant but her smile covers it.

"I see," I smile, letting it go. "So when will this trial be?"

"Two days," she says, shifting papers on her desk. "Gershom has picked someone to speak for him, which was the last piece to put in place."

"Why go to so much trouble?" I ask.

She frowns deeply, shaking her head.

"We've been over this," she sighs. "I've explained it to you the best I can."

I hold my hands up before me. "Rosalind, this doesn't make sense. Everyone knows what he has done. Everyone but you is ready for this to be over. Why drag it out? There is no need for such formality. You are their Commander; your word is law. Do what must be done."

Her cheeks flush a deep red. Rising to her feet, she places her fists on the desk in front of her, leaning over it towards me.

"No, my word is not law," she says. "The Tribe may work on a patriarchal hierarchy, but humans don't. The future I envision for both our people doesn't. Those who are ruled have to have a say in their futures. Those accused have to have the chance to prove themselves innocent."

"But he's not!" I exclaim, exasperated. "Everyone knows it."

"No, everyone has an opinion. A trial will present facts. We will find the truth, and then he will be dealt with."

"It's a long road to get to the same place. Take the short cut."

"No," she shakes her head. "That's exactly it, we can't. What we do, right now, is setting the path for our future."

"You have the best interests of all of them at heart," I argue.

"And if I do? So what? What if whoever comes after me, following in the path I set before us, doesn't? Or the one after that? What we do matters!"

The fire and passion in her words crash against me like the stirring winds of a sandstorm, but instead of pushing me back they draw me in. My first cock is hard and pounding, demanding attention. The jacket of her suit is unzipped, and the shirt she wears under it is low-cut enough to reveal the creamy white of her cleavage. Hearts pounding in my chest, breath short, I can't take my eyes off her heaving breasts. Moving towards her, drawn inexorably in, I know from my bones to my scales—she's my everything.

"Yes," I answer. "Matters."

Her eyes drop then widen seeing the tent in my pants straining towards her.

"You're not listening to me," she accuses.

"I am," I answer her. "Every word, every thought. Your passion is my fire."

When I lean across the desk, my hard cock presses into its cool surface as I take a kiss. Her lips are fire, burning me with her passion. We connect and everything else is gone as wild desire takes us over. One-handed, I undo my pants and let them drop. She crawls over the desk, shedding her jacket. Grabbing her ass, I pull her to me, crushing her against my chest as I try to absorb her into my body.

Together we work her pants off, letting them fall to the floor. When I set her on the edge of the desk, my cock is at her opening. I shove in without preamble. Her wetness welcomes my cock, taking me fully in, and she cries out in surprise and pleasure. Her nails dig into my back as she throws her chin up and lets out a throaty scream.

There isn't even a semblance of control. Desire rules me. I'm thrusting in and out of her hot, wet tunnel, hammering her like an unstoppable force. Grunting with each thrust in, I take her and she gives herself to me. Her chest rises and falls in time with my thrusts. Her perfect, full breasts, exposed and so enticing, push me closer to an orgasm with each heaving.

Suddenly she arches her back, moaning. Her legs clamp around my waist, holding me deep inside her, then her pussy clamps on my cock and I give myself over. Her wetness milks my dick, sucking it dry, until at last she collapses back onto the desk, panting with eyes closed.

My shallow breaths slowly deepen as my hearts slow their racing beat. My cock softens in her and I pull out, eliciting a groan from her, and myself too as it's exposed to the cool air of the room. My second cock rises, ready to go, but Rosalind pushes against my chest.

"No," she says, shaking her head. "I've work to do."

"Ah," I say, unable to hide my disappointment.

"Later," she says with a smile, rising up and kissing me.

"I'll hold you to that," I say and kiss her nose lightly.

"Do that," she says.

"See you tonight," I say, turning to leave.

"Oh, Visidion?" she asks, pulling my attention back.

"Yes?" I ask.

"Don't ever do that again," she says, mouth a hard line.

Black swirling confusion rocks my mind. She can't know … it must be something else.

"What are you talking about?" I ask. Surely she can't mean our lovemaking, can she?

"Send one of your men to handle something I'm already handling," she says, pulling her pants over her hips and fastening them.

"I—"

"No," she cuts me off. "I know why you did it. Don't. Ever again."

"Rosalind," I say. "We need to be done with him and focus on the future, like you say. You know what's out there. We have to get ready."

"Yes, we do," she says. "But as I've said so many times before, how we do it matters. What we do matters."

She walks over to me, laying her hands on my chest, staring into my eyes.

"But—"

"No," she says, placing a finger on my lips. "No buts. You have to trust me. If you don't, this will never work."

I can't argue with the truth in her words. Her soft fingers rest on my lips, her eyes bore into me.

"All right," I say, giving in.

"Good. I know you don't agree, but we discussed this. This is the compromise that protects our future. Give me this, please."

Smiling, she rises on her toes and kisses me. Her tongue seeks out mine, piercing my mouth. When I wrap my arms around her and pull her close, my second cock, ever the optimist, rises again.

"Okay," I say, regret coloring the swelling sensation in my chest. "I'm sorry."

"Don't be," she says. "I know why you did it."

"Do you?" I ask, curious.

"Of course," she smiles. "You love me and want to fix the world, for me. How can I be angry at that?"

Sweeping her off her feet, I twirl her in my arms and extend the kiss until we break, gasping for air.

"I do," I whisper.

"I know," she breathes. "And I love you too."

31

ROSALIND

"*E*veryone's ready," Sarah says, and her voice quavers.

She's nervous and it shows. Moving from behind my desk, I approach, taking her hands in mine, trying to stare into her eyes. Her fear is a palpable thing between us. She can't meet my eyes.

Doubts assail my certainty. Am I doing the right thing?

Her lip trembles, but then she clamps it between her teeth, tightens her grip on my hands.

"Can you do this?" I ask softly.

She hesitates, thinking it over. That alone tells how scared she is.

"Yes," she says, nodding slowly. "I can."

She exhales heavily, bows her head, and then, looking up, she straightens her shoulders and nods again, but with certainty and strength this time. I pull her into an embrace, holding her tight. She stiffens in my arms, surprised, I'm sure, at this display of affection but then she returns it.

"Good," I say. "Remember, be careful."

"I will," she says. "You should go. I'll follow after. We can't be seen together."

I nod my agreement and go to the door where I pause, hand on the cool handle.

"Sarah," I say.

"Yeah?"

"You can say no," I offer, not looking back.

"I know," she says, no hesitation.

The moment grows long, heavy, but she doesn't speak again. I walk out. The decision is made.

Making my way down the broken stairwell, I focus my thoughts in this moment. Decisions made are done, ones to come will come when they do. Focus, here, now. Acutely aware of each step, I'm walking into a turning point. The biggest change in our lives since the ship crashed on Tajss, and possibly the most important. What happens today will set the course for our future.

"Hi," Visidion says, as I turn on a broken landing before I jump the gap in the stairwell.

He's leaning against the wall, arms crossed, waiting.

"Hi," I say, heart rate soaring.

He's incredibly sexy with his nonchalant air and pose. Biceps bulging against his muscular chest where his arms are crossed, his eyes sparkle with delight. My core tightens, feeling like a warm spring ready to explode. Desire rushes through my body, making my cheeks and limbs warm. The way he looks at me, his eyes lit up with desire and more, makes me aware of every nerve in my body. I feel as alive as if I'm walking on air.

"You okay?" he asks, grinning.

It hits me that I'm lost in his gaze once again, like some star-struck schoolgirl with a crush. Pulling my composure back into place, I shake my head.

"Yes," I say, leaping across the gap to land next to him.

He catches me before I can land, strong hands closing on my waist and pulling me in. Our lips meet, and molten fire burns through me at every place he touches. The tension in my shoulders and lower back melts before it, and I meld against him. At last he sets me on my feet.

"Thought I'd walk with you," he says.

"I'd like that," I say.

He takes my hand in his and we resume navigating our way to the ground floor.

"Padraig could probably build something to fix these stairs," he says, watching me cross the beam that covers another break in the stairs.

"That would be good," I say. "Removing the rest of the debris is on my to-do list, once we have things settled."

When we reach the ground floor, I stop before the door leading into the lobby. Once I step through, there's no turning back. I have to do what I set out to do. Gershom must face justice.

"Are you sure?" Visidion asks, no need to clarify the question.

It's the same question he and I have debated over and over. What do I do with Gershom? He wants it done with finality, but I don't know if I can do that. There are too many things to consider. Gershom has followers, people who really believe in him. If I execute him, he becomes a martyr, and the rift between us becomes deeper.

We don't have the resources to jail him, and if we did, how do I make sure he doesn't escape?

There are so few survivors, and I don't have the research available I did on the ship. I can't run computerized prediction models with the DNA of the survivors to find out the minimum viable population. I don't know whose DNA is best suited for the future survival, or if we even stand a chance as it is. We need more bodies, more people to fall in love and have babies and create the next generation. Every single person matters, human or Zmaj. The future I see isn't for two races, it's for one new race. The babies are our future, crossing between the humans and the Zmaj, adapted to their environment but free of the baggage of both races' pasts.

Gershom and his followers are the barrier to that future. Yet they're a vital part of it. Execute him and it will give validity to his ideas. At least some of his followers will become more entrenched in their xenophobic ideas, undermining and destroying that future at every turn. Leave him alive, and he can continue to spread his vitriol and hate.

There is no easy solution to this problem.

Taking a deep breath I put my hand on the door. Visidion puts the palm of his hand on my back, his cool touch offering his wordless support. I open the door and step into the lobby.

Outside the floor-to-ceiling windows, the crowd has already gathered. A makeshift riser has been built in front of the fountain and the crowd is all around it. When we step outside into the pounding heat of the double suns, it seems as if the entire crowd turns to look at me. Silence falls like a blanket over them. They part around me as I walk to the riser and climb the few steps. Three desks are set up on it, simulating a courtroom layout.

Crossing the riser, acutely aware of their eyes burning into me, I take my place behind the largest desk, facing out to the crowd. Before me are the two desks for the defense and prosecutor. On my left are nine seats filled with a split mix of those who were in Gershom's camp and those who were not, including Ormarr and Falkosh, representing the Tribe, and Sverre, the Zmaj of the City. Bert acts as the lead juror, shifting in his seat uncomfortably. He didn't want to take the position, but I was able to convince him.

He's the most neutrally acceptable to all sides and ideal for it.

Gazing across the crowd, I pause on the Gladiators, grouped together around Cenar who stands out in any crowd, being an eight-foot-tall humanoid rock. There is a space around them that doesn't exist anywhere else in the gathering. No one, human or Zmaj, seems sure what to make of them yet. Catching my eye, Mesto smiles and waves.

"Ha! People are many," he exclaims, eliciting laughter from the crowd around him.

The laughter fades away and my shoulders knot with tension.

"Let us begin," I say, rising to my feet. "Gershom, you are accused of betraying your fellow man, endangering the lives of all survivors, and of initiating a coup against the existing government. How do you plead?"

Gershom sits at the defense table, smiling from ear to ear as if he knows a secret. Anger flashes white hot, and I ball my hands into fists. Every fiber of my being wants to walk over and knock that stupid smile off his face. I close my eyes, taking a moment to regain control so I can continue. When I open my eyes he's still smiling, but I'm not going to let him get to me again. He rises to his feet, turns towards the crowd and holds his hands out wide.

"My fellow survivors," he says, voice echoing off the nearby buildings. "This is a preposterous mockery of justice. I did nothing wrong. Is it wrong I want to protect our race? Am I wrong to stand up to a dictator, not for myself, but for you?"

The crowd murmurs and there are a few scattered cheers.

"No, I say I'm not. No matter what happens here today, know this. I did what I did for you. No matter what they accuse me of, no matter what fabricated evidence they might present, I did what I did only for the good of you. My friends, my fellow survivors, my fellow humans."

Random pockets of cheering greet him. He turns to face me, still with that maddening grin on his face.

"To that end and for those reasons, I plead not guilty. I demand that his farce be ended and that fair elections be held for the good of all people."

"All human people!" someone in the crowd yells.

"Your plea is noted," I say, ignoring his grandstanding.

I take my seat and the proceedings begin. The prosecutor rises and makes his opening statements. The suns rise to midday, and I break the proceedings for lunch. Resuming once we've fed everyone, the defense makes its arguments. All of this is a formality and the crowd knows it, but it's an important formality.

Gershom's guilt is clear, and even his defense lawyer seems apathetic, as if he knows he has no chance of winning. As the suns drop to the horizon and the shadows of evening creep across the crowd, the attorneys rest.

"You have heard both sides of the argument," I say to the jury. "It rests on you to decide one question. Is he guilty of the crimes presented? Did he knowingly betray his fellow survivors and work to undermine the existing ruling body in an illegal and subversive manner?"

The jury looks at each other, silent. They stand, file off the riser, and go into the building where a room awaits them.

Food is laid out on tables again, and everyone sets to eating. A plate is brought to me on the riser, and Visidion joins me for dinner. We eat in silence, listening to the murmurs of the crowd as they discuss the case. The gathering looks calm, but tension is zinging in the air like static electricity. I hope that we can resolve this peacefully.

"This is foolish," Visidion says, pitching his voice low for me only.

"No, it's necessary," I reply.

"What if they come back and say he is not guilty?" he asks.

"They won't," I say.

"How can you know that? Half of those debating are his followers," he counters.

"Because I have to believe that," I say.

He shakes his head, chewing on a piece of guster meat.

"I don't understand," he says, swallowing his food.

"We have to put our faith in each other," I answer. "I have to believe that they will make the right choice, given the chance. That they will see the truth and will then make the right choice. If we, as a people, can't do that, then what good is our future?"

"You could take that choice from them," he says. "You know they would follow your word."

"Yes, but then what kind of society would we have? If there is no individual responsibility, what happens when I'm gone?"

"The new leader would take care of them," he says.

"What if the new leader is like Gershom? Interested only in their own power? What if I decide to go that way?"

"You wouldn't," he answers, firmly covering my hand on the table with his own. "You are good."

"Thank you," I say. "That doesn't take care of our future, though. It doesn't create the society I hope to inspire."

Chewing another piece of meat, he leans back on his stool. He turns his hand palm up, closes it over mine, and uses his thumb to make slow circles. Finally, he nods.

"I see," he says.

The murmur of the crowd changes, rises in pitch. The jurors are emerging from the building. The make their way to the dais and take their seats.

"Have you come to a decision?" I ask.

Sweat pours down Bert's face. He looks over at the other

jurors who stare at him, impassive. Rising to his feet, he wavers as if faint before composing himself.

"Yes," he says, voice cracking. He clears his throat, stares at the ground, shakes his head then meets my gaze. "Yes."

"Good, what is your verdict?" I ask, my heart pounding in my chest.

Everything hinges on this moment. My faith in humanity either pays off or we lose it all. The silence lies heavy. The handful of strategically placed guards shift their weapons, and the sound of the metal clicking is deafening. With my eyes boring into Bert, I will him to give me the answer I expect. Please, don't let me down. Eyes drifting across the jury, I try to meet each of their eyes, hoping to see the verdict in their eyes.

"Guilty," Bert says at last.

The crowd explodes. Cheers echoed by cries of despair. Gershom looks surprised and rises to his feet, but a guard steps forward and puts a hand on his shoulder, pushing him back into his chair. I stand and give the crowd their moment, waiting for the initial shock to wear off.

"People!" I yell to be heard over their noise but to no avail.

If anything, they grow louder. A short distance away from the riser, a fistfight breaks out, and the crowd shifts as some try to get away and others try to join in.

"Stop!" I yell.

I'm losing control. Visidion leaps onto the riser, making his way towards me. The mated Zmaj are grabbing their mates and moving them away.

A low, thrumming vibration starts. It's a low bass, so low and deep it throbs in my bones, growing louder until it feels like I'm being shaken apart from the inside. It's affecting everyone. The crowd stops, crossing their arms over themselves, looking around in confusion.

Searching for a source I spot Cenar. He's crouched low,

one hand touching the ground. He's the source of the sound. It continues until the entire crowd has stopped, too busy trying to hold their insides together to be interested in fighting each other any longer. Cenar rises and smiles at me. Arching an eyebrow, I return his smile.

"This isn't fair," Gershom says, sweating for the first time.

Noticing him sweat, I realize something. He's been taking epis. None of his followers can be in this heat without sweating bullets. He's been on epis, probably the entire time. So much for his human-first, reject-the-Zmaj rhetoric.

"Gershom, please rise," I say.

He shakes his head, face pale, hands gripping the desk in front of him. Two guards step forward and pull him to his feet.

"You have been found guilty," I say, letting the words hang in the air.

Tears run down his face.

"No, this isn't right," he says.

Everyone waits, with a quiet so deep I can hear the crowd breathing as if in sync with each other. Judgment has come for Gershom. On one side of the crowd, Sarah catches my eye. She's standing straight and stiff, surrounded by Gershom's supporters. She's chewing on her bottom lip as a tear slides down her face. My heart aches looking at her, but we're doing what we have to do.

"Your punishment must fit your crimes," I say. "And to that end, you will be exiled."

He looks up, shock on his face. Blinking rapidly he looks right and left then back to me.

"Exiled?" he exhales.

"Yes," I say. "Exiled. Those who wish to follow you may. You will be given supplies for a week and sent on your way. You are no longer welcome in the City or at the Tribe."

He shakes his head once more, then looks up and the slow smile spreads across his face.

"Fine," he says.

"Help him out of the dome," I order, then look out at the crowd. "We are at a turning point. Those of you who will not accept that our future lies in our friendship with the Zmaj may follow Gershom. No one will stop you. But if you so choose, you are no longer welcome here. No longer will the City be a place of intolerance and hate. That is the past. We are closing the door on it. Our future is dependent on each of us. Only in working together can we rise above the challenges to our survival and become what we are truly capable of. Only in working together can we create a better future for our children."

The crowd murmurs, turning their attention to each other and discussing their options. I slam my gavel down on the desk, closing the proceedings.

Visidion falls in next to me as I make my way into the building and back up to my apartments.

ROSALIND

"It seems your faith paid off," Visidion says, placing his hands on my waist as we walk into my apartment.

"Yes," I say, turning into his embrace.

We kiss, a long, slow kiss that only whets my appetite for more. Breaking from him, I take both his hands in mine, and walk backwards, pulling him along with me. He grins, following. Elation makes my steps light. Everything has gone according to plan.

Visidion rushes forward, grabbing my waist and lifting, putting me over his shoulder and running forward.

"Hey!" I cry out and he laughs.

I'm Struggling against his grip, but not too hard. He turns and works us through the door to my bedroom. Lifting me with one hand, he pushes me up towards the ceiling and moves me. Holding me as if I weigh nothing he claims a kiss. His tongue, dominant as ever, drives into my mouth, staking his claim with this first penetration.

Lowering me against him, he holds me off my feet and moves to the bed. Hooking an arm under my legs he cradles my body then lowers me to the bed. His kisses are ravenous as he moves across my neck and down. I pull my shirt over my head, letting my breasts fall free. He grabs them in both hands and takes the tip of the left in his mouth.

His rough tongue laps at my nipple, which tightens in response. Sensation pulses out from that sensitive point. He rolls the hard nub with his tongue, sucking and releasing, while his left hand works the other nipple to an erect point.

My pussy is so wet my panties are getting soaked. A familiar, tight ring of fire and the empty ache of need, desiring to be filled, forms inside my core. He works my breasts until I'm in a frenzy. Arching up into him, hips grinding against his pants, I'm begging for the release of his cock penetrating deep.

His lips clamp on my other tit, sucking hard, pulling my erect nipple. Pleasure explodes outward in a blinding rush. His hard cock pushes insistently against the cloth separating my pussy from it. I run my fingers through his hair, and my grip tightens, pulling.

He pulls off my tit, keeping me pinned down with the weight of his body. Rising onto his knees, he grabs my pants and pulls them off my hips, taking my panties along with them. His eyes devour me. He's trailing his hands along my sides and down my legs, making me shiver. I place my hands on his chest, and find that his scales are unusually warm to the touch. Their rough edges excite my fingertips as I trace the lines across him, feeling the hard muscles beneath the protective layer.

RI undo his pants and they drop to his knees. His cock bounces between us, pulsing with desire.

Keeping one hand on his chest, I put my left on my chest, tracing slow circles around my breast, working up to the hard nipple. His eyes follow my hand with an eager intensity. I bite my lower lip as my hand drifts down, across my stomach, towards my core. His eyelids drift down to half, his cock pulses up and down, screaming his desire.

Slowly I slide my hand across my middle and down between my legs. Visidion hisses as my hand passes my thighs. I spread them out so he has an unobstructed view.

Cupping myself in my hand, I rub up and down slowly with very light pressure. It's a pleasing sensation, but my clit pounds needfully, wanting more. Visidion's hand drifts to his cock as he watches me, and slowly he strokes his shaft from head to balls.

"Yes," he exhales, rising to his feet and standing at the end of the bed.

In a blur he grabs my hips and slides my ass to the edge of the bed, bending my legs back and forcing me to open even wider. I'm completely exposed as he lowers to his knees between my legs.

"More," he says, his voice tight and edging towards a guttural sound.

I obey, rubbing my wet pussy with all four fingers. He kisses along my inner thigh but his eyes never leave my hand working myself. My desire climbs as he kisses closer to my core.

Wetness covers my fingers and pussy lips. I increase the pressure of my fingers until my clit throbs. Tightness in my core is overwhelming, consuming me.

Hot breath crosses my working fingers as he moves over to my other thigh, kissing his way back to my knee. I'm moving my fingers faster, my desire increasing, and finally my need is overwhelming.

Reaching my knee he stands up, placing himself between my legs. His massive cock hangs in the air over my pussy.

"Fuck me," I groan.

Glancing up, he shakes his head no, grabbing his huge dick in one hand and stroking it. Eyes roaming over my body, he strokes himself to me. Warmth rushes through my body watching him masturbate to me. The way his eyes roam, drinking me in, makes my desire even higher. I press hard and focus on my clit, edging closer to an orgasm.

"More," he exhales, hand stroking his cock faster.

My eyes drifting closed, pleasure overwhelming all other thoughts, two fingers slide into my wet tunnel, filling me.

"Mmm," I groan, finding some satisfaction in being filled.

"Yessss," he hisses.

Spreading myself open, I move my free hand from his chest to my clit and work it in a frenzy. My hips rise and fall uncontrollably, desire claiming my body. Thrusting up towards his cock. He groans, loud.

Grabbing my hips, he lifts me up. He brings his cock to my opening and shoves it in without preamble. Each ridge sliding in brings pleasure to new heights. I'm swept away on wave after wave of sensations consuming my body.

"Rosalind!" he cries, his huge cock filling my pussy to its limit.

Stretching, my soft, pink walls expand to accommodate his huge girth. He fills me with his pulsating hard member. The walls of my pussy clamp down on him, vibrating in response to the intensity of the pleasure. I'm on the edge and about to fall.

As he pulls back, the ridges of his cock moving out ignite a burning fire deep inside. I'm gasping and his cock is out.

"Visidion!" I scream as he slams it in to me to the hilt.

The hard ridge at the base of his shaft touches my clit, and I'm sent over the edge into total wild abandon. My body is beyond control. Hips move up and down, pushing up to meet his thrust in and retreating in time with him. Heart pounding in my ears in time with the pounding in my clit. Each time he hits bottom, the touch of that hard bone to my clit makes me cry out.

Over and over he slams in, meeting my rising hips, until he slams and holds. His grip on my ass tightens, holding me against him. His cock is buried, I feel it spasm, and my pussy responds in kind. Muscles contracting, quivering as an orgasm rips through my body. Every muscle tightens, my toes curl, and my heart pounds.

Time stops as we join in our mutual pleasure.

It passes slowly, small aftershocks of the orgasm clenching my body, lessening each time until at last he lets me go and I collapse on the bed, feeling like jello.

He pulls out as I drop to the bed, his now-soft cock hanging between his legs, but then his second cock rises, ready to continue.

Smiling, our eyes meet. He trails his fingers softly along my body, exploring, giving me time to prepare before he uses his second dick.

"I love you," he says, soft and tender.

"I love you," I say, hands trailing across his hard abs, down to his massive shaft.

MHe lies down next to me. Hard cock resting on my leg, he lies on his side, running his fingers though my hair. Rising onto an elbow I push against his shoulder and he responds to my intention, lying on his back. His massive dick stands like a flagpole. Ready and at attention. Swinging a leg over him I position his dick at my opening.

If he went in easy before it doesn't compare to how my body accepts him now. It slides in without hesitation, my body drinking in his cock like a man dying of thirst. Hanging my head down, I watch it sliding into me, biting my lip as it does. Shivers run up and down my spine as I grunt and groan, the pleasure rocking my body as he fills me yet again.

His hands land on my hips, making circles on my ass, running up my sides and along my spine. Liquid fire on my skin where he touches, trailing it along with him.

Lowering onto him until I'm resting on top of him, filled to my limit by his huge cock.

Rotating my hips in a slow circle, grinding against the hard nub that fits so perfectly against my clit.

My core tightens with each rotation, my clit responding to the pressure, my pussy filled with his ridged, huge cock. He grabs my tits in both hands, pulling on the nipples. Throwing my head back, I groan.

Panting, I rotate faster, and then he moans, hands clenching my tits tightly as his hands spasm.

Rocking back and forth, I focus the pleasure straight onto my clit, moving it across the bone protrusion made just for this.

Moaning, I gasp with each thrust of my hips forward. Visidion grabs my hips and lifts me up then lowers me down, and we both cry out in pleasure. Loving the sensation, I rise up and down on his pulsating dick, riding him and forcing his cock in and out of my wet pussy.

His hand slaps on my ass as I bottom him out inside me, the soft sting accenting the pleasure of his cock filling me. Leaning over, my lips find his. Passion consumes us both. Our kiss is filled with it. His lips claim me, his tongue drives into my mouth in time with his cock thrusting up into my pussy.

Sensation builds, and once more my body takes over. Pleasure claims every nerve, sensation is overwhelming, taking me. Driving him in and out, moaning into his kiss, I'm overtaken by desire.

My body stiffens. I'm groaning, eyes rolling into my head—I'm shaken to the core by the strength of the orgasm. I'm left panting in exhaustion as small quakes continue after the main wave has hit. I collapse onto his chest and we kiss again, but now its soft and gentle. The bulk of our passion is spent, leaving in its burning wake sensations of satisfaction. In a strange way, I feel complete.

LA hole I didn't realize I had is gone. I'm more when I'm with him. I have in him someone to share my burdens with, a thing I've never had before.

He takes my hand in his as we cuddle together, basking in the afterglow. Soft shivers continue to run through my body as the last vestiges of pleasure unwind.

"You're beautiful," he says, kissing each finger of my hand.

"Thank you," I say, hooking my leg over him.

"You haven't had the tremors," he says, looking at my hand.

FI realize he's right. I've been so busy I hadn't noticed.

"True," I say in surprise.

He smiles.

"Epis has healing properties," he says.

"I know," I agree. "Perhaps it is better."

"It is. The future is ours," he says. "You made the right decision. I'm sorry I didn't see it before but I do now."

Smiling, I lean in and kiss him. The understanding between us is good.

"It won't be easy," I say. "There's a lot we have to do, but we've made a big stride forward."

"Why was Sarah so sad at the trial?" he asks, tracing circles across my skin with his forefinger.

"She is brave," I say. "And she is doing the hardest thing I've ever had to ask anyone to do."

"Oh?" he asks, rising up onto his elbow to look at me directly.

"Yes," I say, frowning. "She is my mole in Gershom's camp."

His smile spreads from ear to ear.

"I knew it," he says. "You always think three steps into the future."

Smiling, I rise and kiss him.

"The future can wait," I say, breaking the kiss. "Today, let's enjoy our victory."

Want to know as soon as the next RED PLANET book is out?
Sign up for my mailing list!
http://mirandamartinromance.com/newsletter/

ABOUT THE AUTHOR

Hi I'm Miranda! xoxo

Country girl, military vet, artistic soul and lover of all things science fiction. I write the heroes of imagination.

Bigger, sexier, and did I mention... bigger? Yeah. That kind of bigger ;)

Are you ready to fall in love with a dragon?

♥♥

Miranda

Get in touch!

mirandamartinromance.com

miranda@mirandamartinromance.com